TAINTED GOLD

LAYNE WALKER

Wild Mustangs Publishing, LLC

TAINTED GOLD

This is a work of fiction.
All characters and incidents are a product
of the author's imagination.
Any relationship to persons living or dead
is purely coincidental.

ISBN-13: 978-0-9883534-0-4

Published by
Wild Mustangs Publishing, LLC
Lake Havasu City, AZ

Visit Layne's website at
www.laynewalkerbooks.com

Printing history
First edition published in September 2012

Thanks to
Anne Cote
for all her hard work
behind the scenes.

Thanks to
Buck Dopp
Jim Veary
and
Mike Wilkinson
for reading an early draft
and giving me their feedback.

Thanks to
Verne Dorn
for being such an enthusiastic fan.

Chapter 1

The driver of the minivan in front of me suddenly swung into the store's parking lot without using a turn signal. I hit my brakes and swerved, narrowly avoiding a rear-end collision. I knew I shouldn't have been following so closely, but I had to get to work. Steve had warned me…if I was late again, I'd be fired.

Without stopping, I slammed the gas pedal of my 1998 Ford Ranger 4x4 to the floor, trying to make up a few precious seconds. Were it not for the flashing red and blue lights of the Lake Havasu City police cruiser suddenly appearing in my rearview mirror, I might have made it on time. *Damn, another ticket.*

Thirty minutes later, I pulled up to the jobsite with the aggravation of having to do some fast talking to convince Steve to let me keep my job.

Steve Wilkes, a tall, husky man in his mid-forties, wearing shorts and a tank top, promptly left his landscaping crew and hurried to the truck before I could open the door. He barked, "Don't bother, Donny. I told you last time what would happen if you were late again."

"I would have made it," I whined. I held my ticket out the window. "I got pulled over. So, technically, it's not my fault."

Steve ran a hand across his sun-bleached, buzz-cut hair, then shook his head sadly. "You'll never change, Donny. You always have an excuse for everything. Nothing's ever your fault. I'm sorry, but for the sake of my business, I can't keep you on."

As Steve walked back to his crew, I sunk down in my seat. *Shit, Donny Jamison screws up again,* I thought. *Another job lost. The fourth one in the last year. What now?* I wasn't in the mood to pound the pavement looking for another job.

Gathering myself, I reached for the ignition key. *You know what? I'm glad Steve fired me. I'll take a few days to explore that new canyon I've been looking at on the map.* I fired up the engine and headed for home.

* * *

After heating a cup of coffee, I spread a mineral survey map out on my kitchen table. I secured the top corners with my smokes and ashtray. My coffee cup and the T.V. remote held the other two corners.

Everybody always said I was a dreamer, that I've always been a slacker. *Hell, maybe I am.* Even in grade school, my teachers had let me sit and stare out the window. They had given up on getting me involved with the class.

Dad had told me I would never accomplish anything worthwhile in life if I didn't have a passion for something. Well, I have a passion…finding a way to make money without working. Hence, the survey map laid out before me. I hoped to find a vein of gold and never have to work again. *I'll show 'em.*

The map displayed an area of the Mohave Mountain Range in Western Arizona, mountains that potentially held gold-bearing quartz. Red marks on the map indicated areas where gold could possibly be found. One little strip of red pointed to a remote canyon high on one of the mountains.

In the past, I had spent a lot of time roaming the desert and hills outside Lake Havasu City. A few years back, I'd even been in the general area of Mount Crossman, the location I planned to explore today. With growing excitement, I double-checked the route, rolled up the map, and stuck it in my pack. Dressed in my usual desert clothes—Wrangler jeans, cowboy boots, and a long-sleeved shirt—I grabbed my cowboy hat off the hook by the door and slapped it on my head on my way out. I threw my hiking gear into the truck and set out for the remote canyon.

An hour later, weaving my truck around creosote bushes, rocks, and an occasional cactus, I slowly made my way up the wash that led to the canyon where I hoped to find my fortune. With the mid-March temperature in the mid-sixties and the windows rolled down, country music blared from my speakers, shattering the peaceful quiet of the desert morning.

Driving as far as I could take my truck, I parked and jumped out. I gathered my equipment, carefully checking to take everything I might need for an emergency. Coming out on the desert alone was risky, I knew, but I'd been out here by myself many times. I figured, as long as I didn't take any unnecessary chances, I'd be okay.

After pulling on my backpack and securing my Ruger .44 cal. pistol in its holster, I locked the door, slipped the keys into my pocket, and climbed out of the wash. Following the ridge of a hill, I made my way higher up the mountain.

Daydreaming about finding the richest vein of gold in history, I almost walked into a patch of cholla cacti. I'd learned on my first trip to the desert to avoid the cholla at all costs. From a distance, the plants look like furry teddy bears. Up close, their tennis-ball-like pods hold hundreds of needles. The pods seem to jump out to attach to clothing and skin, earning them the name "jumping cactus."

Once safely past the patch of cacti, I moved quickly, making good time, reaching the short peak sooner than I'd expected. Slipping off my pack, I pulled out a water bottle and took a few sips while I looked out over the valley. Far to the northwest, I could see the Colorado River, a ribbon of blue, flowing into the twenty-nine-mile-long Lake Havasu. Although impressive, I lost interest after a few minutes and turned to study the next leg of my hike. From here, I had to travel down the back side of the peak and through the saddle, then hike a half-mile or better up the next peak. Returning my water bottle into the pack, I swung the pack over my shoulder and started down the hill.

As I walked, my mind wandered back to the encounter earlier in the day when Steve had fired me. Deep down, I knew he had done the right thing. After all, this was the fourth job in the last year I had lost. It wasn't my fault if I couldn't find a job I liked, was it? *Hell, no.* Either the work was boring, or the boss and I didn't see eye-to-eye. Sometimes, I just flat out didn't like the work. Whatever the case, I'd been moving through jobs faster than most people change the oil in their cars.

Two years ago, I had heard of a guy finding gold out on the desert. I figured, if other people could find gold, why couldn't I? So, I'd started hanging out at the local rock shop and made friends with several rock hounds who had invited me to visit the Havasu Gem and Mineral Club. I joined the club and met a couple of guys who went out looking for gold. With their help, I had learned enough to go searching on my own. With maps, rock hammers, and lots of enthusiasm, I had spent the last two years roaming isolated canyons looking for…hoping for…that big strike so I would never have to work another day in my life.

Today is gonna be different, I told myself. This remote canyon didn't appeal to the guys in the gem club. They avoided it at all cost because it was too hard to get to. Therefore, I'd deduced that no one locally had been up here searching. The possibility of finding a rich vein of shiny gold, running through an outcropping of quartz, loomed large in my mind. *Girls, parties, booze, a big red Dooley with all the bells and whistles in my driveway. Gold nuggets, here I come.* I picked up my pace with eagerness.

* * *

An hour later, I came to a stop in front of my anticipated destination. I stood in the mouth of a steep-walled, rocky canyon. Resting for a moment, I looked out across the valley. A rocky hillside sloped away at my feet.

Not only did I see most of the lake, I caught a glimpse of Bullhead City and Laughlin to the far north. To the west, past the little town of Havasu Landing on the other side of the lake, I observed the thirty-mile stretch of the Old Woman Mountains. Sucking in my breath, I stared in awe, duly impressed by the wide span of the valley from this vantage point.

Behind me in the canyon, a rock rolled and bounced, thumped off other rocks, then stopped with a solid *thunk*.

I turned with my hand on my gun. Starkly aware of my isolation and distance from help, I shifted my gun into a more accessible position on my hip. I swallowed hard, listening for more movement. *Rocks fall all the time*, I told myself. *It's a natural event.*

Curious to find out if I was alone, I slowly made my way forward with my right hand remaining on my gun. I wove through the boulders, heading cautiously into the canyon.

My head and eyes constantly scanned the crevices and rocks. If someone else was in the canyon, I wanted the advantage of seeing that person…or persons…first. At my slow pace, I also checked for outcroppings of quartz that might bear a vein of gold.

Fifteen minutes later, a smaller canyon branched off to the right from the main canyon. I didn't remember this area from the maps.

Not seeing or hearing anyone in the vicinity, I decided to explore the first part of this smaller canyon, which seemed to be less steep than the first one. After two hundred yards, it leveled out. I found myself walking in a sandy wash interspersed with occasional boulders and rocks.

Rounding a bend, I caught sight of a flash of brown skin disappearing behind a large rock. My eyes widened in alarm. I stopped and grabbed the smooth, wood grips of my gun. Son-of-a-bitch, if that hadn't looked like a person's leg. I listened carefully and looked around. Who'd be up here? Was someone else looking for that vein of gold? What if somebody had already found it and was mining it? Mining *my* gold?

For the first time, I noticed tracks in the sand of the wash…not tracks really, but evenly spaced indents about the size of a human foot. The tracks couldn't have been made by an animal. One set of tracks seemed to indicate only one person in the party. *This must be the person who had dislodged the rock that fell earlier,* I told myself, not sure what danger may lay ahead if I encountered this person.

Cautiously, I followed the tracks up the wash. The walls of the canyon slowly rose steeper and grew narrower, turning into solid rock only ten feet apart on each side. Feeling trapped and claustrophobic, I paused. I wondered if it was wise to go any farther. Reconfirming the sight of only one set of tracks ahead of me, I swallowed down my fear and decided I could handle one person, if need be. With my hand still on my gun, I continued forward, one silent step at a time, checking behind myself occasionally. Up ahead, I saw a turn in the wash where the rock walls veered sharply to the left.

As I peered around the corner, I found myself facing a solid rock wall, twenty feet away, that rose straight up for at least seventy or eighty feet. A dead end with no one in sight. My eyes shot to the tracks in the sand, which stopped at the foot of the wall. Turning in a complete circle, I checked for a place where a person could climb out of the canyon. Without ropes and rock-climbing gear, or at least hand-holds, that would be impossible, and there were no signs of an escape route.

The section of the wall where the foot prints ended suddenly shimmered, looking liquid for a moment.

I blinked in surprise, fearing I was seeing things, like a mirage in the heat. When the same thing happened again, chills ran down my spine. "What the hell?" Glancing around to make sure I was still alone, I stepped up to the wall. I reached out to press my hand against the surface. The seemingly solid rock not only gave way, my hand disappeared through it. I jumped back and screamed, "Son-of-a-bitch." I studied my hand to make sure it wasn't damaged. It seemed to be okay.

The wall shimmered again.

I stared in disbelief. *Did the other person go through there? Where does it go? Is it safe?* These questions flashed through my mind as I stood frozen in place.

Finally, I picked up a rock and threw it at the wall.

Instead of bouncing, the rock disappeared as the wall shimmered again.

I stood for a long moment, wondering if I dared investigate the wall further. Was this some kind of portal, like in the movies? Maybe it went into another world, to some other planet, or to another dimension in time.

My heart raced as I considered what I should do. *This could be big*, I told myself. What if this *was* a way into another world? What would that world look like? Did people live there? The tracks seemed to be made by someone walking on two legs…or *something* walking on two legs.

I paced back and forth, keeping my eye on the wall to catch the illusive shimmers. It seemed dangerous to go through a portal without knowing what was on the other side. I could die or disappear forever. Movies portrayed portals as moving, shifting, opening, and closing. That was science fiction and fantasy. The strange wall before me seemed real enough, but the way it worked was a fearsome mystery.

Still, how could I *not* investigate? This might be a once-in-a-lifetime opportunity.

I stared at the wall one more time.

What the hell? What do I have to lose? There's not much waiting for me in town. I might as well see what happens. Maybe I'll get lucky.

I took a deep breath to calm my pounding heart as I stepped toward the wall. I stuck my hand through first. I felt no pain, just a tingling feeling. The weirdest part was watching my hand and forearm disappear up to my elbow. Drawing my arm back, I once again found no irregularity or apparent change in my hand.

The faint roar of an airplane overhead pulled my attention upward. In the thin line of blue sky visible beyond the canyon walls, I saw multiple jet streams and one dark speck of a plane flying overhead, probably at thirty thousand feet.

I shook myself. *Enough distractions*.

Facing the wall just in front of me, I squared my shoulders and stepped into the unknown.

Chapter 2

My shoulders dropped in disappointment as I found myself standing in the same wash, looking at the same rock walls. Everything appeared exactly the same, except I faced *away* from the wall, not into it.

Confused, I sat down on a convenient boulder. Staring at the ground, I noticed only one set of tracks, the same tracks I had seen walking up the wash. I gingerly glanced around as my brow tightened. I had created a second set of tracks coming up the wash, left dozens of my own tracks everywhere in the area, so where were they now? I leaned forward and studied the tracks more closely. The indents appeared as though someone had walked over the same tracks in both directions. Now, the single set of tracks seemed to be going *down* the wash, away from the wall, not into it. How could that be?

A small rock caught my eye. The sand beneath it had been disturbed, as if the rock had been thrown and rolled to a stop.

I jumped up. It was the rock I had thrown at the wall. I must be on the other side. I spun around. Other than the tracks, nothing looked different. I shot a look up at the clear blue sky. No plane. No jet streams. An eerie feeling shivered through my body.

Tentatively, I walked down the wash, following the footsteps, watching for anything unusual. The canyon walls, the rocks, the dirt, everything, except for the footprints heading in the opposite direction, seemed to be exactly the same. Was I losing my mind?

As I stepped through the opening of the main canyon, I stopped dead in my tracks and blinked twice, trying to process what I saw.

The geography of the land looked generally the same, but the lake and the towns were gone. A river, eight to ten miles away, flowed through the virgin desert land. Everything man-made was gone.

Wait, that wasn't totally true. In the distance, near the river, a haze of smoke hung just above the valley floor. It had to be a settlement of some kind, maybe a village or a camp. Could it be an Indian camp? Did I go back in time somehow? Is this another dimension or a parallel world?

I blinked again and rubbed my eyes, but only saw the same panorama.

Spinning in place, I tried to grapple with the situation. I'd heard about this kind of stuff, but I'd never imagined it was real, or that it could happen to me. I wasn't sure what to think. I'd done a lot of daydreaming in my lifetime, but nothing like this. My breath caught in my throat at the thought I might be stuck in this new reality. I had to get back.

As I turned toward the canyon, a movement on the hill below me caught my eye. I quickly pulled out my binoculars and focused on the hill. A man in a loincloth and sandals darted from one boulder to another, moving downward toward the valley. Bits of leather-like material had been braided into the man's long, black hair.

My heart raced as I lowered my binoculars. It looked like an Indian. Was I really seeing this? I lifted my binoculars again. I suspected this Indian had been the one in the canyon, the one I had glimpsed briefly, the one who had disturbed the rock, the one making the tracks.

The Indian headed toward the area in the distance where the smoke rose, re-affirming my belief there could be a tribe of natives living there. I wondered if they were friendly.

Glancing around nervously, I hoped no other Indians would pop up nearby and catch me by surprise. The one set of tracks gave me fleeting confidence the Indian had been alone. I started back, my feet hurried and my heart pounding in my chest. When I reached the wall, I stopped and gulped, hoping against hope I could get back to my own world.

I stuck out my hand. It passed easily through the wall. I closed my eyes and moved quickly to the other side.

Hearing a plane overhead, I looked up. Jet streams crisscrossed the busy blue sky from the many jets flying to and from the west coast. An airplane moved southward in the same spot I had seen the airplane earlier. A flood of relief washed over me. I was back in my own world. At least, I was pretty sure I was back in my own world.

I turned and studied the rock wall. It shimmered slightly, appearing again briefly as a pool of water.

Wow, I'd seen movies where people had gone through gateways and portals to a different time or a different dimension. Until now, I'd never really taken it seriously or even thought it was possible.

I sat down on a rock similar to the convenient rock I'd found on the other side. Sipping from my water bottle, I studied the wall and considered the other world, how much it resembled my own with the layout of the land, the location of the river, the hills and mountains around the valley, the vast stretch of desert, the wide river bed where the water flooded during rain storms. The main difference between the two worlds seemed to be that the other world lacked development, lacked civilization as I knew it. No houses. No lake. No London Bridge. It had been like stepping back into the past, maybe two hundred years or more ago, and seeing the area as it had existed before the white man had taken hold and changed it.

The wall shimmered again.

I stood up. Excitement began to build within me as my imagination started taking over. New possibilities crossed my mind. This new world offered potential opportunities that might give me an edge on life. If this new world happened to be the same world as my own, just hundreds of years earlier in time, then the Gold Rush had never happened over there. The prospecting of the western states never took place.

And, if by chance, it wasn't the same world…well, gold probably still existed over there in the same places as here, just like the mountains and the valley still existed over there, just like here.

As the implications dawned on me, I felt a rush of adrenaline pump through my body. The gold could still be there, all the gold I could ever use. As far as I knew from history, the Indians didn't mine gold for profit. They never equated gold to money like the white man. It was just waiting for me to go and get it. I could taste the sweet notion on my lips.

I restrained myself from walking back through the portal right then. Even though I ached to return and check it out more thoroughly as soon as possible, I worried about how the natives might react to a stranger showing up. I needed to make preparations for the trip, and more importantly, I needed help.

Throwing my water bottle into my pack, I hurried down the canyon wash. This thing was too big to let leak to the public. Everyone would be swarming into the new world. I had to keep it under wraps, be careful about who found out. I'd talk to my brother, Eric, the successful business man. I was sure

Eric would be interested in this new world and its financial possibilities.

Arriving at my truck in half the time it took me to get up the mountain, I tossed in my gear, revved up the engine, skidded through the desert brush, and pulled into town forty-five minutes later.

* * *

Sitting in the living room of Eric's million-dollar home, I leaned forward on my legs and shifted uneasily. "Come on, Eric, just take a look. It's really amazing." I hadn't yet mentioned the "portal" for fear Eric would kick me out of the house. Already, the grievance on Eric's face told me that maybe coming to him had not been such a good idea.

"I don't care what you found out there," Eric said with exasperation. "I'm not taking time out of my busy schedule to go running around the desert for some wild hair of yours."

I cringed inside at Eric's rebuff. Eight years younger, I had always felt inferior to his natural charm and good looks. Although we stood the same height, about five-foot-seven, and both had the same wavy brown hair, the similarities between us ended there. My plain, brown eyes contrasted sharply with Eric's ever-changing hazel irises. My skin was a lighter tone and burned easily, while Eric's skin tanned evenly and naturally during the many hours he played sports and boated. My chin wasn't as firm as Eric's, and my nose and ears were larger. It wasn't that I was ugly, but my features weren't arranged as attractively as Eric's. And being Mr. Popularity his whole life, Eric had never had a problem getting dates or making friends in high school and later. Not like I did.

Taking a silent breath, I kept my tone even, trying to sound convincing without seeming half-cocked, the way Eric always made me feel. "I promise, this is worth going to see.

And with your nose for business, you could even make money. Lots of money."

Eric's glare flashed a look of interest. "What do you mean? What did you find out there? Gold?" Although Eric owned a thriving construction company that allowed him and his wife, Cindy, to live extravagantly and not have to work, Eric always sought alternative ways to make money. He had a nose for money. It was his passion.

I grinned, a little hope rising in my heart. "The only way you're gonna find out is to come with me."

At first, Eric shook his head. He got up, went into the kitchen, and came back with another beer. "Where is this place?"

"The Mohave Mountains."

As Eric dropped down in his easy chair, he narrowed his eyes on me.

I held my breath, hoping it would be a go.

Eric popped open the beer can and took a long swig. To the can, he said, "Something tells me I should go. I don't know why." His hazel eyes looked up and bore back into me. "If this turns out to be another one of your hair-brained schemes to make money, I swear, I'll disown you for good this time."

"Don't worry," I said eagerly. "I guarantee you'll be glad you went. You can't even imagine the opportunities you'll have."

"I better be glad," Eric bellowed. He took another swig. "When do we go?"

"I want at least one more person to go with us. What about Pat, do you think he'll go?"

"Probably. He's always up for an adventure."

A surge of excitement rushed over me. "Call him. See if he's free tomorrow. I want to get back out there as soon as possible."

As Eric dialed the number on his cell and spoke to Pat, I could hardly sit still. Nervous energy coursed through my veins.

Unknown to Eric, I had an ulterior motive for inviting his friend Pat Brinkman, a twenty-eight-year-old, full-blooded Mojave Indian from the reservation in Parker, a small town just down the river from Lake Havasu. Pat spoke his native language. While I couldn't be sure about the language of the natives on the other side of the portal—natives who might have existed thousands of years earlier and, for all I knew, spoke Swahili—I hoped they might be related to the Mojave Indians or be Pat's ancestors and speak the same language or something close. If so, Pat would be able to understand them and translate, maybe smooth things over with the Indians and get useful information about locations of gold.

I jumped up and paced the floor, my mind now racing through the items I would need to take on the trip. For sure, I'd take my pistol and lots of ammo. I didn't want to take any chances with the natives. Neither Eric nor Pat ever traversed the desert without guns, so I didn't have to suggest they bring weapons.

When Eric gave me a nod that signaled Pat would join us, I pumped my arm in the air. *Yes*.

"Tomorrow morning at seven," Eric said as he snapped the phone shut. "The gas station at the southern edge of town."

Saying my farewell, I grabbed my keys off the coffee table and headed for the door. My mind filled with fantasies of bringing home loads of gold, purchasing a shiny new truck, and surrounding myself with bathing-beauty babes. I itched to get back to the portal.

* * *

I could hardly sleep that night. This portal, this new, untouched world was my ticket to the big-time: fame, fortune, and babes. Lots of babes, all of them begging me to pick them out of the crowd. Yeah, that's what I wanted.

I tossed off my covers and lay staring at the ceiling. I was tired of dead-end jobs. Hell, I was tired of working, period. I wanted to be one of those guys I had watched down at the lake on weekends, the guy with a one-hundred-thousand-dollar, forty-foot boat, decked out with seven or eight girls wearing skimpy bikinis, dancing to hip-hop, falling over each other to see to his every need.

Mmmm, yeah.

I drifted off to sleep with big boats and sexy girls on my mind. Soon, the dream darkened. Dark-skinned native Indians chased and captured me, along with Eric and Pat. After many days of torture, we became their slaves.

I woke briefly, then shifted into another dream.

A horde of screeching, half-naked natives chase the three of us across the desert. Sharp rocks and cactus needles bloody our bare feet. The sun blisters the skin on our backs. We run for days on end, the bloodthirsty natives constantly hanging at our heels. Straight ahead, on a small rise, a tall Indian stands next to a large black pot. Bending over, the Indian sticks his arms into the pot and pulls out two handfuls of gold. He holds the gold out toward me, as if he dares me to come and get it.

Suddenly, I find myself in an Indian camp standing next to a fire. In the distance, drums pound out to the beat of BOOM, boom, boom, boom, BOOM, boom, boom, boom.

One of the natives, a pretty girl with big brown eyes, smiles at me. "We're having a feast tonight to celebrate the arrival of Eric, Pat and you, Donny."

I smile back. "Good, I'm starving. What're we eating?"

She laughs and pulls out a large butcher knife. "You, silly," she says as she plunges the knife deeply into my chest.

I screamed, fighting to get free from the sweaty sheets tangled around my body. I jerked upward in my bed. Catching my breath, I plopped back down. For a long time, I wondered if the dream was trying to tell me something, a premonition of things to come. When I finally convinced myself it was just another bad dream brought on by pizza and beer, I drifted off into another restless sleep.

Chapter 3

The sun, rising over the mountains the next morning, brought me a great sense of relief. I had to admit, my dreams throughout the night worried me about the upcoming trip to the other side. I considered taking two or three more people with us, just in case we ran into trouble, but in the end, I settled for making sure all three of us had our guns with us and at the ready.

When I arrived at the gas station, I found Eric and Pat dressed in jeans, boots, and long-sleeved shirts for the cool morning weather. Eric wore a cowboy hat while Pat's silky black hair hung down his back in a ponytail, tied with a strip of leather decorated with small pieces of brightly colored cloth, beads, and little bells.

I smiled to myself. If Pat wore a loincloth, he'd look just like his ancestors two hundred years before. My smile disappeared when I realized that, if Pat did have on a loincloth, he'd look just like the Indian I had seen on the other side of the portal.

We filled our gas tanks and I led the way in my truck. Eric rode with Pat in Pat's Jeep. The day promised to be sunny and warm, with temperatures in the mid-seventies.

Thoughts of seeing the portal again filled me with excitement. I couldn't wait to see the expression on Eric's face when he watched me put my hand through the rock. What a kick. *Even better, wait until he sees the virgin land and all the gold that hasn't been found.* I slammed on the gas pedal and headed up the dusty terrain, avoiding the scattered cacti and large rocks.

As I slowed my truck to enter the wash that led to the canyon, my excitement began to dampen. What if the portal had disappeared? Doubts assailed my mind. The closer I got, the more worried I grew that I would find a solid wall of rock where the portal had been. Worse, maybe I'd dreamed the whole thing. Maybe it was just another figment of my imagination.

I quickly shook the misgivings from my head. No. It was too real for a dream. It happened. I refused to think about how angry Eric would be if the portal wasn't there and I had nothing to show for bringing him all this distance. Distracting my thoughts from this dreadful scenario, I cranked up the radio and blasted country music into the open desert.

Finally, we arrived at the spot where I had parked the day before. Anxious to get going, I grabbed my gear and nervously paced back and forth, while Eric and Pat took their time getting ready for the long hike up the mountain.

Not five minutes after leaving the vehicles, a huge mule deer buck jumped up from where he'd been sleeping under a tree and crashed through the thin desert brush.

My heart jumped to my throat. I clumsily tried to draw my gun as I yelped in fear. Visions of the previous night's dreams—the natives coming to attack me—flashed through my mind. I stumbled backwards and bumped into Eric.

Pat laughed. "Jeez, it's just a deer, Donny."

Lightheaded from the sudden rush of adrenaline, I took a deep gasping breath and slowly let it out.

"Yeah, Donny," Eric said, "you seem awful jumpy today. What's up?"

"Nothing, I just…I just didn't sleep very good last night." Suddenly aware of how uptight and jumpy I had been acting, I realized my dreams of being the main course at a celebratory feast must have had more of an effect on me than I'd thought. As I sensed Eric was about to ask me why I'd had a restless night, I cut him off. "Don't worry about it, Bro. I'm okay." I hurried up the hillside before anything else could be said, then stayed well in the lead to discourage talking. I wasn't in the mood to explain about my dreams or anything else. I just hoped the portal was still there and I wasn't making a total fool out of myself on this whole trip.

When we reached the top of the first peak, Pat whistled. "Wow, what a view. You can almost see Bullhead City from here."

"You can see it a little further up," I said, stopping for a rest. Breathing heavily from the steep hike, I took off my hat and wiped the sweat from my forehead with my shirt sleeve. After returning the hat, I pulled a pack of cigarettes out of my shirt pocket and shook the pack until a single cigarette popped out. Sticking the smoke in my mouth, I lit it with a BIC Lighter.

"When you gonna give those stinkin' things up?" Pat asked waving a hand in front of his face even though the smoke wasn't coming anywhere near him.

I didn't smoke a lot, maybe five or six cigs a day. One of the main reasons I did it was to make Eric mad. He hated me smoking, and I didn't care he hated it. I used it to rebel against his authority. Since our dad had died ten years before, Eric had tried taking over the paternal role in my life. Naturally, I resented it.

I inhaled deeply and slowly blew out the smoke. "When I'm good and ready," I stated flatly. If I didn't put an end to the conversation right away, Eric would get involved, and I wasn't in the mood for one of his fatherly lectures.

Eric took the hint, giving me a disgusted shake of his head. "How much higher do we climb?"

"See that canyon over there?" I pointed to the opposite hillside. "That's the main canyon. A smaller canyon branches off of it part way up."

As we continued forward, my nervousness grew about what we were going to find.

* * *

Around ten o'clock, I stopped a few feet in front of the wall where the portal had been the day before. The sunrays hadn't reached the bottom of the narrow canyon yet. In the shadowy light, the wall looked normal, solid, just like a rock wall should be. Dare I touch it?

Eric and Pat studied the sheer walls of the dead-end canyon. Eric put his hands on his hips and spoke with irritation. "Okay, where's this great discovery you made?"

Fearing the portal would be gone and I'd look like a fool, I swallowed hard, but I wasn't going to lose face in front of my brother until it came to that. I stepped up to the wall with fledging confidence and said boldly, "Right here." I pushed my hand into the wall. Relief flooded through me when it disappeared behind the illusion of solid rock. With my hand and arm up to the elbow still invisible, I turned to look at my companions over my shoulder.

Eric's mouth dropped open without a word. His eyes held shock and confusion, as though he couldn't believe what he was seeing.

Pat remained silent, also, but he stared with intense interest, as though he found the whole thing intriguing. His mind seemed to be racing a mile-a-minute.

I casually pulled back my hand. After a couple of seconds, the wall shimmered.

"What the hell's going on?" Eric cried out. "How did you do that?" He moved closer to the wall, studying it intently, but he didn't make a move to touch it.

Pat's dark eyes squinted as they shot from the wall to me. "He didn't do anything," Pat said, staring at me. "He was just lucky enough to stumble onto it."

"Stumble onto what?" Eric asked in a disgusted tone.

"Tell him, Donny."

I suddenly sensed that Pat had suspected all along what we might find when we got here, but then again, I shouldn't have been surprised. Being an Indian, Pat had always believed in spirits, hoodoos, and all kinds of mystical happenings.

Looking Eric squarely in the eye, I said, "It's a portal to another time or dimension." The words seemed strange, even to my ears, but I stood my ground before Eric's obvious anger.

Eric pursed his lips in silence. His piercing hazel eyes darted from me to Pat and back to the wall. He shook his head in disbelief...or maybe denial. "This is a bunch of crap, Donny." His voice rose in anger, bouncing off the rock walls. "I can't believe you dragged us up here for *this*." He walked back down the path, then swung around. "Dammit, Donny, I canceled an important meeting today because you assured me you'd found something amazing and unique that would make us money. Then you show me some stupid magic trick. What the hell were you thinking?" He glanced at Pat with anger. "What'd you do, pull Pat into your little scheme, too?"

"It isn't a trick," I shot back. "If you don't believe me, watch." I turned and stepped through the wall.

On the other side, I sat on a rock and waited for Eric and Pat to follow me. I looked at my watch to check the time. The watch had stopped working. I tapped it a few times, but the battery must've died. Rather than spend ten bucks on a new battery, I'd probably just buy another seven-dollar watch from Wally-world.

After what seemed like about five minutes, I got tired of waiting and walked back through the wall.

Eric and Pat stood in the exact same places I had left them.

"I waited for you for five minutes," I whined. "I thought you would come through. Aren't you gonna try it?"

Pat chuckled. "You were only gone for a split second, Donny."

"No," I insisted, "I know I was over there for at least five minutes, but my watch stopped." I glanced at my cheap watch. Surprise, surprise. It was working again.

Pat piped up. "My turn. I'll be right back."

Before I could speak, Pat disappeared into the wall, then reappeared almost instantly with his face filled with awe. "Wow, that was amazing. So, Donny, how long was I gone?"

My eyes widened. I looked timidly at Eric. "It's a little spooky seeing it from this side."

"You can say that again," Eric replied.

I turned back to Pat. "You were only gone a split second." Sarcastically, I added, "Just like me."

Pat smiled. "I was gone at least a minute." He looked at his watch. "Hmmm, that's weird. My watch had stopped working over there, too, but now it's working fine."

"Mine, too," I exclaimed. I turned my head slowly upward toward the blue sky above with a few jet-stream trails. I felt a tug at the back of my mind. On the previous day, when I'd made my first trip through the portal, an airplane had been passing overhead before I had entered. Afterward, I had seen another plane in the same place. Now, I realized it was the *same* plane, the *same* moment as when I had stepped into the portal.

Filled with a sense of awe, I looked at my companions. "Time on this side stops when you go through. It stops until you come back." My mind reeled with the possibilities. "That means, we could stay over there for days, weeks, or months, and no one on this side would ever know."

Eric stood in a stupor, his eyes full of suspicion and fear. "I don't know how you two did that. I'm not sure I want to have anything to do with this. It's too weird." He looked at us warily. "I'm going back to town. You coming with me, Pat?"

Studying the wall and seeming lost in his own thoughts, Pat hesitated a little too long to satisfy Eric's impatience.

"Pat, give me your keys," Eric barked as he held out his hand. "If you and Donny want to stay here to fool around with this hocus-pocus, that's fine. He can give you a ride home. I'm outta here."

I felt a sudden desperation to have Eric's support and knowledge for future trips into the portal to find gold. I couldn't do it alone. Eric had a lot more experience, expertise, and foresight. He would make a better leader and know what to do when things got rough. Pat would be useful, but Pat didn't have the power of leadership like Eric. I had to convince Eric to stay.

"Wait," I protested as Pat drew the keys out of his pocket. "Let me prove this to you, Eric. Give me a chance. You're already here, so what have you got to lose? There's something you want on the other side. Something we all want...gold. Lots of gold. Come on, I dare you to go through that portal to get it."

Not giving Eric a chance to respond, I crossed in front of Pat and stepped into the shimmering mass.

* * *

I turned around to find Pat right behind me. "Do you think he'll come through, Pat?"

He put his keys back in his pocket. "I don't know, but if you're right about time standing still, we could be on this side for years while Eric's waiting over there. When we go back, he'll think we've only been gone a split second."

As I pondered this quandary, Eric stepped through the wall. He paused and looked around in confusion. "That's weird. All of a sudden, I'm facing the opposite direction. What happened?"

I didn't want to bother to explain.

"I thought you were going home," Pat commented.

"You two went through. I figured I might as well give it a try. Besides, you didn't give me your damn car keys."

I laughed, glad to have a chance to show Eric what I'd found. I took off down the wash.

"Where's the gold?" Eric yelled after me.

"Come on. You'll see."

As I came to the mountain ledge at the end of the canyon pass, the deserted desert valley below still came as a shock to me. The missing lake, missing houses, and missing roads made it seem like a master hand had wiped civilization off the face of the earth. I blinked a few times to make sure my eyes weren't playing tricks on me.

Smoke rose from the unseen camp in the distance. I hoped the Indians, or whoever lived there, were friendly. I put my hand on my gun to make sure it was still at my side.

Pat stepped next to me on the ledge. Excitement glittered in his eyes as he gazed across the valley. "Amazing."

"You didn't seem all that surprised by the portal," I said, dying of curiosity. "Why?"

Pat continued looking across the valley. "Among my people, we have a legend about a portal up in these mountains. We call it Blind Man's Gateway." He shook his head in amazement. "I never thought I'd be a part of that legend, but here I am on the other side."

"What do you mean? What's the legend about? Why do they call it Blind Man's Gateway?"

As Eric approached, he stood next to us and looked out over the valley.

Pat leaned closer to me and whispered, "I'll tell you later."

I wondered how much Pat and his tribe knew about the portal. Maybe Pat had important information that would be vital to our success, or even prevent our failure. Since Pat seemed so intrigued with the portal, I decided it had to be good news. Maybe the name Blind Man was to scare people off. At any rate, I couldn't wait to hear more about the legend.

Eric's reaction to the new world seemed tempered by suspicion and doubt. His eyes scanned the horizon with a deepening frown.

I stepped closer to him and gave him time to study the valley for a few minutes. Finally, I said, "Well, what do you think?"

"I'm not sure," Eric replied slowly. "Where's the town? Where's the lake? I'm still trying to figure out how all of this can be possible."

"Don't worry about *how*," Pat said reverently, "just know that it is and go with it."

"Let me tell you what happened yesterday," I said with growing eagerness to share my story. "It might help you understand what's going on a little better." I motioned to an array of large rocks where we sat down and took a swig of water from our water bottles.

Over the next ten minutes, I told them the details of what had happened to me the day before. At the end of my story, both Pat and Eric remained silent for a long time.

Finally, Eric said, "It just seems so unbelievable. I'm here, so I know it's real, but…"

Pat stood up. "Maybe it'll seem more real if we go down to the Indian camp. I want to know if these are my ancestors."

"That camp has to be at least ten miles away," Eric complained. "It'll take us all day to get there."

"So what?" I said, secretly hoping we could explore this new world a little more before going back. "We can be gone as long as we want. When we go back through the portal, no time will have passed. So, what difference does it make?"

"He's got a point," Pat said as he threw his pack over his shoulder and started down the hill.

"What if we don't get back before dark?" Eric called after him. "We don't have any gear or sleeping bags. We don't have food for the night. Let's come back another time."

Pat kept hopping downward from one rock to another.

"I'm going with him," I said eagerly, grabbing my pack and adjusting it on my back.

Reluctantly, Eric picked up his pack. He still seemed to be in a daze, like he couldn't quite get a grip on this new reality.

"Just make sure you have your guns available," I advised as I took off down the hill.

Even though the Indians could turn out to be unfriendly, the adventure excited me. Plus, if anything went wrong, Eric couldn't blame me for making the decision to go to the camp. That was Pat's doing.

Chapter 4

As the sun fell toward the west in the mid-March afternoon sky, I figured we had trudged over the rocky, hilly, brush-covered desert terrain for a least five hours, maybe six. My watch still didn't work and my feet ached in my boots.

The smoke from the Indian camp rose just over the next sandy bluff. Modern Lake Havasu City inhabitants called this area Crystal Beach, even though it sat mostly on a bluff and didn't have a real beach.

As we climbed up the gully toward the top of a ridge, I heard a dog bark in the distance.

Pat stopped. "Let's go cautiously. We don't want to frighten them."

We came over the ridge and walked across the hard-packed dirt of the bluff. A fifty-foot deep gully lay between our party and the next bluff, where the Indian camp sat, at least a half-mile away.

As we got closer, I could see more details in the camp: dozens of Indian men and women moving about their daily lives around a maze of low-roofed mud huts. Children played in the dirt. Some clung to their mothers, who carried large pots or woven baskets through the streets. This was a village, not a camp.

A dog barked again, then a loud yell came from the village proper.

Boom, BOOM, boom, BOOM.

The sudden beat of the drum sent chills down my spine. I wondered if this was how Lewis and Clark felt the first time they had encountered a tribe of Indians.

"They know we're here," Pat said casually, as though nothing seemed unusual.

We came to a stop at the edge of the bluff. A quarter of a mile away, even if we couldn't make out their faces, we could see their forms and they could see us.

A group of warriors moved toward the front of the village. Slowly, in small groups at first, men, women, and children began to gather in a wide line behind them.

I swallowed hard. In the open gully between us, there was no place to hide. Turning and running across the bluff and into the gully behind us was our only option, if it came to that. "What do we do now?" I asked.

"I think they're friendly," Pat said, his dark eyes studying them with interest.

"Maybe we should go meet them," I said, trying to show some leadership skills in the face of Pat's calm assessment and Eric's unexpected lack of direction. The fact that the Indians weren't whooping and hollering in a war dance added to my feeling that maybe they wouldn't attack. The sooner we got this over with, the sooner we could go home and make plans to get to the gold. "Let's go meet them." I took a deep breath and started down the hill.

Pat grabbed my arm. "Wait a minute, Donny. It might be best if we don't go toward the village just yet. They might feel threatened. Let's let them start toward us first, then we'll meet them halfway."

"Good idea," Eric readily agreed. "We'll also be able to run if they don't turn out to be friendly." His hand rested on the butt of his pistol.

A consultation took place among the Indians. A group of ten males broke from the crowd and began heading down into the gully between the village and our group.

"Okay," Pat said, "let's move slowly into the gully to meet them. Let them know we are friendly."

As I skidded down the sandy hillside, I mumbled, "I sure hope you're right about this, Pat." I left my gun in its holster, but, without being too obvious, kept my hand nearby and on alert.

* * *

As the ten Indians drew closer to us, they fanned out in a semicircle, reaching halfway around us.

I heard a scuffling noise behind me. Over my shoulder, I saw fifteen more Indians pour out from behind a knoll. So much for running away if things went sour. My hands began to sweat. I nudged Pat and nodded my head in the direction behind us.

Pat whispered, "I know. Don't worry. Everything's gonna to be fine." Pat's easy-going attitude seemed more convincing to me when the Indians were further away. Now, I didn't understand how he could remain so cool.

Twenty-five tall, big-boned, heavily built Indians surrounded us. Their strong facial features, dark skin, large noses, and broad foreheads, gave them a slightly Negroid look. On their faces, arms, and bodies, they sported tattoos, ranging from basic lines and swirls to intricate full-faced patterns, giving them fierce, menacing looks. They all wore loincloths and sandals. Slightly different patterns of shells, beads, and small dried animals had been woven into their long, black hair. Most of them carried what looked like clubs and tomahawks. Though these weapons wouldn't be as quick as guns, twenty-five of these big guys against three outsiders didn't put the odds in our favor.

A skinny old man with sparse gray hair stood at the forefront of the Indian group. He wore the most intricate tattoo I'd ever seen. Overlaying circles, triangles, and spirals, in various soft-toned colors of nature, filled his entire face and most of his chest. Horizontal stripes covered the rest of him, including his legs and arms. The old man raised his claw-like hands to his chest, then started singing and chanting. He shoved his arms, palms up, toward our group.

"I think he's trying to get us to leave," Eric muttered out of the side of his mouth.

Pat whispered, "I think he's their shaman. He seems to be praying to the ones who have passed on to the other side. He's asking for a sign…about…something…I'm not sure. I'm having trouble understanding some of the words."

Eric shot Pat a look of surprise. "You can understand him?"

"Why do you think I wanted to bring Pat along?" I boasted, taking credit for something I did right for a change.

A mean-looking six-foot-four Indian without any markings on his face or body stepped forward. He held a tomahawk with an obsidian head in his right hand and a wicked-looking war club made of deer antlers in his other. He stopped directly in front of Pat and spoke in an angry tone. "He's not sure if you are good or evil, so he's asking the old ones for guidance."

"Wait a minute," Eric blurted, "you speak perfect English."

Surprised, too, I kept silent, sensing things might not turn out so well with this guy, who I judged to be in his early thirties. I still kept my hand near my gun.

Pat stood his ground placidly, probably ticking off the Indian even more.

Ignoring Eric's comment, the enraged Indian glared at all three of us, with his eyes stopping on me. "I don't need the old ones to tell *me*. I say you're evil. I say we kill you. Right here and now." The muscles in the Indian's chest and arms tightened as he slowly lifted his war club and tomahawk in my direction.

My dream of the Indian slaughter flashed through my mind. I was about to draw my gun.

The old man immediately quit chanting, pulled a two-foot braided whip from the waistband of his loincloth, and, with fire in his eyes, slapped the younger Indian twice across his bare back.

The enraged Indian, still holding his weapons, dropped his hands and turned around. His face distorted in fury and shock. Blood oozed from the welts made by the whip.

The old Indian spoke sharply in his native tongue, eyes glaring like sharp needles at the younger Indian.

The angry one flinched and stiffly walked back to his original place in the line. As he stood there, his black eyes stared directly at me.

I wondered if he was the Indian I had followed into the portal. He made me uncomfortable so I looked away.

Facing us, the old man said in a raspy voice, "I sorry…O-cha…" He pointed his whip at the Indian, now standing with a sour look on his face. "O-cha no speak bad no more." The old man's English sounded like dialogue out of an old western.

A sense of relief washed over me that the Indians knew at least a little English. I wondered if there were other members who spoke as well as O-cha. If so, we would be able to communicate with them directly, rather than rely on Pat as an interpreter. I felt relief, too, that the old man, appearing to be the chief of the tribe, would keep us safe from harm from disgruntled Indians like O-cha. Still, I didn't want to cross the old man and bring down his wrath. Trying to make friends, I shifted toward the old man and braved a question. "How come you speak English? How did you learn it?"

With dark, intense eyes, the old man studied me closely. He looked me up and down. Finally, he smiled, raised his eyebrows a couple of times, and licked his lips.

I almost crapped in my jeans at the memory of being served for dinner in my dream.

"I tell later. Now…come…eat." He turned and said something to the other Indians. They tightened their circle, forcing us to be escorted into the camp.

I leaned close to Pat. "I'm not sure if we're prisoners or not. What do you think?"

Pat shrugged. "The old man seemed friendly enough. Then again, maybe he's just acting. All we can do now is wait and see what happens."

While Pat didn't sound all that worried, I wasn't so sure. I feared the old man's offer of food might be to fatten us up before we were served as the main course.

* * *

O-cha, the whipped Indian, led the procession up the gully toward the village on the bluff, which overlooked the river and flood plain.

Walking through the street, I got a better look at the homes: squat mud huts with slightly domed roofs that flattened out on top. Smoke rose above most of the roofs. The four-foot high openings into the huts seemed to contrast strangely with these tall Indians, who had to do a lot of stooping to get inside their homes.

As we passed one of the huts, I crouched down to look inside. From what I could tell, the twenty-foot-wide floor had been formed by digging a hole in the ground, maybe three or four feet deep. A mixture of mud and grass created the ceilings and walls. Next to the door, I noticed a flat, raft-like object that was made of poles lashed together and covered with grass and reeds. Being a little larger than the door opening, it looked like something that could be lifted into place if the weather got cold or the occupants wanted privacy.

A little further up the street, I saw a group of Indians building a new, much larger home. The sunken floor had a span of about forty feet. One group of Indian workers stuck ten long poles into the ground in a circle around a center pole. They placed a pole horizontally across the top of each pole to connect them, creating a header for the wall. They lashed poles from the header to the center pole, creating the support beams for the roof. Another set of Indians lashed together shorter poles and stacked them along the perimeter, forming the walls. It reminded me of building a wooden cabin, using poles and sticks instead of logs. When they finished, no doubt, the Indians would slather the walls with their mud-and-grass concoction.

The workers eyed us cautiously as we passed, but kept working on their tasks.

I noticed a three-foot-wide by ten-foot-long ramp extending from the roof of each dwelling to the ground. "What do you think those ramps are for?" I asked Pat.

"They give the occupants access to the roofs. There, they work on projects or keep an eye out for danger. They might use it as a stage to talk to crowds assembled on the ground for important meetings. We have a few of these huts on the reservation. Built just the same way. In fact, these people look a lot like some of the members of my tribe. Their facial features are familiar enough to make me want to look for some of my relatives." He scanned the faces of the Indians in the vicinity and seemed to be in a state of constant amazement.

Curious women, wearing only short skirts woven from grass or tree bark, stopped their weaving and meal grinding to watch us walk by. Naked children stood in slack-jawed awe or ran to hide behind their mothers' legs. We must have looked strange to them.

Fierce-looking wolf-dogs, seemingly upset by the intrusion of strangers into their territory, ran restlessly through the streets of the village. They barked and howled but, thankfully, kept their distance.

We came to a large hut built like the other dwellings, but much larger in size, with a door in each of the four walls. It had to be some kind of community hut, an Indian version of a convention center.

By this time, much to my relief, O-cha had disappeared.

Ducking under the door and entering the large room, it took my eyes a few moments to adjust to the dimness of the interior. A fire pit sat in the middle of the sunken floor. Grass mats and a couple of sets of mortar and pestle had been laid next to one of the back walls. I figured the women used them to grind up corn and nuts to make flour for their bread, or whatever they ate. I suddenly hoped they wouldn't feed us. I couldn't stomach the thought of eating snakes, lizards, or even worse, dog. *Yuck.* We still had some travel rations, enough in our backpacks for dinner this night and a light lunch tomorrow. We'd be okay without any Indian food.

A whole slew of male Indians entered from all four doors of the hut and stood around the room.

The old man motioned with an arc to the ground around the fire pit. "Sit, sit. Eat soon." He barked an order in his own language.

Two nearby Indians ran off, while two others stoked up the fire in the pit. The rest of the Indian entourage squatted on their heels against the walls or stood around the periphery.

Eric and Pat sat cross-legged on the dirt floor.

I sat down with my legs stretched out in front of me, relief for my aching feet. Despite the cooler weather over the desert at this time of year, the hike across the rocks, hills, and desert scrub had been long and arduous. Right now, a chilly late-afternoon breeze passed through the hut doors, making me grateful for the fire.

The old man squatted across from us on the other side of the fire.

Pat leaned forward, the first to speak. "What is your name?"

The old man smiled and tapped his chest. "Ku-mad-ha." Catching the puzzled looks on our faces, he called out to an Indian who stood on the fringes.

The Indian looked to be about thirty, one of the few men with no tattoos on his face. His narrow jaw, long beaked nose, and delicate features contrasted with the other members of the tribe and made him look more like the modern Indians I knew. In his long braided hair, he had woven what looked like a string of red, white, and blue beads, along with a strip of a red cowboy bandana.

Wow, that's strange, I thought. *None of the other men wear anything like that in their hair. He looks like an American patriot.*

The Indian squatted next to the old man and listened to him speak in his native tongue. He turned to Pat and said, "This is our shaman and chief. His name is Ku-mad-ha, which roughly translates as Iron Cactus."

Ku-mad-ha grinned from ear to ear, showing his three teeth, black nubs in his lower jaw.

Pat nodded in greeting. "I'm pleased to meet you, Iron Cactus. I'm Maspatamho. This is Donny and Eric."

Eric and I both nodded our greetings to the old shaman, then looked at Pat in shock.

"Hey," Pat said sheepishly, "it's my Indian name."

Eric chuckled. "No wonder we just call you Pat."

"Iron Cactus welcome you me home," the old man said. "Talk no good. He talk better." Iron Cactus added something in his own language to the younger man.

"Iron Cactus wants to welcome you to our village. He says his English isn't good and will talk through me, Beaver."

"How did you learn to speak English so well, Beaver?" Eric asked.

Beaver consulted briefly with Iron Cactus, who nodded his head.

"We have a group of warriors who are called the Keepers. It's our job to watch the Gateway you entered. We are allowed to cross over and spend time on your side in order to keep an eye on you. As a result, some of us are fluent in English, and most of our tribe can speak it a little bit."

That explained where he got the beads and bandana.

With unconcealed surprise, Eric leaned forward. "You're telling me that you and some of your friends here have been living among us? Studying us?"

"Yes."

Pat asked, "How long has this been going on?"

"About a hundred and fifty years," Beaver stated.

I suddenly wondered if anyone else from my own world had ever crossed to this side.

Before I could ask, two women entered the hut. One set down a platter filled with ears of corn, squares of squash, a large bowl filled with small brown beans, a stack of tortillas, and a pile of some kind of meat that had been cut into thin strips. The other woman handed each of the men around the fire pit a flat piece of wood to serve as a plate and a cup. The cups, about the size of an orange, seemed to be made out of a dried gourd that had been cut in half.

I feared the cups would tip over until I checked out the bottom. Apparently, the Indians only used the top half of the gourd where the stalk had been broken off. This left a flat, natural platform that made the cup unusually stable.

It had been a long time since breakfast, but when I was offered the food, I only took corn, beans, tortillas, and squash.

Seeing this, Beaver said, "Don't you eat meat?"

"I do, but…"

"But you're not sure what kind of meat this is, so you don't want to try it, right?"

I felt my face turn red. "Yeah, I don't want to eat dog meat or anything like that."

Beaver chuckled and shook his head. He turned and said something to his fellow warriors in his native tongue. When he was done, they hooted and laughed. Some of them barked like dogs at me.

I ducked my head in shame.

"Don't worry," Beaver said lightheartedly, "it isn't dog meat or rat meat or even lizard. It's rabbit and quail, and it's really quite good." He popped a piece into his mouth and chewed slowly, as if he was savoring the flavor of a steak he'd ordered in one of the finest restaurants in New York City.

Pat nudged my arm. "Donny, even if this was dog meat, it's rude to refuse their offer of food. So just eat whatever they put on your plate and pretend to like it."

One of the women poured us a clear liquid drink from a jug.

I pretended to take a sip, but instead, simply smelled it. I didn't care what Pat said, I wasn't going to eat or drink anything unless I knew what it was. Thankfully, my cup held only water.

Chapter 5

After the food was served, the warriors sitting along the wall and standing on the sidelines began to leave.

When only Iron Cactus and Beaver remained, Beaver began the conversation while we ate. "We did not know about the Gateway until the year 1852. That's when a man came through with a burro. He was looking for gold."

Somebody did have the same idea, I thought, paying more attention. *I wonder how that worked out.*

Chewing on a piece of rabbit, Eric said, "He must have been a prospector, wandering around the hills and looking for gold, and he just happened to stumble onto the portal."

"Our ancestors could not talk to him. They were curious where he had come from. They watched him closely. When he left, they followed him to the other side." Beaver picked up a stick and stirred the fire back to life. "What our ancestors saw over there scared them. Your kind were taking over the world by moving onto the land, setting up towns, making roads, building forts for your armies. Your kind had things they'd never seen or even dreamed of: iron pots, knives, woven cloth, and, of course, guns. These things could have made their lives easier. It would have been easy to get these things and bring them back, but when our ancestors saw how your people were treating the Indians on your side, they decided they didn't want anything to do with your kind."

I could relate to that. I felt a little embarrassed by the white man's behavior toward the Indians. But all that had changed years ago, so I didn't see why the Indians wouldn't want to update their primitive living conditions to something better now.

Beaver went on. "They formed a clan of warriors whose job was to keep an eye on your kind, to make sure you never found the Gateway."

Pat asked, "You and O-cha are part of this clan. That's why you don't have tattoos on your faces, right?"

Beaver nodded. "Our ancestors believed the Gateway could be used for good or for evil. We, the Keepers, guard it because we're afraid that one day evil men will come through. Then, our people and all the other tribes on this side could be wiped off the face of the earth."

I wasn't sure how a group of Indians with bows and arrows could keep a large, determined force like the U.S. Army out, but hey, who knew what the Indians could do? I had a feeling they knew a lot more about the portal than they were telling us.

"And you're afraid that we're these evil men?" Pat asked evenly.

Beaver smiled. "No. We have had visitors from your side a few times before. We have always been able to tell the ones who are going to be a threat."

The haunting images of my violent dreams flashed in front of my mind. "What would you do if you thought we were a threat?" I asked.

Beaver looked me square in the eye and said sharply, "We would have a ceremony and sacrifice you to the river gods."

I gulped, almost choking on the beans I was eating. I hoped Beaver and Iron Cactus would continue to believe we wouldn't be a threat. Even though Iron Cactus had protected us from O-cha, I sensed the chief, with those piercing brown eyes boring into me through a mean-looking face covered with tattoos, wouldn't hesitate for a moment to sacrifice us if he thought we were a threat to his village or way of life.

Pat interrupted my thoughts. "Donny, remember when I told you I'd explain about the legend later?"

I nodded.

"Everything he just said is exactly what I was gonna tell you."

"I'm fascinated by all of this," Eric broke in. His manner seemed freshly renewed, like he was back to his old self. He directed his words to Beaver. "You've been using the portal all this time, going back and forth between the two worlds whenever you want?"

"Not really," Beaver said. "The portal, as you call it, isn't always there."

Alarmed, I blurted, "What do you mean, 'it isn't always there'? We will be able to get back, won't we?"

Beaver shrugged, undaunted by my concern. "It comes and goes. Sometimes it's there for years. Then it will disappear for a while."

Eric shifted forward. "How long is a while?" He squinted at me with an if-we're-trapped-here-you're-dead look.

"Usually, it will disappear for around six months. Sometimes as long as two-and-a-half years. The timing seems to be determined by solar eclipses. On the day of an eclipse, it will open and stay open until the next eclipse, then it will close."

Pat groaned. "When was the last time it opened?"

Beaver seemed to be counting in his mind. "Three weeks ago."

"That's right," I said brightly. "I remember now. There *was* an eclipse three weeks ago."

Eric said, "You said *solar* eclipses. They are rare, right?"

"Not really," Pat offered. "I think they happen about every six months, don't they, Beaver?"

"Yes, but the Gateway doesn't open every time."

"Why not?" I asked. It seemed ironic that men from an advanced society like mine had to ask questions about eclipses of someone who lived like a barbarian.

"We're not sure. We think it has to be a total eclipse, not just a partial. All we really know is that it will be open sometimes. Then it will close."

"I assume," Pat interjected, "if you're on the other side when it closes, you have to stay there until it opens again. Right?"

Beaver nodded. "It happened to me once. I was stuck on your side for almost three years. That's one of the reasons I speak English so well. While I was there, I went to school and learned everything I could about your people, the language, the history, especially information involving the Indians and their customs."

Eric, finishing up his food, set his empty wooden plank on the ground and stared at me. "As soon as we get back home, I'm gonna do some research and find out when the next eclipse occurs, because I don't want to spend three years over here."

I looked to Beaver for a further explanation. "But even if we're trapped on this side, it doesn't matter, does it? Time stopped, didn't it? When we go back through, time will start from where we left off."

Beaver nodded. "That's right. And if you're hurt, your injuries will be healed when you go back to your own time. Also, if you d-"

Iron Cactus grunted and gave Beaver a dirty look.

I got the distinct feeling Iron Cactus had understood everything that had been said all along, and he didn't want revealed whatever little bit of information Beaver was about to part with. I glanced at Eric and Pat, who didn't seem to put any stock into what Beaver had just said, that injuries were healed. I considered it a bonus. I wanted to ask Beaver what would happen if someone from the other world died on this side, but with Iron Cactus listening in and censoring Beaver's words, this didn't seem to be the right time.

Iron Cactus said something to Beaver, who translated. "Ku-mad-ha wants to know why you came through the Gateway."

I explained in detail how I'd accidently found the portal and followed an Indian through. "I've been looking for gold up in those mountains. The area is marked on my map as potentially being a good place for finding gold. After I came to this side and saw how this world looked exactly like mine, other than the fact that the white man had not yet settled it, I began to think that maybe all the gold found later in my world, might still be here. That's why I came back. I wanted to find out more about this world and to look for gold."

"Have you ever had contact with the Spaniards?" Eric asked Beaver.

"Spaniards came through this world back in the 1600's and again in the 1700's. For some reason, they didn't stay long and never established missions along the California coast like they did in your world."

"Are there any white men in this world yet?" Pat asked.

"A few thousand live on the east coast. But you must understand something, we are not your past. We exist simultaneously with you."

The idea jolted me. "Are you saying this is an alternate world?" I had misconstrued this world as being hundreds of years earlier than my own. Going back in time seemed more plausible that perceiving this primitive world being un-evolved after so many years.

"Yes, and we don't know why our world developed differently than yours." Beaver shrugged. "Maybe Columbus never made it here. Maybe something happened overseas in England that changed the course of our history to make it different from yours. Whatever it was, it left this land alone. We do know from word of mouth across the Indian grapevine, there was never an Industrial Revolution here. Even though it is the same year here as in your world, this whole world is stuck in what you think of as the Middle Ages, though it pleases us to have our freedom."

Eric looked solemnly at me. "Now, I understand why you said your discovery could be worth money. You were planning to find gold here all along, weren't you?"

"Yeah, but I knew you'd never believe any of this unless you saw it for yourself."

"Okay, I'm here and I believe it." He turned to the tribe's leader. "Iron Cactus, do you or your tribe have a problem with us gathering up gold and taking it home with us through the portal?"

Beaver immediately answered for him. "No, we don't have a problem. We know the value of gold on your side. In fact, that's how we are able to stay on your side and watch you. We have been taking gold to the other side for more than a hundred years. We invest it and use the profits to support our warriors who spend time over there. Your biggest problem is going to be finding the gold, at least as much as you want."

"What do you mean?" I asked. "There's gold around here, isn't there? If this is the same world, and just the people and events are different, then the gold should still be in the same places that had been mined in our world."

"Not that much around here," Beaver said. "We've done our own mining and there's not much left around here. What we possess right now we had to get from other tribes that live north of here. What we have now will be traded on your side of the Gateway."

Eric looked gingerly from me to Pat, then set his expectant hazel eyes on Beaver. "That shouldn't be a problem. We'll bring goods to trade."

"That only works for small amounts," Beaver responded. "To get the amounts of gold you are looking for, you're going to have to go a long way to get it."

"How far is a long way?" Pat asked.

"At least four or five hundred miles north. We send out scouts, stay in touch with many tribes, keep an eye on where gold is found. As one of the Keepers, it is my job to know where we can get gold when we need it for our investments on the other side."

"I'm thinking Northern California," Pat said. "Sutter's Mill area."

Beaver nodded.

"*Damn*," Eric said, snapping his fingers. "That's a long ways."

"But it's doable, right?" I asked, looking at Eric hopefully. Just seeing Eric back in the leadership role gave me comfort that things would work out well. If Eric decided to do something, it would get done.

"Sure, I suppose. As long as Beaver and his people are willing to help us. Beaver, are there Indians living in the Sutter's Mill area? How would they react to us coming in and taking large amounts of gold?"

"Just as it used to be in your world, there are many tribes across the land here. Fortunately for you, they don't put much value in gold. To them, gold is just a pretty yellow rock that's heavier than a normal rock."

"Not to change the subject or anything," Pat interrupted, "but aren't you worried we'll go back to our world and tell someone where we got the gold?"

"Not really," Beaver said with a hint of a smile. "Who is going to believe you?"

Eric chuckled. "He's got a point. I'm having a hard time believing all this myself. And I'm here, seeing it firsthand."

Iron Cactus spoke a few native words to Beaver.

Beaver rose and helped Iron Cactus to his feet. "The chief invites you to spend the night here in the village. You can go back home tomorrow."

For the first time, I realized it had gotten dark. I had been concentrating so hard on the fascinating information and the talk of gold, I had forgotten about time.

Eric stood up and stretched. "I'd like to stay. It's too late to hike across the desert. We don't have any nighttime gear. That okay with you, Pat?"

"Sure." Pat got to his feet and brushed the dirt off his jeans. "I've always wanted to spend the night in a mud hut like this. See what it would be like to live like my ancestors."

Iron Cactus called out and the two women who had brought the food quickly returned. After a few words from the old man, the women hurried away, probably to get a hut ready for us.

Turning to Eric, Beaver said, "Come with me and I'll show you your hut." As an afterthought he added, "Come back here for your breakfast in the morning. The women find it easier to use the community hut to fix most of our meals. Plus it gives them a chance to sit around and gossip while they make the food."

I thought of it as kind of a precursor to restaurants in my world. Except here, you didn't have to pay to eat.

As we left the community shelter, I saw O-cha standing in the street with two other Indians. All three glared at our party as we passed. For some reason, O-cha's angry face stayed glued on me.

I hoped Chief Iron Cactus and Beaver could keep control over O-cha and his friends. Otherwise, I feared my nightmare of being killed and eaten might turn into reality by morning. Despite my exhaustion, I would have to keep vigilance through the night.

Chapter 6

The next morning at dawn, I found myself still alive after a heavy sleep. I turned my attention to getting back home and planning the expedition to find gold. My stomach churned with excitement.

Sitting in the community hut alone with Eric and Pat, I picked at the leftover rabbit, quail, and corn that sat before me. I edged closer to the fire, taking off the chill of the morning air. As the village men and women went about their tasks outside, I felt relieved to see no sign of O-cha.

"When we get back home," I exclaimed to my companions, "I'll do some research and find the locations of the largest gold strikes. That way, we'll know where to go when we come back." My mind raced forward, ready to formulate a detailed plan. I wished I had my computer to start my research now.

"Make sure you don't pick places where the gold will be hard to get to," Eric advised. "We don't want to be doing a lot of hard-rock mining."

"Good idea," I added thoughtfully, pushing my food away. "I didn't think about that."

Eric gobbled up my remaining rabbit and quail, as though he hadn't eaten for ages. "That place in Northern California, Sutter's Mill," Eric said between bites, "might be a good place to go. I think most of that gold was taken from rivers using sluice boxes and gold pans."

My eyes lit up. "Yeah, that would be a great place to go."

"As long as the Spaniards that came through didn't take the gold," Eric added.

"I hate to throw water on your fire," Pat said to me, "but have you considered how we're gonna get there and how we're gonna haul all this gold back?"

"Nooo, I didn't." I suddenly realized I hadn't seen any horses or animals, other than dogs. We couldn't drive a four-wheeler or Jeep through the Gateway. The passage was too narrow and inaccessible. Plus, the lack of roads and fuel made that option unfeasible.

"We'll bring our own horses, if we have to," Eric announced.

"We have horses," Beaver said, entering the hut. The cold air didn't seem to bother his bare skin. He didn't even have goose bumps.

"Can we borrow some for our trip?" I asked hopefully.

"I don't see a problem. They aren't used to riders, though."

"We'll figure that out," Eric said as he finished off the last of my meal and stood up. "We'll need one or two of your people to go on this trip with us…for a guide and camp helper. Do you think that's possible?"

Beaver nodded. "We can make arrangements."

I jumped up and threw my backpack over my shoulder. "Great. Let's get going." I wanted to get out of there before O-cha caused more trouble. Maybe by the time we returned, O-cha's steam would be cooled.

* * *

Hours later, after the rigorous, uphill hike under the beaming sun, now high in the sky, my body ached as I approached the portal with my companions. Daydreams of being rich and surrounded by beautiful babes had followed me all the way up the tough climb, keeping my mind distracted. Now, coming up on the portal, I crossed my fingers that we could get through to the other side.

Eric in the lead, back to taking charge, slowed as he approached the rock wall. "Let's hope it's still open. If not, we might be here for a long time."

"Wait a minute," I called out. I stepped up to the "convenient" bolder I had sat on a few days before, balled up my fist, and punched the rock hard, splitting the skin on my knuckles.

"Why the hell did you do that?" Eric asked in his condescending, parental tone.

"I'm doing an experiment," I responded caustically. My knuckles burned. Blood seeped through my skin. "I'm gonna see if I'll be healed after I go to the other side, like Beaver said."

Pat rolled his eyes in disbelief, stepped forward, and disappeared through the portal.

"I guess it's still open," Eric said as he followed.

"Of course, it's still open," I mumbled to myself. "I never once had any doubt about it." I hurried through to join the others before it closed on me, leaving me behind.

Arriving on the other side, I looked at my hand first thing. No blood. No burning. No pain. It was healed. Holding it out, I said self-righteously, "See?"

Eric took my hand and examined it closely. His jaw dropped as he looked on in awe. "I didn't really believe Beaver when he told us about this."

Pat's eyes, wide with surprise, studied my hand, too. "To tell you the truth," he reluctantly admitted, "neither did I. I figured it was just a part of the legend, too good to be true."

"This whole thing is too good to be true," I said as we started down the canyon. Filled with renewed enthusiasm, I didn't see how we could go wrong on our adventure. "We need to take advantage of this opportunity while we can. Think about it guys, this is like winning the lottery...only better...because nobody else knows about it. If we play our cards right, we can have the best of both worlds."

Pat glanced at Eric. "He's right. Imagine the vacations we could take over there when we want to escape."

"Yeah," I added excitedly. "And hunting trips. No game wardens to harass us. No limits on how many animals we can take."

"Even better," Pat added, playing along with my fantasies, "we could take a trip down through Mexico to the tropics. Can you imagine spending a month in Puerto Vallarta? Nobody around except the natives, catering to our every need?"

Eric laughed. "Now, that would be great."

When I exited the canyon and looked out over the valley, I sighed with relief to see the familiar, manmade landmarks of the lake, roads, and town. I couldn't wait to get home to plan the next excursion through the portal. So far, with Eric enthused, Pat intrigued, and the Indians being friendly enough, everything was going better than I had expected. Now, just to figure out the eclipses and how to time the entries and exits through the portal so that we could get in and out without being stuck.

Meanwhile, I buried the potential problems with O-cha and my dread-provoking nightmares in the back of my mind. I had others things to think about.

* * *

Later that night, I slouched in one of the cushioned chairs next to Eric's lighted pool. Eric and I drank beers, while Pat preferred whiskey.

"Did you find out when the next eclipse is, Eric?" Pat asked, setting his glass on the table.

"In five months…mid-August."

"That's good," I exclaimed. "We'll have plenty of time to get our gold and be back before the portal closes."

"Yes," Eric stated, looking at me with a slight glare. "And we'd better be back by then, because I don't want to stay over there for two-and-a-half years,"

I sat up. "Two-and-a-half years? You're kidding me, right?"

"Nope. That's when the next total eclipse occurs." Eric left his beer can on the table and stretched out in his chair, his hands locked behind his head. "From what I read, eclipses come in cycles, roughly every six months, usually two a year. Only *some* of those can be what they call a 'total eclipse,' meaning the sun and moon are exactly aligned. The others are partials.

"Assuming Beaver's right, that the portal isn't affected by partial eclipses, I only checked the dates for total eclipses. I learned they have a cycle of their own. A total eclipse will be followed by another one six months later. The next pair won't occur until another twenty-eight to thirty months after that."

Pat stared into his whiskey and spoke with a dour tone. "So, three weeks ago, an eclipse opened the portal. In five months, another one will close it. That doesn't give us a whole lot of time to do our thing over there, barring that Beaver is right about the eclipses."

Anxious to keep the excitement about the trip from fizzling out, I said eagerly, "Five months. That's plenty of time if we go right away. Besides, we can always go back for more gold later if we have to cut the trip short. We can use some of the gold from this trip to better prepare for the next one."

"Maybe so," Eric said, sitting up and reaching for his beer. "I'm really concerned about the time. I sure don't want to spend three years living over there in a mud hut and eating quail and fish every day."

I pulled out my smokes and lit one. "How long would it take? A month to go north, two months to collect the gold, and a month to get home. No problem."

After a long pause, Pat shrugged and looked at Eric. "We could probably do it in four months. I estimate we could cover twenty-five-miles a day on horseback. If the distance is around six hundred miles from the village like we figured, we should make it in about twenty-four days."

Warily, Eric ran his hands through his thick brown hair. "We won't make that kind of time the first few days. None of us is used to riding. Been a long time since I've been on a horse. We're gonna be sore as hell for the first week or so."

"Yeah," Pat admitted. "But even if we only make ten miles a day the first week, we'll still be able to make it up there in less than a month."

Eric downed the last of his beer and slammed the can on the table. "I don't know...maybe." He turned to me. "Steve told me what happened the other day. Do you think you can get your shit together long enough to get everything on your end ready in the next couple of days? If so, I'll consider it. Pat and I have other responsibilities, so it's up to you to help take care of a lot of the details. I don't want to be dallying around and losing time because you can't get your act together."

"You don't have to worry about me," I snapped resentfully, my old anger at Eric's authoritative bullshit rising again.

"Okay, if you're ready and if we all agree that, should we run out of time, we stop collecting gold and head back. Rather than push our luck, I'm willing to end up with a little bit of gold and make it home. Are you with me?"

Pat nodded.

I followed with a weak nod, still bitter about Eric's putdown.

"Good," Eric said, slapping his hand on the table. "Let's make some plans. I've got a long list of things on my mind that have to be accomplished, starting with how many other people we need to take with us."

"What?" I cried. "Why do we need to take anyone else?" I didn't want other people knowing our secret about the portal. I had found the golden goose, and someone else could screw it up. The government could come in and take control.

"We need some backup over there, Donny. In case we run into trouble."

"What about Steve and his landscaping crew?" Pat offered. "They know how to use picks and shovels."

"Not Steve," I whined. I wanted nothing to do with the man. I especially didn't want him to come along with us on this once-in-a-lifetime money-making trip, not after he had fired me.

Eric and Pat ignored me and began discussing the options of who to invite and the importance of not telling anyone about the portal closing in five months. Next, they discussed the supplies we would need, including the gear that I was to pick up for them and myself.

Knowing that I wouldn't be able to pay for what we needed, I worriedly asked, "Who's gonna pay for the supplies?"

Eric sighed. "I suppose I'll have to foot the bill, since I know *you* can't."

"I can help with part of it," Pat offered.

"That's okay," Eric said, holding up a hand. "I'll give Donny one of my credit cards to use to get the stuff."

Pat smiled. "I guess we now know who's in charge of our supplies."

"Can you handle that, Donny?" Eric asked with arched eyebrows.

"Yes," I said grudgingly, "I can handle it."

"Good," Eric replied sharply, dismissing the subject and pissing me off. "If you have any problems, let me know."

Like usual, Eric was already taking over everything and bossing me around like one of his employees, not listening to my ideas or giving me credit for my contributions. I almost wished I had never told Eric about the portal in the first place. Now, I was stuck with my big brother's arrogance for the whole trip.

I dropped angrily back in the chair. *This is my discovery...my plan. How come this always happens to me?*

Chapter 7

Once I got home, I was actually looking forward to finding suitable locations for gold mining and mapping out our route. I spent half the night researching the biggest gold strikes I could find. I looked for ones close to Lake Havasu first, hoping to limit our travels, but, unfortunately, almost all the gold recovered in Arizona came from the byproduct of mining for other minerals like copper, silver, and lead. Also, most of the mining was hard-rock mining.

Aware that the most famous gold strikes occurred in Colorado and California, I decided to check out California first, which turned out to be a literal gold mine, with Sutter's Mill being at the top. On January 24, 1848, James Marshall spotted pea-sized nuggets in a mill raceway on the South Fork of the American River. Once word got out, thousands of prospectors rushed to the area to seek their fortunes. Some, like the Murphy brothers, succeeded. They struck gold a few days after arriving and, by the end of the year, had taken out $1,500,000 of gold. The website claimed that, in 2005 dollars, with gold at $400 an ounce, the Murphys' take would be worth over $37 million. Now, seven years later, with gold jumping to over $1600 an ounce, I calculated it to be worth over $148 million.

Eager to collect my share, I listed the sites in order from south to north, starting with the Murphy-brothers site, then moving north to Weber's Creek. If we could carry more gold than we found in those locations, we would move on to Sutter's Mill. Two more sites in the northern part of the gold fields, Bidwell's Bar and Rich Bar, looked to be the most promising. Rich Bar, one of the sandbars located on the North Fork of the Feather River, had produced huge amounts of gold. Rich Bar alone produced enough gold to be worth over $561 million in 2005. That came to over two billion in today's dollars.

Wow. Soon, some of that very gold will be mine.

I pushed my chair away from the computer and headed for bed. I made a mental note to order topographical maps off the internet so I could plot out our course. I needed to identify the exact coordinates of the strikes. With limited time, I didn't want to be wandering around the general area, hoping I'd stumble onto the gold. I had to know exactly where to look.

Lying on my sunken mattress, I thought about what I could do with all that money: a cabin in the Pacific Northwest, the latest hunting gear, high-powered rifles, girls in the local bars. As I turned over, I decided a new mattress was going to be one of the top items on my list.

* * *

I stood proudly with self-confidence on a stage and waved to a crowd of thousands of people. They cheered and called out to me.

An old Indian, with an intricate tattoo on his face, made his way through the crowd. He came to stand in the front row, right below me. Lifting his hands, the Indian said something I couldn't understand. He made a shoving motion with his hands as if he was trying to shove me away.

No, *I thought,* he isn't shoving me away. He's holding something in his hands.

The old man motioned for me to take it.

Bending down, I reached out.

The Indian held up a gourd-cup.

Accepting it, I put it to my lips to take a drink. The cup was empty. Not sure what the Indian wanted me to do with an empty cup, I leaned back toward the him. "What am I supposed to do with this?"

"Answer it," the old man replied.

The cup started to ring like a phone.

Confused, I held the cup up and studied it. When it rang again, I put it to my ear.

The old man started laughing. The people standing around the Indian started laughing. Pretty soon, the whole crowd was laughing so hard, they had tears rolling down their cheeks

"Not the cup, stupid," the old Indian said. "Answer your phone." In a puff of smoke, he disappeared.

* * *

I jerked upward in my bed as my cell rang, vibrating on the bare wood of the nightstand.

"Yeah," I croaked into the phone, my voice gravelly from drowsiness and too many smokes the night before.

"Rise and shine, Little Brother. It's seven o'clock. We've got a full day ahead of us, so get your ass out of bed. Be at my house in an hour."

It pissed me off that Eric could sound so cheerful this early in the morning. It was barely light outside. "And what if I'm not there in an hour?" I shot back, just to be annoying.

"Don't cop an attitude with me, Donny. This thing was your idea. If you want to be involved, you're gonna have to conform to a schedule, just like the rest of us."

"What schedule?" I swung my legs out of the bed, slid on my slippers, and lit up my morning smoke.

"Whatever schedule I make," Eric barked.

I cringed at the thought of getting another one of Eric's lectures. I figured I might as well start getting ready while I listened. I activated the hands-free speaker and set the phone on the bathroom counter while I used the toilet.

Eric's voice erupted from the speaker. "We need each other's help to pull this off….You've never been a team player….Don't screw this up…." *Blah, blah, blah.*

I finished, then flushed.

"Are you listening to me, Donny?"

"Yeah, Bro, but I'm getting ready, too."

"You'd better be. This is too good an opportunity. I won't stand by and let you screw it up."

"I won't screw it up," I snapped as I picked up my phone. "I've got to get ready. See ya in a bit." I ended the call and slammed the phone down so hard the plastic cracked. *Another cheap phone*. Luckily, I always bought the extra insurance with my phones, because I ended up breaking at least two or three a year.

As I brushed my teeth, my anger at Eric melted away and the memory of my dream of the old Indian floated into my mind. It wasn't the weirdest dream I'd ever had, but something about it bothered me. The old Indian had been trying to tell me something important before the phone rang.

I shrugged it off, put coffee on to brew, dressed, and drank a quick cup of sugar-laden coffee before I grabbed up my keys, gold-strike notes, and took off.

* * *

As I entered Eric's kitchen, a large box of donuts and pastries sat on the marble countertop. The smell of freshly brewed coffee filled the house.

I nearly cringed when I saw Steve sitting at the table with Pat and Eric. *So, that's what this is all about.*

Steve's squinty blue eyes gave me a passing glance as he sipped his coffee leisurely.

Eric got right down to business. "Donny, tell Steve what happened the day you found the portal."

Yeah, right. I poured myself a cup a coffee, loaded it with sugar, picked up a chocolate-covered donut, and sat down at the table. Over the next ten minutes, I shared my story while Steve watched, a mixture of disbelief, uncertainty, and curiosity crossing his rugged face.

Eric filled Steve in on the second trip. When he finished, he said, "We'd like you and your crew to go over with us."

Steve's brow raised. "That's quite a tale." Looking from one to the other, he tapped his fingers nervously on the table, as if deciding what to say.

Eric sat back without a word.

Pat leaned his forearms on the table while his hands caressed his coffee cup.

The only sound in the room came from Steve's constant *TAP, tap, tap, tap.*

I remembered the Indian drums in my dream. The one where the young Indian girl had pulled out a knife and stabbed me in the chest.

TAP, tap, tap, tap. BOOM, boom, boom, boom.

I shifted uncomfortably, thinking this might be another bad omen.

Steve's voice finally shattered the tense silence. "If Donny was the only one telling me this story, I wouldn't believe a word of it."

I groaned inwardly. *Nobody ever believes me. The story of my life.*

"But since you, Eric, and Pat seem to believe all this happened, I'm convinced you're either telling me the truth, or you're playing a cruel practical joke on me."

"This is no joke," Pat stated flatly, his brown eyes serious. "We'll take you through to the other side and introduce you to Iron Cactus in person, if you want."

Steve's husky six-foot frame fell back in his chair. He sighed heavily. A look of indecision sat on his face. He shook his head. "I don't know. It sounds crazy. I guess, if I saw it for myself…"

This was exactly what I had feared. Nobody would believe the portal existed until they'd gone through and seen it for themselves. I was willing to bet that Eric would stick me with taking them through, forcing me to be their tour guide, while he and Pat stayed home and did nothing. Yeah, right, he and Pat had *other* responsibilities. He just wanted to dump all the work on me.

Pat said to Steve, "The workers you choose will need to go through also."

"I don't think we need more than ten people," Eric said, "maybe twelve people."

I interrupted sharply. "Counting the four of us, we only need six more."

"Okay," Steve said, leaning forward against the table, "I've got six guys working for me that I'm pretty sure will be interested in going with us." He shook his head and chuckled. "Jeez, listen to me. I sound like I really believe we're actually going somewhere."

"We *are* going somewhere," Pat declared.

Eric got up to fill his coffee cup and get another donut. "I want my doctor, Kathy O'Neal, and her nurse, Trish Mattea, to come. We may not need medical assistance, but it would be nice to have them along…just in case."

"That brings us up to twelve," I complained, trying to hold back my irritation that the party was getting too big. The more people involved, the longer it would take to get everyone organized. "That's enough."

"Steve," Eric said, ignoring me and taking control, "talk to your guys. See who's interested. Arrange a time with Donny for him to take you through the portal."

See. I knew it. He's gonna make me do the dirty work while he sits at his computer and plays games.

Eric continued. "I'll try to convince Kathy and Trish to go on the same trip, so Donny doesn't have to go over twice."

I couldn't believe Eric actually considered the inconvenience it would be for me to cross the portal multiple times.

Then, Eric added, "We don't want to offend Chief Iron Cactus and his tribe by making too many trips."

I wanted to shout, *What about me? Don't you care how I feel?* Instead, I shoved half a chocolate donut in my mouth, earning me a disapproving glare from Eric. I chomped noisily, silently daring Eric to reprimand me in front of his friends.

As Eric gave Pat instructions, I reached into my back pocket for the locations of the gold strikes. "You want to know what I found in my research?"

Pat shook his head. "I don't think we need to cover that today, do we, Eric?"

"No. We've got more important things to do. We can look at them later."

I angrily shoved the papers back into my pocket. *Maybe I shouldn't be here. Maybe I shouldn't tell them where to find the gold. They can go sightseeing while I split off on my own with a couple of Steve's workers. When I come back loaded down with gold, they'll be sorry. They'll beg me to show them where I found my cache. I'll just ignore them like they ignore me.* I knew this was childish, but I hated being forced to the periphery. If it wouldn't have been for me, they wouldn't even be having this discussion, let alone planning a trip.

"Donny," Pat said, pulling me back into the conversation, "when you take the group through the portal, keep a close eye on them. Don't let anyone do anything stupid to make Iron Cactus and his people mad at us. We need their help to pull this off."

"It's also gonna be up to you," Eric added, "to convince the group to go back with us for the gold. Unless we have at least nine or ten other people, I'm cancelling this whole affair until a future date. Got it?"

"Okay," I agreed halfheartedly, resenting the fact that this trip was spiraling out of my control.

As usual, Eric held the reigns, especially now since he was financing the trip.

Eric's such a tight-ass with his money, he'll probably send a bill out to everybody that goes with us, hoping to be reimbursed for his expenses.

I couldn't wait another two or three years for the portal to open again. I had to make it work now because I didn't what to get another job. I'd seen enough of the other side to know I couldn't do it alone. For one thing, O-cha scared me. O-cha was in the prime of his life, in excellent physical condition, and seemed determined to keep my world separated from his own. If O-cha challenged me to a fight, I wouldn't last thirty seconds.

As Pat and Steve got up to leave, Eric dialed Kathy and made an appointment. When he got off the phone, he said, "Donny, I want you to go with me to talk to Kathy and Trish. I'll meet you there this afternoon at two."

I nodded in agreement, dragged myself up from the table, emptied my coffee cup in the sink, and strolled out to my beat-up truck, which was sitting next to Eric's shiny Lexus. I pulled out of the driveway, distracting myself from my troubles by thinking about what kind of sports car I'd buy when I got back with all my gold.

Chapter 8

At home, I made a list of supplies on my word-processing program. Switching back and forth between my list and the internet, I compiled an impressive inventory of tools and equipment I thought we would need to collect gold. I made sure everything I chose was small, portable, and light-weight.

Two or three people could share a sluice box, so five Keene folding sluice boxes topped my list, followed by gold pans, shovels, picks, rakes, hammers, and chisels. I included a book on how to find and recover gold from rivers and streams and a scale to weigh the gold.

What else? Hmmm.

I almost forgot to add sacks to carry the gold in. A quick internet search brought me to a site selling heavy-duty canvas money bags.

Eric wouldn't be happy about the $150 price tag, but we needed the best we could find, and it'd pay off in the end. Cheap bags would break open, spill our hard-won gold all over the ground. Besides, Eric could afford the best. He'd made a few million bucks since he'd started his construction business. He always told me, "If you're gonna buy something, spend the money to buy the best."

Of course, for myself, I only bought the cheapest items I could find. *Yeah, if I had Eric's money, I'd splurge, too.*

Nothing cheap for this trip. Armed with Eric's credit card, I was going to take his advice and go for the best of everything.

At noon, my stomach rumbled. Shutting down the computer, I wandered into the kitchen to find something quick and easy: a peanut-butter-and-jelly sandwich and a box macaroni and cheese. As I waited for the water to boil, I realized I had forgotten to put topographic maps on my list. I made a mental note to add them later.

While I ate, I started a handwritten list of personal items I'd need to take along. I started with clothes, including a coat and gloves, in case the weather was cold in Northern California. Rather than take cigarettes, I'd take a pipe and a couple of large pouches of tobacco. That would take up less room than the three or four cartons of smokes I'd need for five months. I definitely needed my pistol and extra boxes of ammunition. I planned to take my 30.06 hunting rifle, too. Assuming we would be living off the land, I'd help supply the camp with a deer or an elk now and then.

I decided to make sure everybody had a rifle. Judging from the little I'd seen on the other side, we could run into a bear or other dangerous creature, four-legged or two-legged.

A knife, a sharpening stone, and a couple of BIC Lighters topped off my list. I didn't know how the Indians made fire, but I wasn't about to sit around rubbing two sticks together. I added a flint and steel fire-making kit to the list, just in case the lighters got lost or broken.

I looked at the clock. It was time to head to the doctor's office. Although I liked Eric's idea of having medical aid available, I found the idea of bringing women along repulsive. *If they're like most women I know, they'll be whining and complaining every inch of the way.* I hoped they would decide not to go.

* * *

The receptionist led us down a hallway to a door marked *Private*. As I entered Doctor Kathleen O'Neal's office behind Eric, I was pleasantly surprised. The woman sitting behind a small wooden desk was a fox. Eric introduced her as Kathy. In her mid-thirties, her shoulder-length brown hair framed a perfectly proportioned tanned face. Although she looked athletic, I couldn't see her full body behind the desk, stacked with manila files and papers, but her big brown eyes and seductive mouth left me wanting to see more.

A tall, big-boned woman in purple scrubs sat in a chair next to the desk. Eric introduced her as Trish Mattea, Kathy's nurse and good friend. Her short blond hair, chubby cheeks, and pudgy nose made her face look piggish. She represented what I referred to as "hefty."

Eric dove right into the story of the portal as I sat in a chair and continued to study the doctor. She didn't have the glamorous looks of a supermodel; more like the girl next door, eye-catching and attractive in a natural sort of way. Glancing at her hand, I noticed she wasn't wearing a wedding ring. *I wouldn't mind spending a few months in a tent with her.*

My overactive imagination kicked into gear. As Eric rattled on, I fantasized finding romance and adventure with the decadent doctor on the upcoming trip. Out in the wilderness, we would pitch a tent away from the camp and explore our own personal escapades.

"I've got to admit, I'm intrigued," Kathy said, jarring me back to reality. "But I'm having a hard time believing there's an alternate world and that you've found a portal into it."

Trish's eyes glimmered with excitement. She seemed to almost bounce off the chair. "I believe you, I believe you," she exclaimed in a high-pitched, squeaky voice that sounded like nails on a chalkboard.

I cringed as her shrill continued.

"I've always thought alternate worlds existed. But I never thought I'd get the chance to see one for myself."

God, if she goes along, I'm gonna have to stay as far from her as possible. I gave her a surly stare.

"I don't know," Kathy said, folding her arms across her chest in doubt. "It sounds a little farfetched to me."

Eric's voice dropped a little in disappointment. "I was hoping we wouldn't have to take you through the portal in order to convince you. We already have a large group going over, and I don't want to impose on Iron Cactus and his village."

Kathy tucked a strand of brown hair behind her ear and seemed hesitant. "If you're so concerned about upsetting these so-called Indians who live on the other side, why not make two trips?"

"Same problem," Eric responded. "We don't want to interrupt the Indians' lives any more than we have to."

I sensed Kathy didn't believe a word of what Eric had told her. Knowing how badly Eric wanted her to go, and feeling an urge of my own to convince her to go along, I got an idea to appeal to her medical side. I sat forward and put enthusiasm into my voice. "We thought you'd be interested in seeing how these people live. They seem pretty strong and healthy, but you could talk to them about the medicines they use, how they heal someone who is sick. They might have some tricks or special herbs that you could use in your practice."

A look of interest flashed through Kathy's golden-brown eyes.

Trish jumped in. "You're always telling me anything's possible, Doctor O'Neal. Were you just saying that, or do you really believe it?"

In silence, Kathy stared at Trish with a look of perplexity, as though she had been caught off-guard. It occurred to me that Kathy was trying to figure out how to get out of going on the trip without looking like a liar.

"Come on, Kathy," Eric pleaded, "give us a few hours of your time. What can it hurt, just to go take a look at the other world?"

"Please?" Trish begged, sitting up in her chair with her hands folded like in a prayer and her eyes bugging out.

Finally, Kathy held up her hands in resignation. "Fine. I'll go. I need a break anyway, and I've been thinking about taking a hike on the desert. This way, at least, I'll have some company."

"When can we go?" Trish asked, squirming in her chair like a little kid needing to go the bathroom. "I don't think I'll be able to sleep until we go."

"Steve said he would have his guys at the rendezvous location tomorrow morning at seven," Eric said. "Can you make it that soon?"

Kathy picked up the phone and spoke to her receptionist. When she finished, she announced, "Okay, I've cleared my schedule for tomorrow. I'll be ready to go."

After Eric gave her the details of where the group would meet, Kathy stood up and stepped from behind the desk

I resisted the urge to whistle. Her form-fitting black skirt accentuated her curves and ended at mid-thigh, allowing me to see her shapely, well-tanned legs. A neatly pressed white doctor coat and white blouse topped off her outfit. I smelled her light perfume as she moved closer to shake my hand. "Thank you, Doctor O'Neal," I said, giving her my best smile.

She cocked her head slightly to the left and smiled warmly. "Call me Kathy."

A wave of nervous excitement flooded me. "You can ride in my truck with me if you want to. I could pick you up around ten minutes to seven…if that's okay with you?" I quickly added. My hands started sweating.

"Fine. We'll see you here tomorrow morning." She escorted us to the door, picked up a clipboard, and with an excited Trish right behind her, headed down the hallway to an examining room.

I stared after her, lost in a haze of lust.

"Forget it, Donny," Eric said, pushing me toward the exit. "She's way out of your league."

"Maybe…maybe not," I replied, following Eric out the door. I felt I might not have a shot at her right now, but things were going to change after I got the gold. I'd be able to buy her a big house and take care of her. She wouldn't have to work. I'd show everyone, especially Eric, that I could be responsible.

* * *

When I pulled up the next morning, Kathy and Trish stood in the parking lot next to a newer car. They each had a small backpack sitting at their feet and looked ready to go. Kathy wore tight jeans and a tight blue t-shirt, showing off her trim figure. I liked the way she had her hair pulled back a ponytail. It made her look young and innocent. *Oh, yeah.*

For some reason I suddenly felt awkward. Insecurity began replacing the confidence I had felt in the office when I had met Kathy. I was glad Trish was there to act as a buffer.

"Morning," I said as Kathy slid across the bench seat and settled in next to me. To Trish, I also said, "Good morning." To cover up my lack of knowing what else to say, I turned up the stereo and pretended to be deep in thought about the upcoming trip, all the while, thinking about how sexy Kathy looked.

I slipped the truck in gear and pulled out of the parking lot. The tight squeeze of three people on the bench seat forced the warmth of Kathy's thigh against mine, making it hard for me to think of anything else. I hoped I could concentrate enough on my driving to get us to the designated meeting place without wrecking my truck.

After a ten-minute drive, with no conversation, I pulled up to the parking lot. As I jumped out of the truck, I was glad to see that all the men wore pistols strapped to their waists.

After I introduced the women, Steve began introducing the men. Because I had only worked for Steve a short time, I didn't know any of them well. I decided to use this opportunity to study them closer as potential future companions.

"The two oldest men are brothers, James and Tory," Steve said.

The two fortyish men smiled shyly and nodded to the two women.

"They're originally from Wyoming and are as solid and reliable as they come. If we need them, they'll be our horse wranglers, since they know about everything there is to know about horses."

Other than being dressed alike in jeans, boots, and cowboy hats, the two men didn't look much like brothers. James stood taller by a couple of inches and outweighed Tory by at least twenty-five pounds. Even though both had sandy blond hair and blue eyes, Tory's face was chiseled and rugged while James's face was rounder and softer. James wore a short mustache and long sideburns, while Tory's clean-shaven face added to the sharpness of his features.

Steve moved on to the next guys. "These two muscle-bound goons are Chad and Travis."

Obviously the youngest members of the group, each mumbled a quiet hello. They looked to be in their early twenties, with the easy camaraderie of best friends. Well over six-feet tall, they both exhibited the classic physique of bodybuilders, men who worked out regularly.

If I had to guess, I'd say they had both come from California. They had that west-coast, beach-bum look: tanned, muscle-bound, and good-looking...every girl's dream. Just the kind of guys I always lost the girls to. Even though I didn't know Chad and Travis, I disliked them already and hoped they'd stay away from Kathy. I thought she was too old for them, but with guys like that, you never knew.

"Next," Steve announced, "are my two foremen, Sergio and Juan. They've been with me since I started my business and they're like brothers to me."

In their mid-thirties, neither Mexican displayed the bulging muscles of Chad and Travis, but both looked to be in excellent condition.

I had worked with a few superstitious Mexicans in the past. I hoped these two wouldn't balk when it came time to go through the portal.

"Okay, now that we all know each other," Steve said, "let's go see this portal to another world." He sounded like he really believed the portal existed, while the other guys smirked and seemed to be going along just to humor Steve. I had to wonder if Steve was paying them their normal wages for the day. It was highly likely, which explained their good spirits. Getting paid to go for a hike on the desert sounded like a perfect day at work to me.

I felt confident that once I disappeared into the portal, they would all become believers. I just hoped the portal was still there. If not, I would be making a serious fool of myself in front of the men and, especially, in front of Kathy. My dreams of bringing back gold and never working again would also go up in smoke.

* * *

Approaching the portal for the third time, I felt a sudden panic attack starting to come on. I took a deep breath, turned around near the wall, and waited until the group had finished coming up the wash. I knew they needed some kind of instruction before I disappeared. "Listen up. This is it. After I go through this wall, I want each of you to come through, one at a time. I'll be waiting on the other side."

Trish's enthusiasm had evaporated with the hike up the mountain. Now, her excitement to go through to the other side seemed to be wavering. "It doesn't hurt, does it?"

I laughed, my tension briefly easing. "No, it doesn't hurt. It feels more like a tingle." I turned and stretched out my hands in front of me, just in case, to keep my face from smashing into the hard rock. *Please be open.*

Slowly, I walked into the wall, my hands disappearing first, tingling with that strange sensation. "Follow me," I said as I forced myself to move slowly for the benefit of the others.

Gasps of astonishment echoed behind me.

"No way," I heard Chad say just before I transitioned through. His voice sounded distorted and faint, as if he was talking through a big hollow tube far away.

Alone on the other side, I sat on a rock. Curious as to who would have the guts to come through and who would chicken out, I waited patiently. I decided to wait no more than a couple of minutes. If nobody showed up, I'd go back to check on them and hope they hadn't all turned and run for home. To my surprise, Kathy and Trish were the first to arrive.

"Wait a minute," Trish squeaked, her green eyes flicking in every direction. "We're still here."

"I'll explain that after everybody comes through," I said, elated to be in Kathy's presence again.

Steve showed up next, followed by the two brothers, James and Tory. The three of them glanced around with confused looks, but none said a word.

Chad and Travis came next.

A little while passed as I waited for Sergio and Juan. I held my breath, hoping they hadn't already turned and bolted.

Shortly, the two came through, both jittery. They seemed to calm down as they caught sight of the rest of us and looked around at the familiar rock walls.

"Things don't look any different," Steve said. "Are you sure we're on the other side?"

"Follow me," I said with a wave of my hand. "You aren't gonna believe we're here until you can see it for yourselves." I led them down the wash to the overlook.

"Son-of-a-bitch," Steve mumbled with awe. "I was hoping it was true, but until this moment, I didn't really believe it could be possible."

Gazing out across the valley, I once again found myself shocked at the missing town and lake. I stood in silence, letting the others study the landscape and come to their own conclusions.

The faces of my companions ranged from shock to disbelief to outright fear. I assumed their lack of speech reflected the fact they were still trying to come to terms with being in an alternate world. I hoped they wouldn't freak out and run across the desert while pulling out their hair.

Kathy pointed to the column of smoke rising in the distance. "Is that the Indian village?"

"Yeah." Turning to the group, I said, "It's a good hike, so let's get going."

"Wow. It's an awfully long ways to get over there," Kathy said, her eyebrows furrowing in concern.

"Yeah," Steve concurred. "There's no way we're gonna make it there and back before dark."

"Oh, that's right," I replied, "we didn't tell you that when you go through the portal, time on our side stops."

Confusion and surprise shot across the faces of the group. I explained about the time factor. Then I told them how I had split my knuckles open and how my hand had healed when I returned through the portal.

Some nodded numbly. Others remained in a stupor, apparently overwhelmed by the changes they were seeing. I was surprised nobody questioned me. I figured they either believed what I'd told them, or they were waiting to find out for themselves.

"Let me warn you," I said, looking over the group before making the descent, "don't be alarmed if the Indians act hostile at first. Everybody stay together and let me do the talking. Keep your guns holstered unless I tell you to take them out. I don't want to scare the Indians." I didn't mention O-cha's name, but the angry Indian jumped to the front of my mind.

I turned and headed down the rocky hillside. As much as I enjoyed being in charge for once, I suddenly felt the heavy weight of responsibility for these nine lives. Glancing back often to make sure everyone followed safely, I wondered if I could be held responsible if one of them died over here. Could the courts back home prosecute me for something that happened in a different world? If the courts could prove I had convinced these people to go, would they have a case?

Well, they can't be run over by a car or crash in an airplane here. Maybe this is a safer world.

As I trudged through the brush and dusty sand of the desert floor, my first nightmares of being tortured and eaten flashed into my mind. Fear prickled at the back of my neck like porcupine quills. I quickly turned to look at Kathy, treading close behind me. Her tight jeans, slender waist, and attractive face brought other thoughts to mind. I decided to occupy myself with her image to keep the scarier things at bay.

Chapter 9

Boom, BOOM, boom, BOOM.

We had made better time than my first trip and the sun was high in the sky. Standing now in the middle of the gully that separated the Indian village from my party, I watched as the formidable tall male Indians surrounded me and my nervous group. Loud shouts from the village and a fast, persistent rhythm on the drums had warned the Indians of our arrival. This time, I sensed a mild panic among the villagers. Perhaps they felt threatened by my larger group. Oh, how I wished for the reassurance of Pat's pacifying presence and Eric's take-charge attitude. This time, I was on my own.

I took a deep, calming breath and looked into the tattooed, stern face of Iron Cactus and the expressionless face of Beaver, both standing at the front of the encompassing circle. My voice, slightly shaky, called out, "Chief Iron Cactus, Beaver, my friends. It's me…Donny." I stepped forward, holding my hands out to my sides and expecting a peaceful meeting.

A smile appeared on Iron Cactus's face.

I felt a sigh of relief until I saw O-cha and his two pals, coming late down the hillside from the village and glaring at me with threatening looks. Unfortunately, Iron Cactus didn't see O-cha's enraged face and hostile march forward, at least not in time to pull out his whip and give O-cha and his followers twenty lashes before they attacked.

Barely fifty feet away, O-cha bolted in front of Iron Cactus. Screaming a piercing war cry and raising his wicked-looking antler war club, O-cha rushed at my small group, now trapped in the circle of natives.

Spontaneously, I jerked out my pistol and fired a shot into the ground at O-cha's feet.

He slid to a stop, his eyes wide with shock as the roar of the shot echoed off the surrounding hills. His buddies quickly backed away with palms up, seeming not to want to have anything to do with this now.

As the rush of adrenaline shot through me, I stood my ground, holding my pistol at the ready. I quickly surveyed the rest of the Indians to make sure they wouldn't attack from another side. No one in the stunned group dared approach me. I waited to see what O-cha would do next.

O-cha hesitated, indecisive, giving me a growing feeling of confidence and control. I pointed the gun directly at O-cha's face. "Is today a good day to die?" I said evenly in my best Clint Eastwood impression. My vision narrowed until I only saw O-cha's intense brown face and killing glare. We stared at each other for a long moment.

The sound of leather slapping against bare skin and O-cha's sudden grunt and look of pain drew me back to my surroundings.

O-cha spun away as Iron Cactus's whip struck again.

What sounded like obscenities erupted from Iron Cactus's mouth.

Shocked expressions on the faces of the other Indians surrounding me seemed to say that the chief's words must have been pretty harsh. When O-cha yelled something back, they gasped and looked at each other in awe.

Iron Cactus's face turned red with fury. Locked eye to eye, the two stared one another down until one of O-cha's friends grabbed him by the arm and whispered something in his ear.

With a loud grunt, O-cha whirled around to face me. He snarled, "I will kill you, all of you...soon." He and his two friends hurried back to the village.

Now that the danger had past, my whole body shook so badly I had to use both hands to get my gun back into the holster. Worried about how my charges had taken the situation, I turned to look at them.

All the men, alert and prepared, had guns in their hands.

I had to admit, I was impressed. *Wow, these are the kind of men I want to travel with. Men who won't run when threatened. Men who will stand next to me and fight alongside me.*

Kathy stood close behind the men and looked scared. She seemed pensive about what might yet happen.

Trish's green eyes flitted from one Indian to another. They locked on Beaver's placid face as he approached with Iron Cactus.

I felt a shift in the Indians mood and somehow knew the danger was over. "It's okay," I said to Steve and his crew. "You can put your guns away now. Those three Indians are the only ones who will make trouble for us." Pat's warning about not letting anyone do something stupid, flashed through my mind. I hoped Iron Cactus wouldn't blame me for causing the trouble and make the whole group go home. Eric would never forgive me, and worse, the gold trip would be off.

"I'm sorry about that," I said, taking Beaver's hand in a friendly handshake. "I didn't know if he was really gonna attack me or not."

"Not your fault," Beaver said. "O-cha is in big trouble."

"He pay," Iron Cactus said, nodding vigorously, his braids bounding on his forehead. "He pay big." He looked at my companions with wide, child-like eyes. "Friends?"

"Yes, friends from my world." I introduced each of them to Iron Cactus and Beaver. The other Indians watched with interest.

I liked seeing the looks of awe and shock on the faces of my group. They glanced around curiously, trying to take everything in as they walked through the dusty village streets toward the community hut. Bits and pieces of whispered conversations confirmed to me that reality was finally settling in for them.

"Unbelievable."

"Can you believe this?"

"Look at that."

Although my companions had said earlier that they believed we were in another world, seeing the actual Indian village seemed to drive that belief home with a vengeance.

I still had a hard time believing this was all real and not some weird, off-the-wall dream.

Behind me, Travis and Chad, the two youngest members of the group and the two macho bodybuilders, laughed quietly as I caught snatches of their conversation about the half-naked women living in the village. "No clothes...naked...easy...get lucky tonight."

I sighed with concern. I couldn't let this kind of problem get started. The Indians would be at their throats immediately. Slowing my pace, I let the two younger men catch up to me. Clearing my throat, I said nervously, "Hey, guys, I couldn't help but overhear part of your conversation. I want to warn you...don't do anything that will cause Iron Cactus or any of his villagers to be mad at us. We need them to help us on our trip to get the gold. Don't let your raging hormones spoil a good thing here."

"Don't worry, Donny," Travis said quickly. "We was just kidding around. Right, Chad?"

"Oh, yeah, right." Chad hurriedly replied. "We wouldn't jeopardize the mission. We want our share of the gold as much as you want yours." Chad eyes shifted constantly to the naked breasts of the women standing by their huts and watching us go by.

"Well, make sure you don't," I snapped with as much authority as I could muster. "Remember, this is a different world. Look at what happened to O-cha. Over here, there are no cops, no lawyers, and no courts. If you do something to displease the Indians, they'll punish you right away, and they have no qualms about the death penalty."

Travis slapped me on the back like I was his best friend. "I promise you, we aren't gonna do anything wrong, so stop worrying. We were outta line and it won't happen again."

Not trusting they would stay out of trouble like they promised, I made a note to keep an eye on them. I returned to the front of the group just as we arrived in the center of the village. Entering the main hut, I called out, "Everybody sit on the ground in a circle around the fire pit. If things happen the same way they did last time, we'll be offered food and drink while we visit."

As I sat down, I remembered my concerns about the food during my last visit. Now that I was in charge of making sure the Indians were not displeased with us, I informed the group, "Last time, they fed us corn, squash, beans, and quail meat rolled in corn tortillas. It was really good. It would be an insult to not eat at least something."

Trish's shrill voice brought the muted conversations to a halt when she announced, "I'm a vegetarian, so I'll eat the corn and the other stuff, but I won't eat the meat. I don't care if it offends them or not." She glared defiantly at the brown faces assembling around us as everyone else settled to the ground.

It appeared that most of the Indians didn't understand what she'd said, or they didn't care. A few, though, seemed to take offense at her blatant disregard for one of their customs.

I wasn't sure what to do or say. I couldn't make Trish eat the meat if she didn't want to, but I didn't want her refusal to jeopardize the trip either.

Beaver eased the situation by saying, "No problem. You don't have to eat meat. Some of us may think it's weird, but you won't offend us." He said something in his native language to his fellow tribesmen, which sparked nods of approval and grunts of acceptance. "I told them your spirit helper forbids you to eat meat of any kind."

Steve, sitting cross-legged next to Trish, looked at her and said, "You being a vegetarian could be a problem on our trip. We'll probably be living off the land most of the time, which means eating what we kill or collect along the way. Are you gonna be able to survive on whatever seeds and berries you can find?"

Trish immediately grew defensive, her voice screeching more piercingly. "I'll have you know that, as a vegetarian, I don't need as much food as the rest of you. Beaver will help me." She looked at him and smiled. "I'm sure he can arrange to get some dried corn and squash for me to take along. That, and whatever I can forage along the way will be more than adequate to sustain me." Smugly turning away, she glanced down at the dirt on her hands and grimaced.

I couldn't help but wonder how she would handle living five months in these conditions.

The Indian women showed up with the promised food. Everyone was given a serving platter and cup, just like the last time. When the food came by, I didn't hesitate to take a large portion of meat, earning me a grin from Beaver.

During the meal, Kathy came to Trish's defense. "Don't worry about Trish, Steve. She'll be fine. I'm sure we'll be eating plenty of native plants along the way. I'll make sure she does some research into edible plants so she'll have some idea of what to look for as we're traveling."

I had been so involved with everything going on around me and my responsibilities, I hadn't paid much attention to Kathy. I looked at her now with her brown hair and tanned skin, darker from the day's long hike across the desert. She seemed to be holding up well, a strong, thoughtful woman. I hoped to spend more time getting to know her as time went on.

"Speakin' of travelin'," James said between bites, "I assumed we was gonna be ridin' horses on this trip. I ain't seen none." He looked at Beaver. "Ya do have horses, right?"

"Yes," Beaver answered. "We keep the herd in a sheltered valley. About a mile north of here." He turned and asked a question of one of the men squatting against the wall. After a short conversation, Beaver said, "Last count, thirty-five head. All in good shape. We don't have tack…saddles, bridles, that kind of thing. You're going to have to bring your own."

Tory, the quiet brother who hadn't said more than a few words since I had met him, spoke up. "Gittin' the tack ain't no problem, but gittin' the horses used ta wearin' it might be." He looked at me. "We'll probably have ta spend at least a week, maybe two, workin' with the horses before we can git outta here."

I almost said something about needing to be back before the portal closed, then remembered they hadn't been told that little nugget of information. I wondered why Eric and Pat wanted to withhold it from them. Who knew, but I wasn't going to be the one to let it slip. "That's not a problem. Take as long as you need. Remember, when you come through the portal, time on our side stops."

"Um, could you tell us about that time-stops thing again?" Travis asked. "I'm not sure I was really listening when you told us about it before."

"Yeah," Steve said, "we were kind of overwhelmed by what we were seeing."

I repeated what I'd told them about the time factor and how time stopped on our side when a person went through the portal. I also told them again about how I'd split my knuckles open and how my hand had been healed when I'd returned to our side of the portal.

Iron Cactus, Beaver, and a couple of the other Indians exchanged worried looks, giving me the distinct feeling there were more things about the portal the Indians hadn't told us yet, or didn't want us to know. I made a mental note to myself to ask Beaver about it later.

"Anybody have any questions?" I asked at the end of my speech.

This time, questions flew at me from all directions.

"Whoa, whoa," I said, holding up my hands. "One at a time, please. And remember, I don't have all the answers. Hell, I don't know much more about the portal than you do now."

Steve said, "Personally, I don't think we need to know any more about the portal. It's not important."

"What do you mean, it's not important," I snapped. "It's *very* important. If it wasn't for the portal, we wouldn't be here right now."

"I didn't mean it wasn't important that way, Donny," he responded in a condescending tone. "What I meant was, it's not important to *understand* it. As long as it's there, and we can go back and forth, that's all that matters. The important thing is the trip we want to take later. We need to think seriously about everything that could happen and prepare for the worst."

"Like what?" Juan asked, his dark eyes wide as saucers. "What could go wrong?"

"Plenty," Steve replied. "This is a world without laws, except for the law of survival."

"Only the strongest will survive," Sergio said quietly.

"That's right," Beaver said, breaking into the conversation. "Steve's right. You must think long and hard about this trip. It's a different world. You'll see sights you've never seen on your side. Some aren't pretty. Some of the tribes on this side still believe in slavery, torture, and human sacrifices. If you're not willing to witness these things, you should stay on your own side."

At the mention of slavery and torture, Kathy's mouth drew into a pinched, straight line. Her eyes narrowed in a self-righteous glare.

I swore I could almost see smoke coming from her ears. Fearing she was about to blast Beaver and his tribe for allowing these atrocities to be committed on fellow human beings, I broke in. "No matter how we each feel about these things," I said firmly, "we have to remember that this isn't our world. It's theirs. We can't come over here and start changing things. Hell, look at what we did to the Indians on our side when we took their land and forced them to live on reservations in shacks with no electricity or running water."

Softening my voice a little, I added, "Besides, we're only gonna be here for a few months at the most. Then, we'll go back to our world. Maybe with our new-found wealth we can make a positive difference in somebody's life back there."

James stood up. "I'd like ta see them horses. That okay, Beaver?"

"Yes," Beaver responded. "Someone will take you out there. The rest of you can wander around the village and get to know the tribe members. It might help you feel more comfortable and help them accept you. One word of caution. Don't go outside the village or walk alone without an escort. No one has seen O-cha since your arrival."

Kathy and Trish both paled slightly and traded nervous looks.

I quickly said, "We'll make sure we stay in the village." I stood up and stretched my hips and lower back, stiff from sitting on the hard ground. "What are you gonna do, Steve?"

"I'm going with James and Tory. I want to see the horses for myself. Anybody else want to come along?"

Chad, Travis, Sergio, and Juan all volunteered.

I saw a restlessness in the eyes and mannerisms of all the members of Steve's crew. Without a T.V., video games, or a refrigerator full of beer, they had no way to occupy their minds or alleviate their boredom. I hoped Beaver wouldn't get the wrong idea about us not intermixing with the Indians, but I didn't blame the guys for wanting to get out of the village to see the horses. I didn't relish the thought of trying to carry on a conversation with someone using pidgin English.

I turned to Kathy and Trish, now standing beside me.

"Trish and I want to spend time with Iron Cactus," Kathy said, "to look at the medicines he uses in his healing."

"Good," I said, relieved that the woman would be kept busy. I figured they'd be safe with him, but then again, I really didn't know for sure.

Beaver motioned to one of the Indians to lead the women to Iron Cactus. He bid several other males to take Steve's group to the horse herd.

I waited for Beaver to finish up with the men. I had some important things to ask him.

So far, it looked like everyone in my group was handling the challenge of being in an alternate world pretty well. Nobody had freaked out or had insisted on going home. I wasn't going to hold my breath, but it looked like they might all be willing to come back for the trip north to get the gold. I hoped they would all stay busy and interested enough to keep from getting in trouble or offending the Indians. We still had a night to get through and I noticed Chad continuing to eye the half-naked women.

Chapter 10

From the top of Beaver's flat roof, I waited nervously for him to show up. I wanted to know more about the peculiarities of the portal and potential dangers concerning the future trip to find gold. I also wanted to know what the tribe would do to me if I killed O-cha, either in self-defense or otherwise.

I looked out across the valley and watched the group of men going to see the horse herd as they headed toward the jagged peaks north of the village. As they disappeared out of sight, I felt a sense of panic. I knew it was foolish. Other than O-cha and his buddies, I hadn't seen any signs of danger from any of the Indians, but, still, if anything happened to Steve's group while they were gone, I would be accountable for them as well as be on my own with the women, who I also had to worry about.

Iron Cactus still made me uncomfortable with his facial tattoos, piercing stare, and raspy voice. I feared that, should I do anything wrong, Iron Cactus wouldn't hesitate to whip me or kill me. For some reason, Iron Cactus hadn't raised a hand to have his Indians attack when I had pulled out the gun and shot a warning to O-cha. This still amazed me.

I fidgeted as I recalled my dream. I started picturing the Indians taking my companions into the canyon and killing them. I could see myself and the women dragged through the streets, tied to the stake, and Kathy glaring at me with hatred at having brought them into this deadly world. Beads of perspiration formed on my brow, even though clouds covered the sky and a slight chill hung in the air.

The sudden appearance of Beaver coming up the sloping ramp, snapped me out of my negative reveries. A young woman, who I surmised to be Beaver's wife, followed him up the ramp with a large gourd full of water and two homemade gourd cups.

I did a double-take when I saw her. Her long black hair looked greasy and full of dirt, snarled with snatches of reeds and dead mesquite twigs. As she glanced up at me forlornly, her dark eyes seemed to be barely alive on her face, caked with mud. Numerous scabs from small cuts covered her arms and bare chest.

I sensed that the wounds were self-inflicted. I'd heard about people called "cutters." If I remembered right, they were usually teens who couldn't cope with their circumstances and grew depressed. They would cut themselves on purpose as a kind of self-punishment, then hide the cuts from other people. With the minimal clothing worn in this environment, a cutter wouldn't have a way to hide the wounds. But how could such a psychological disorder affect a primitive, isolated Indian village like this.

The woman set the gourd and cups down, then quickly retreated down the ramp.

I stared after her in shock and concern.

"She's in mourning," Beaver said casually as he sat down on a hand-woven mat and poured us both a drink.

Not sure how much I should say about the matter, I sat down in silence and took the cup of water Beaver offered me.

"She lost her child a month before it was to be born," Beaver explained without emotion. "Our traditions say she can't bathe or change her clothing for one moon cycle. She must cut herself twice each day, at sunrise and sunset. To release the demons living inside her, the demons that killed the baby."

"I'm sorry," I said, confused about Beaver's dispassionate attitude. "I didn't realize the two of you were going through something like that."

"It's okay. Today makes her last mourning day. She'll wash tomorrow and be back to normal."

"Is *she* the only one required to do that?" I asked hesitantly, wondering at Beaver's role as the father of the child. At the sight of bewilderment on Beaver's face, I added, "I mean, aren't you supposed to do something, too?"

"No. She lost the baby before it was born." Seeing my look of confusion he said, "She's not mourning the loss of a child like in your world. She's morning because she allowed an evil spirit to invade her and steal her unborn child before it was allowed to become a person."

I wasn't sure I understood. "So, your tribe doesn't acknowledge a baby as a person until it's actually born?"

Beaver shrugged and looked out over the valley. "It must sound strange to you, but that's what we believe. Just because our customs are different, doesn't make them wrong. Your people have their own customs. They tend to be narrow-minded in how other people live. That's why I warned your group earlier there are many things on this side they won't agree with. We expect you to respect our way of life and not interfere with it. In return, we allow you access through the Gateway to achieve your own goals."

Feeling uncomfortable about the abuse forced on Beaver's wife for losing a child, I shifted on the mat and changed the subject. "I want to ask you a question about O-cha."

Beaver shot me a look of interest. This was the first time Beaver showed any kind of reaction since he had arrived on the roof. "Go ahead."

I fumbled around in my mind to find the right words. "Well...actually...what I want to know is...how would the tribe have reacted if I would have shot and killed O-cha earlier today."

Beaver looked out across the valley again as though he were contemplating an answer. "Most of my tribe would accept you protecting yourself. Those siding with O-cha would want you punished."

I gulped. "Your laws and customs are alien to me. I don't want to do something, like kill someone, and end up tied to a burning stake in the center of a bonfire."

A rare chuckle erupted from Beaver's mouth. "We aren't as barbaric as we may seem to you. We don't burn people at the stake, and we aren't cannibals." It was almost as though Beaver had read my mind.

"So, what would they do if I killed O-cha in self-defense?"

"Some would want to see you punished. Most, like me, would stand for your right to protect yourself."

I picked up my cup and poured myself more water. "It's just…I don't know…I guess I feel like O-cha has a vendetta against me for some reason that I don't understand."

"O-cha hates your world and the people in it. He lived there many years as a child and saw much evil. Now, he fears that evil ones will enter from your world and destroy ours. He wants to kill everyone who discovers the Gateway and comes through, even if they have no ill intentions."

"Does he think I am one of the evil ones?"

"He thinks all from your world are evil ones, but you are the one who followed him through the Gateway. For this, he is responsible. In his own mind, he must reverse what he has done. As you bring more of your people into this world, you increase his fears that he must stop what he had started."

Wow, I suddenly realized I might not even be here had it not been for O-cha being in the canyon that day.

"If it were up to O-cha," Beaver went on, "the Gateway would be closed permanently by creating a rockslide or putting up a barrier of some kind."

"What about the rest of the tribe? How do they feel about closing the Gateway?"

"That is not Nature's plan. It is not our plan. We must honor Nature's way. It is the first rule of our tribe."

I pondered this a long time. Now, I could see how I was a threat to O-cha, a threat that he had to resolve. "I'm curious," I said tentatively, encouraged by Beaver's nonchalant attitude and openness, "what else do you know about the portal that you're not telling me?"

Beaver squinted, obviously debating what he should say. Iron Cactus probably had a rule about how much could be revealed.

After a long pause, Beaver finally said, "No one fully knows the workings of the Gateway. Our ancestors studied it for over a hundred years and passed that knowledge down. We know some of its secrets, but it catches us by surprise sometimes. We don't have your advanced scientific instruments and knowledge, but I doubt even with those, no one will ever learn all the Gateway's secrets."

"I know you know something else," I insisted, looking pleadingly at Beaver. "Come on. Tell me. I want to know."

Beaver stared hard into my eyes for a moment, then looked away. He pressed his lips together in silence.

"Okay, then, tell me this. Does what you know have any bearing on the trip we will be taking to find gold? Is there anything that could affect what happens?"

Beaver sat so still, I thought he might be meditating.

"As long as we get back to the portal before it closes, and if we are healed of wounds when we get there, what other problems could we have?"

No response.

Growing more curious and worried, I refused to let Beaver off so easily. I blurted, "Will we be able to take the gold back through the portal? You said your tribe used gold to finance their lives on the other side, so they must have taken gold over there. This won't be a problem, will it?"

Beaver cracked a smile. "Whatever you take to the other side will stay there, unless you bring it back."

"Then what?"

Beaver's face sobered up quickly.

I leaned forward, pleading one last time. "Tell me."

"Time," Beaver said.

"Time? What do you mean?"

"The Gateway must keep time equal."

I opened my palms upward and rolled my fingers in a gesture for Beaver to get on with the information.

Beaver let out a quiet sigh. "You know, when you're on this side, time stops on your side, right?"

I nodded in agreement.

"And, you also know that, when you go back through, you are exactly the same, even if you've been injured?"

I nodded again. *Come on. Get to the point.*

"So, say you come over here at twenty years old and stay fifty years. You could marry, raise a family, and have kids. Later, when you went back through the Gateway to your original home, you would be twenty again."

"I don't see a problem with that," I said, thinking it was pretty cool to be young again in my world. "If time stops when I come through, who would know I'd been gone?"

"That's true," Beaver said somberly, "but, if you come back here the next day, you would be twenty again." He paused and studied my response.

I tried to work it out in my mind. I still thought it would be pretty cool to be twenty again on the other side, but not so cool to come back and see everyone else fifty years older, even my kids. That didn't make sense. "Well, if I did come back, wouldn't I be the same age over here as I was when I left from my own world again?"

"Yes, you would, but it's not so simple. You have to wait *fifty years* to come back."

My brow furrowed. Now, *that* didn't make sense.

"While the Gateway remains open between the solar eclipses," Beaver explained, "it closes for individuals in order to keep time equal on both sides. If I'm on the other side for a week, then come back home, I can't go through the Gateway again until a full week has passed."

"Wow," I said, thinking back to my experiences going through the portal. The first time, I had waited about five minutes for Eric and Pat to come through. When I'd returned to the other side, I'd spent a few minutes talking to them before going back through the portal again. After the three of us had spent over twenty-four hours hiking the desert and staying with the Indians, I hadn't returned with the new group until almost forty-eight hours later. I couldn't verify that what he said wasn't true.

Seeming to sense my lingering doubt, Beaver said, "We've tested it. Many times."

"Why do you and Iron Cactus seem to act funny about us knowing these things? It seems like it would be helpful to know, especially since we are coming back."

"While Iron Cactus accepts that there will be people who will stumble upon the Gateway, for whatever reason, and make their way through, he fears that some of these people will abuse this gift." He paused to take a drink. "If someone knows he can be healed just by stepping through the portal, he might think he is like your Superman and not worry about getting injured or killed. That would be a bad mistake."

Killed? I hadn't really stopped to think about the repercussions on the other side if I or one of my companions were killed on this side.

"Getting injured is one thing," Beaver went on. "If you get killed over here, you stay dead over here. The Gateway can't bring someone back to life."

"Would I just cease to exist on the other side or what?"

Beaver said no more, just shook his head noncommittally.

Wow. I wondered if the world on the other side would change if I died in this world and disappeared in the other. Eric wouldn't have a brother. I would disappear from all the family pictures. My life would mean nothing to anyone. The idea nauseated me.

Beaver pursed his lips again, maybe regretting he had told me more about the portal. I strongly sensed he was leaving out something important.

I sat quietly and pulled out my pipe, chewing on the stem. I didn't want to admit that I'd begun to envision myself and my group as invincible. I figured if we got hurt or killed, as long as we were taken back through the portal, we'd be back to new. This new bit of information changed things drastically, especially since I could see this new world wasn't totally safe. That scared me. There were no police, armies, or search-and-rescue teams to call for help if we got into trouble. The lack of a hospital, equipped with a state-of-the-art trauma center and skilled surgeons, ready to spend hours repairing bloody wounds, gave me pause.

Eric had been wise to convince Kathy and Trish to make the trip. Even in this primitive environment, their services would be an invaluable asset. I hoped they wouldn't be frightened off by my concerns.

The gold. My desire for the gold still weighed heavily on my mind. I could almost feel the soft metal in my hand. It would solve all my problems: pay my bills, allow me to have nice things like Eric, give pool parties, take trips, wear nice clothes, drive a big truck with all the trimmings, buy nice things for Kathy. I wanted that gold.

Well, I reasoned, both worlds had their pros and cons. Both had positive aspects and negative aspects. Both could be dangerous in their own ways. Like everything else, we'd just have to be careful, make sure everyone had guns and plenty of ammunition. Besides, once we got out of this Indian village and away from O-cha, things would be a lot better.

Chapter 11

Shouts rang out from a small group of people coming from the direction of the northern peaks. Sensing something was wrong, I stood up from my mat on Beaver's roof and scanned for Steve and his crew. One person was being carried on a crude stretcher. My heart jumped into my throat as I turned and hurriedly followed Beaver down the ramp.

At the edge of the village, I pushed through the small crowd of men, women, and children to see Travis and Chad carrying the improvised stretcher, a plank of mesquite limbs bound together. An Indian with an arrow in the side of his upper thigh and an arrow in his shoulder, lay sprawled out on the stretcher, his face contorted with pain. The two muscle-bound men carried the stretcher into the village and gently laid it on the ground.

I looked at the three Indians who had come along with Chad and Travis. I recognized one of the Indians as having gone off with Steve's crew. I wasn't sure about the other two. "Where's Steve?" I asked Travis as I anxiously looked toward the northern path. "Where's the rest of the crew?"

"They're still back with the horses. Trying to round them up."

"What happened?"

"As far as we can tell," Travis said, catching his breath from the run, "this man and two other hunters were attacked by a group of warriors from another tribe. When they reached the canyon with the horses, we helped them bring this man back."

Beaver approached the injured man, squatted next to him, and spoke quietly in his native tongue.

Multiple cuts and scrapes covered the arms, legs, and body of the wounded man. It looked as though he had been dragged across the scrub-ridden desert or rolled down a rock-covered hill.

"Are these the other two hunters?" I asked, looking at the young bare-chested Indians standing over the stretcher with somber faces made fierce by their geometric tattoos.

With a note of self-righteous indignation, Chad said, "No. The other two hunters are dead. These two dudes went with us to see the horse herd. They volunteered to help bring the stretcher in. So, on the trail, I'm trying to convince them to let us go back with them to get the bodies, but they don't seem to understand what I'm saying."

"I don't think it's a good idea for you to go back with them," I said firmly. "You don't know what might happen. The other tribe might attack again and the whole rescue party could get killed."

"So what?" Chad stated recklessly. "If I get killed, just take my body back through the portal, and it'll heal me."

I sighed as I looked down at the wounded Indian. "It doesn't work that way." Ignoring Chad's inquiring look, I turned to observe more tribe members gathering with shocked looks and quiet murmurs. "We need to get our crew back here before someone else is injured or killed," I said to no one in particular.

Iron Cactus, accompanied by Kathy and Trish, came quickly up the path. The village on-lookers moved aside for them.

Kathy stepped forward, her brow slightly furrowed, her brown eyes seriously intent on the task at hand. She immediately took charge, pushing some of the gawkers away and inspected the man's injuries. "We need to take him where he can be close to a fire." She stood up. "Chad, Travis, let's get this man inside Iron Cactus's hut."

Chad massaged his bulging muscles. "Sorry," he said, "but someone else has to take it from here. My arms are shot."

Kathy glared at him with disgust.

Before I opened my mouth to scold Chad and force him to lift the damn stretcher, Beaver called to two men nearby. Picking up the stretcher, they followed Kathy and Trish, heading to Iron Cactus's home.

Irritated with Chad and frightened about Steve's crew being in danger, I turned to Travis and said, "You and Chad go back to the canyon and get Steve and the rest of the men. They'll have to deal with the horses when we return on the next trip."

Chad's defiant eyes remained a long moment on mine before Travis pulled him away and the two started down the trail. The two Indians who had come with them, accompanied them back toward the canyon.

I felt a deep shiver well up from inside me. I would worry until I saw all the men back safely in the village. What would I tell Eric if someone died? Would anyone on the other side even know that person had existed?

* * *

I jumped when Beaver came up beside me.

His eyes held a new intensity. An aura of pensiveness pervaded his normally laid-back presence.

"What is it? Are we in danger? Are we gonna be attacked? Did one of my people do something wrong?" The questions shot out of me like popcorn kernels out of an uncovered pot.

Beaver took me by the arm and led me toward his hut. "You go up. I must talk to my wife first." He disappeared inside.

I climbed up to the roof and sat down. I was worried about the lives of my men, worried about being attacked, worried about what my men might do to jeopardize our relationship with Iron Cactus's tribe. I also wondered what was going on in Beaver's mind. Luckily, I hadn't seen O-cha.

I hoped none of this would discourage Eric and Pat from going forward with the trip. If they backed out, I might have to convince some of Steve's men to go with me, but I had no financial backing. *Strange*, I thought, *that I need someone else's money to find gold to have my own money.*

I thought about Kathy. Could I protect her in this world? My minded drifted to a future wilderness where the members of our group were riding horses across an open plain as we made our way north to find gold.

Out of nowhere, I hear the war cry of Indians coming from the edges of the plain. Eric takes the lead, charging forward on his horse. I follow, along with Pat, Steve, and all the crew. I check back over my shoulder to make sure Kathy stays safely with the group when I see her horse stumble and fall to the ground. I turn away from my stampeding companions and head back to the fallen horse. As the Indians draw closer, I lean to the side of my horse, grab Kathy under her arms, and lift her to sit sidesaddle in front of me. I turn sharply and race to catch up with the rest of my group as arrows fly over my head and all around me.

I was jolted from my daydream as Beaver sat cross-legged next to me. He seemed calmer.

"My wife's brother died," he said flatly.

I stared at him, trying to reconcile the emotional content of the spoken words with the cold manner. "What do you mean?"

"He was one of the hunters who was killed. I wanted her to hear it from me. We have some pretty mean women in the tribe, jealous women who would spring this kind of news on her, then laugh at her reaction."

I had never thought of Indian tribes as having internal conflicts. "I guess every society has their evil people."

"The man on the stretcher is called Sunman…"

I cut him off. "Sunman? What significance does that have? Is he bright and happy or something?" I laughed at my own joke, trying to make things lighter in my apprehensive state.

"Actually, yes," Beaver replied, not seeming to pick up on the humor, but rather, appearing agitated. "He's always joking with people, making them laugh. He brightens our day, so he's called Sunman. Is there anything wrong with that?"

I quickly decided not to push my luck. "No, not at all." I shrugged. "I assumed it was something like that. I'm sure you know that, in our world, we give people nicknames if they have traits like that. I guess it's kind of the same thing."

"Yeah, kind of."

Through the opening in the roof, I heard the faint sounds of Beaver's wife crying below. I couldn't imagine what it must feel like to lose your child and your brother. Wanting to keep Beaver distracted from the sounds, I said, "Did Sunman tell you what happened to the hunting party?"

Beaver sighed. "Yes. It involves you and your group."

I shuddered involuntarily. I'd had a feeling something was going to go horribly wrong on this trip and, sure enough, here it was. I just knew Beaver was going to tell me that we were all going to be sent home and never allowed back.

"The tribe that attacked the hunters lives to the east of us, near where the town of Kingman exists in your world."

In my mind, I pictured a map with Lake Havasu City lying south of Interstate 40, which passes through Kingman to the east and into California to the west. It took about forty-five minutes to reach Kingman from Lake Havasu by vehicle. I couldn't imagine how long it would take by foot, especially having to go around the Mohave Mountain Range.

"Our tribes used to be friends. Lately, with their new chief, they've been abnormally aggressive. We think it has something to do with the Gateway being open and people being allowed through. They have always possessed the idea that they are superior to us. Because we are the closest in proximity to the Gateway, they want us to prevent other-world people from entering, although they, too, have sent their own people over to your world for their own purposes."

"What do they do over there? Spy on us?

"In a manner of speaking."

"Are they afraid of us?" I asked. "Is that why they don't want us over here?"

"Yes. You have a very poor record of dealing with the natives in your world."

I wondered how many tribes on this side of the portal knew it existed. "You are the Keepers, aren't you? Don't you control who goes through?"

"Remember, we don't look at the world the same way you do. We don't believe in owning and controlling the land like you do. The Gateway is open to anyone who desires to use it. We won't try to tell anyone not to use it."

"Okay, so you're telling me that this attack today is because Eric, Pat, and I came through the portal?"

"Yes."

"And this other tribe is pissed off because I'm here again with another group?"

"Yes."

I wondered if these Indians were in cahoots with O-cha. "Does that mean you are gonna deny us the use of the portal now?"

"No." Beaver's short, blunt answers made it sound as though he was angry at me for everything that was happening.

"So, I take it your tribe wants us to go home and never come back again. Is that right?"

"Some do. Most feel the way I do."

"And how's that?"

Beaver smiled wryly. "We're curious to see what you and your group will do…how you'll handle life over here."

"Kind of like a school science experiment, right?"

Beaver chuckled. "Yeah, only on a grand scale."

I felt relieved to see Beaver lighten up, but dreary feelings lurked under the surface of my thoughts. How would Eric and Pat react when they discovered our presence here had cost two Indians their lives? On the other hand, everything in life was a risk, wasn't it? Driving on the highway could get someone killed. This new world just offered different opportunities and different dangers. Anyway, how could I help it if some of the natives had a problem with our presence?

Remembering that the men hadn't come back from the canyon yet, I stood up to look toward the canyon.

Beaver stood beside me. "My tribe will deal with the problems that arise from your presence on this side. Just know, this is how our world works. It's always been this way and will be so, long after you're gone."

Even though I still felt guilty about two men dying because of us, I knew, deep down, I wasn't going to let it get in the way of my ultimate goal of coming back for the gold.

Beaver gripped my shoulder. "Everyone makes choices. It's not your fault that someone died. Whatever comes of all this, we are all in it together." Turning away, he descended the roof.

In the distance, I saw movement along the path from the canyon. A dozen men appeared. Two stretchers were being carried. The men drew closer, the clothing separated my own people from the Indians. It looked like Steve and all his crew members were walking on two feet at a healthy pace.

Feeling relieved, I wanted to be alone for awhile to get my mind around all the things that were happening. With everyone now safely in the village, I looked toward the river bed that lay west of the bluff. Water always seemed to soothe the restlessness in me. It wasn't too far from the village. I figured I'd be safe. I decided to escape to the river and take the opportunity to be alone.

Chapter 12

Lost in thought, I wandered out of the village. I followed the dry wash that ran to my left as I headed for the mighty Colorado River, now a wide expanse across the valley. Without dams to control the water from the north or the south, the river wound in a squiggly pattern across the harsh desert plain.

A strange pile of rocks, obviously not arranged by nature, caused me to stop at the top of an embankment. I looked down the hill to my left. Here the river had backed up into the mouth of the wash, leaving a calm lagoon lined with reeds and tall water grasses. Ten or so ducks floated atop the water among the reeds.

Sitting on the mound overlooking the lagoon, I thought about the day—firing a warning shot at O-cha, Indians being killed, possibly dying in this world and *staying dead*. I wondered what my companions were thinking about this world now. Would they want to bow out of the gold trip? Would it be my fault if one of them got killed over here?

Everything I've ever done always turns out to be a disaster. I can't hold down a job. I've never been able to concentrate long enough to finish up the projects I start. I live from day-to-day, barely surviving. I hate the thought of working. The gold is the only thing that can solve all my problems.

I picked up a rock and angrily threw it in a long arc toward the center of the calmly flowing water. As the rock disappeared with a splash, I shouted, "It's not my fault if these stupid Indians want to have a war with each other over the portal and kill each other."

The ripples spread out and died as they hit the shore.

Even if I wanted to end the trip, I couldn't stop it now that Eric was involved. He was going to be the one to make the decision. No matter what I wanted to do, Eric would take over, just like he had sent me over here while he did all the fun things at home. Hell, everything was out of my hands. Even if I stayed home, Eric would come back with the rest of the group and I'd miss out on the gold. *No way, they're not gonna get the gold without me. This is my idea.*

As my anger roiled, I thought about Kathy, her big brown eyes, her cute, tilting head when she said, "Just call me Kathy." I so liked how she took charge with the injured Indian, knowing her business, showing concern for the injured man's wounds. A smart lady. I could imagine her just now, gently caressing compresses against the man's wounds and talking to him softly to relieve his pain.

I stared out over the river as I imagined myself lying on the mat in Iron Cactus's hut with Kathy wiping a cool towel across my forehead.

"You'll be okay," she whispers soothingly, her soft lips close to my face. "I'll take care of you. Don't worry. We'll get you back through the portal and everything will be back to normal. I'll hold your hand the entire way."

I moan, feeling her hand grip mine more tightly as she draws a little closer. I smell the faint perfume of orange blossoms in her hair.

The squawks of a flock of ducks startled me. They landed on the stretch of water near the patch of reeds where the other ducks milled around.

Still frustrated with my current situation, I picked up a rock the size of a baseball and stood up. "How come things always have to be so complicated?" I hurled the rock at the ducks.

When the rock hit the water with a loud plunk, the mass of ducks lit into the air with wild warning shrieks. At the same time, a naked Indian exploded up out of the water.

As the ducks and their calls faded into the distance, I stood frozen in place, trying to grapple with why this man would be underwater, and why some of the ducks remained calmly floating along the reeds as though nothing had happened.

The dripping-wet figure waded toward the shore.

Fearing my rock might have hit him, I made my way down the embankment to the edge of the water. As I grew closer, I could see the Indian was a woman, not a man. She held a dead duck in one hand.

When she reached the bank, she threw the duck on the ground at my feet and glared at me. Water dripped off her dark-tanned face, shoulders, perfect breasts, and youthful body, creating a puddle in the sand at her bare feet. "Thanks to you, White Man," she said in clipped, precise words that attested to her well-spoken English, "I have only one duck for dinner tonight, not two."

"I…um," I stammered, not sure what to say to the soaking-wet, extremely beautiful, completely naked woman standing before me.

She stood about five-foot-two-inches, maybe in her mid-thirties. Her long, dark-brown hair fell into a single drenched braid. Strangely, she didn't have the large body and strong facial features so common in the rest of the tribe. Her lean, firm figure and delicate facial structure gave the impression she had the blood of two different races running through her veins. With her clear English, I wondered if she had been to my world.

"Well," she demanded, her hands on her hips, "aren't you going to say anything?"

Looking into her large brown eyes, I managed to say, "I…I'm sorry. I didn't realize you were hiding in the water." I looked around, realizing now that the remaining ducks were stuffed decoys. "I've never seen anybody hunt ducks that way before."

"That's right," she blared. "You're one of *those* people…from the other side." Her eyes ran down my body to my boots, then back up to my face and cowboy hat. Shaking her head in disgust, she turned her back to me. "I guess I can't expect you to know our signs. But I'm still mad at you for interfering with my hunt."

"What signs?" I said, looking around, half-expecting to see big sign saying: *Caution! Beautiful, sexy woman hiding in water hunting ducks. Don't throw rocks.*

She pulled her long braid over her shoulder, gathered it in her hands, and wrung out the water. "Didn't you see the pile of rocks up there?" She tipped her head in the direction of the hill where I had been sitting.

"Yeah," I said, trying to figure out how a stupid pile of rocks could be a sign.

"That's my sign, telling people I'm hunting ducks. But like I said," she added in a lighter tone, "I can't expect *you* to know that." She reached down and picked up her leather skirt, which had been stuffed between two rocks.

"That's right," I blurted, sensing her forgiveness and wanting to get on her good side. "Let me make it up to you."

She laughed as she pulled on her skirt. "What are you going to do? Take me to dinner? Buy me flowers?"

"Well, um.," I mumbled, not sure what to say, not sure how she knew about such things as dinner and flowers, unless she'd been to my world. I felt my face turning red so I looked toward the river and pretended to be thinking about the problem.

She came up behind to me and placed her soft hand gently on my arm.

My heart raced. Electricity shot through me.

Leaning closer, she whispered seductively in my ear, "That's okay, I forgive you." She slid her hand from around my arm to my chest.

My breath caught in my throat when her hand continued upward, her fingers brushing up my neck and caressing my cheek.

"Ahhh...I um...I'm not...." I stammered. No woman had never come on to me like this and, to tell the truth, it made me a little nervous. I wasn't sure what to do.

She giggled. "Come to my house for dinner tonight. We'll share the duck."

"I...don't..." I cleared my throat, struggling to get out the words. "I don't know where you live."

"Beaver can tell you," she said coyly, her hand softly brushing my neck under my ear.

I closed my eyes and took a couple of deep breaths. By the time I got myself together and turned to face her, she was gone.

I whirled around and listened intently for nearby noises. I heard only the gentle lapping of waves against the shoreline and an occasional dog barking in the distance back at the village. Seeing no sign of her in the water or the weeds, I wondered if she had gone back under the water. I moved closer, trying to see through the murky undergrowth, but I couldn't tell if she was under the water or not. I couldn't stand there all day, so I decided to climb the hill and return to the village.

As I came over the mound, I saw a small figure, a flopping duck in her hand, running toward the village. She had slipped away like a ghost.

I ignored the brief knot forming in my stomach about having a date with a beautiful woman right under Kathy's nose. But, I was still a free man, wasn't I? I could still picture this Indian woman coming up naked out of the water. I couldn't wait for dinner.

* * *

That evening, I leaned back against the pile of deer, elk, and bear furs in Butterfly's hut. "Ahhh, that was the best duck I've ever had," I said as I stretched out my legs. The late afternoon sun, coming through the doorway, gave the room a warm, soft glow as if it was lit by candles. The smell of dinner lingered in the air.

With a slight edge of annoyance, Butterfly said, "It would have been better if we'd had two of them."

Earlier, after I'd returned to the village, Beaver had showed concerned when I told him the events at the river. "Her name is Kuwanyamtiwa," he'd said "and I'd be careful if I were you. She may be more than you can handle."

"Kuwana…whata?" I asked, having trouble pronouncing her name.

"It means 'Butterfly showing beautiful wings,' but you can just call her Butterfly."

Now, as I watched Butterfly putter around the fire pit and clean up from dinner, I had to admit she was beautiful with her long silky hair, tanned skin, and delicate features. She wore a thick necklace made of small white beads, strung together and layered to form a choker that completely covered her neck. What I didn't see was what Beaver had meant about her being more than I could handle. Smart, charming, and attentive, she'd been the perfect hostess all evening. I couldn't remember when I'd had such a good time.

The question that had loomed heavy in my mind all afternoon was, did I want to have a one-night stand with this beautiful woman? Thinking about Kathy made me squirm in the furs. What if she found out about it? True, Kathy and I had nothing going...yet. Given the chance, I hoped there would be something between us. Deep inside, my intuition told me that Kathy would be worth waiting for. I quickly made a decision. I didn't want to ruin any chance I might have to get involved with her. I just hoped she wouldn't be mad if she found out I'd had dinner with a beautiful, sexy, single woman...who I'd seen naked.

Butterfly sat down close to me. "I realize we come from two different worlds and we can't have a normal relationship." She paused, taking my hand in hers. "But that doesn't mean we can't enjoy a night of passion, does it?"

I almost choked. This was the first time a girl had come on to me so directly. How easy it would have been to give in to a night in her bed as I looked into her big brown seductive eyes. As tempting as I found her to be, though, my gut kept telling me that sleeping with her would be one of the biggest mistakes in my life.

Swallowing hard, I gently pulled back my hand and slid away from her. "Listen, Butterfly," I said, getting to my feet and trying to be reasonable, "normally, I'd jump at the chance to go to bed with someone as beautiful as you..."

Her eyes suddenly bored into me. "But?" she forced out between clenched teeth.

I stepped back. Five seconds ago, she'd been a cheerful, sexy woman, openly flirting with me. Now, she glared daggers at me. The word "bi-polar" flashed through my mind. I'd known a girl in high school with the disease. One second, she'd act like my best friend; the next, she'd tear into me like her worst enemy.

I had to come up with a good excuse not to have sex with this woman. Mentioning my feelings for Kathy would probably not be a good idea. I didn't even want her to know about Kathy. Knowing from history lessons and TV shows that Indians were spirit-oriented, I decided to blame it on religion. "In my world," I said carefully, "my religion forbids two people from having sex unless they're married, and…"

"You don't have to explain it to me," she snarled as she jumped to her feet. "I've lived in your world. In fact, I was born there."

Even though I'd half-suspected something like that, I found the revelation shocking. I wasn't sure what to say. I had to admit, it did explain why she spoke such good English and seemed to know so much about my world.

She pointed meanly to the door. "Get out."

Feeling like I'd made a grave mistake in angering her, I wanted to make things better. "No, you don't understand. I was gonna say…"

She reached down near the fire pit and grabbed a butcher knife. "I said, get out," she screamed, swinging the knife in my direction.

Backing toward the door, I almost stumbled as I made a hasty retreat. I was pretty sure this was the worst date I'd ever had.

* * *

Safely outside, I realized what Beaver had meant about her being more than I could handle. Feeling embarrassed about being forced out of her hut, I glanced around to see if anyone was watching. In the dimming evening light, the few Indians outside seemed to be looking in other directions.

I immediately headed for Beaver's hut. Not seeing him outside, I knocked on the side of the hut door.

Beaver's wife hollered something to me.

I didn't understand, so I hollered back. "I'm looking for Beaver. Do you know where he is?"

The dirty, scarred woman suddenly appeared in the doorway with a knife in her hand. Pieces of dried reeds and desert brush still clung to her long grimy hair. Her brazen brown eyes glowered from behind the mask of mud on her face.

I took two quick steps back. *Man, today's not my day to deal with women.*

"No. Go now," she spat, waving the knife in front of her face.

Needing no more encouragement, I hurried away, wandering through the village to look for Beaver and keeping an eye out for O-cha. I saw a woman cooking dinner over a fire outside her hut. Across the way, another woman ground meal, while a younger woman tended to a couple of children. Around their necks, most of the women wore thick chokers made from strands of beads. Their faces bore tattoos, just like the men.

The men busied themselves with whittling wood for bows or arrows. Some scraped stone against stone to make arrowheads. The older Indians simply sat on mats near their huts and quietly talked. Most of these people waved or nodded to me, as though they were getting used to us being among them.

Even though the Indians had different activities, it surprised me how closely life here resembled life in my world, like people everywhere had the same basic needs. They just satisfied them on different levels and in different ways.

I found all the members of my group in the community hut talking among themselves. I assumed they were discussing everything they'd experienced throughout the day. I didn't feel like interrupting them and, unable to find Beaver, I returned to the hut that had been allotted to us for our stay.

Lying on my furs and blankets with my hands under my head, I looked up at the mud ceiling. This world in the Indian village scared me. I wasn't sure what to expect or how to deal with the problems. In my world, I could call the cops and have a woman arrested for pulling a knife on me. Here, I had to figure out what to do on my own. I wasn't sure I was comfortable with that.

As I rolled over, it dawned on me how much I'd depended on other people...especially Eric...to take care of things. I didn't know if I wanted to change that much and become responsible for handling everything myself.

I guess I'm gonna have to cowboy up and learn to take matters into my own hands, I thought wearily as I drifted off to sleep.

Chapter 13

The next morning, barely before dawn, I awoke from a dark dream about an Indian maiden standing over me with a butcher knife. I knew it stemmed from my experience with the two women the night before, and I hoped it wasn't a premonition of more to come. I jumped up from my makeshift bed and gathered my things, glad to be heading back to my world where I'd feel more secure.

I rustled the others out of their sleep. "Come on, let's get something to eat and get on the road. We've got a long hike to get back home."

No one seemed to resent my waking them. In fact, they all looked eager to get going, too.

I made my way to Beaver's hut with the dream still hanging over me like a dark moon I couldn't shake.

Beaver sat alone outside the entrance of his hut as though he had been waiting for me. He chewed on a piece of the tortilla-type bread. Arching his eyebrows in interest, he asked, "How did you and Butterfly get along last night?"

"That's one messed-up lady," I replied, sitting next to him and leaning my back against the wall. I took a slice of the food he offered. "What's her story? She told me she was born in my world, so how come she's living here?"

As Beaver swallowed his last bite of food, he answered, "When she was eight, she lived with her father on the Indian reservation near Bullhead City. One of our warriors and his son lived in the trailer house next door. She made friends with the son and, one day, the boy confided in her, told her about this world. His dad was angry when he found out, but there was nothing he could do.

"The girl insisted she wanted to come here to see this world. The father eventually gave in and brought her here for a week. She didn't want to go home and live with her own drunken dad, but the warrior made her return. A few months after her trip, her dad skidded off a road in a drunken fit and landed in the Colorado River. He drowned. Quickly seeing the dilemma of the girl being left on her own, the warrior gave her a choice: to go into the custody of the state and live in foster homes or to live on this side. She chose this world and she's never returned to the other side."

"How did they explain her disappearance to the police?" I asked.

"The warrior told the police she had been with her father when the car went into the river. They searched for days. Never found her body. Said it would wash up downriver, sooner or later, but it never did. I think eventually they forgot about it, wrote it off as an unsolved case."

"That explains how she knows so much about my world."

"So, last night didn't go very well?"

I swear, even in the dim light of dawn, I saw a faint smile cross Beaver's face as he asked the question. Ignoring his amusement, I related the events of the previous evening.

Beaver chuckled lightly. "I think there's more to this than meets the eye."

Puzzled, I shot him a look.

"The more I think about it," he went on, "the more I think last night was a setup."

"What do you mean?"

"Butterfly's behavior doesn't fit. She hates everything from your world. She hates everybody from your world. She wouldn't come on to you unless it was part of a bigger plan."

A gnawing pang started growing in my gut. "Like what?"

"Here's what I think." Beaver leaned his head back against the wall. "She was supposed to seduce you. Get you all hot and bothered. Then, she would scream…like you were raping her. Her boyhood friend would rush in, save her from the horrible foreigner."

Now, it was my turn to chuckle. "That's pretty farfetched."

"Not when you consider her boyhood friend."

"Who?"

"O-cha."

As the picture suddenly became crystal clear, I slammed my fist into the hard-packed earth. "That bitch." Rubbing my hand, I turned back to Beaver. "Do you really think O-cha would go to that much trouble to get even with me?"

"He's out to get you. When you come back, you watch yourself around both of them."

I couldn't believe how stupid I had been. "Don't worry," I said bitterly, "I'll definitely stay as far from them as possible."

Seeing the morning sun rise over the Mohave Mountains and hearing my travel companions heading in my direction, I stood up and bade farewell to Beaver.

It was time to turn my attention to the next leg of this journey and get my companions home safely. Even with the events of the previous day, we were all still alive.

* * *

As I led the group out of the village, I thought about Eric's threat to call off the trip if I couldn't convince the group to join in the search for gold. Listening to the men talk excitedly among themselves about the experiences they had had the night before and hearing them make plans for the next trip, I got the feeling they wouldn't miss out on it. Even Sergio and Juan seemed to be going along with the others.

Kathy and Trish hiked in high spirits behind me.

I slowed my pace to join them. "What do you think, Kathy? You've seen the dangers in the wilderness here and had to assist with the wounded Indian. Do you think you would want to come back again to make the trip across the country to find the gold?"

"I wouldn't miss it for the world. I'm anxious to see where all this goes."

Secretly, her words thrilled me. *See where all this goes.* I twisted it to mean our relationship. Thinking about it, I felt my face turn red. I still felt a little nervous and tongue-tied around her.

She continued forward, watching the ground for rocks and brush as she marched at my side. "I learned so many things from Iron Cactus about how the tribe heals wounds and takes care of their people. It's pretty primitive in some ways, but in other ways, they have herbs that seem magical in their healing properties." She looked at me and spoke in an apologetic tone. "I don't know how much I will be of help on the trip. My medical skills will only go so far without all the equipment and drugs available on our side. But as far as I'm concerned, the adventure of the trip excites me. And since I won't lose a day of work when I get back, I don't see that I have anything to lose by going."

"That's great," I blurted. A shiver of excitement ran through me at knowing we would have more time to get to know each other. The thought scared me, too. *I'll get over my fright once I get to know her better,* I told myself. *I'll be her protector. We'll take walks together and share our food. She can sleep in my tent.*

"I want to come back, too," Trish squealed into my ear, destroying the moment.

Rubbing my ear and hurrying ahead, I said, "Okay, then, let's get moving."

As we hiked across the desert, all of us anxious to get home, I crossed my fingers. *Portal, still be open.* No way did I want to return and live in this village with Butterfly and O-cha for an indefinite period of time.

* * *

That evening, I awoke on the couch in my apartment at the insistent ringing of my cell phone.

The long hike across the desert and into the mountains had been relatively uneventful, but totally exhausting. Luckily, we had passed easily through the portal, but we had lost a few hours by crossing to our side. In the Indian-world, the sun had moved past high noon, while in own world, we found ourselves at late morning, the exact moment we had left. We hiked down the canyon and descended the bluffs in silence. Hungry and thirsty, we all climbed into our vehicles and made haste across the desert floor.

Kathy, sitting next to me in the truck, seemed too tired to talk.

I liked her thigh touching mine, but I thought I would leave her to her own reveries. Again, I didn't know what to say. I turned up the music and tore out across the desert, the dust flying behind my truck and a cold case of beer and hot shower waiting for me at home.

Now, the cell phone pierced into my groggy mind. "Hello," I mumbled.

"Why didn't you call me?" Eric screeched.

I woke up quickly as my hackles rose. "I'm sorry, Oh, Supreme Commander. I thought my report could wait till I'd taken a shower and had a much needed rest."

"Don't get smart with me, Donny," Eric chirped. "You should have called me the minute you had service on your phone." Before I could respond, he announced in an autocratic tone, "We're all meeting at my house in an hour. I expect you to be there."

"And what if I'm not?" I blasted back.

"Come on, Donny. Don't do this," Eric reprimanded. In a softer tone, he added, "I don't have time for one of your moods. We need your report before we can make our final plans."

I rolled my eyes. *He's always right and I'm always wrong.* "Okay, fine," I said belligerently, "I'll be there." I flipped my phone closed so hard, I almost dropped it.

Kathy will be there, too. That gave me motivation to get up and get going.

As much as I hurried to arrive at Eric's on time, I was still the last one. When I entered the house, Eric gave me an irritated shake of his head, but at least he didn't embarrass me in front of the crowd.

Eric's wife, Cindy, had laid out a smorgasbord of finger-foods, snacks, and drinks on the kitchen table. Everyone, including Sergio and Juan, sat outside around the patio with paper plates of food and pops or beers.

Figuring I had plenty of time before Eric started his "meeting," I popped open a cold beer and sipped. I scanned the food options. My stomach rumbled. I hadn't realized how hungry I had become. After filling my plate, I stepped outside to join the others. I balanced my plate and beer in one hand, while I shut the door with the other. Looking around the patio for an empty chair, my eyes stopped on Kathy's trim figure.

She gave me a friendly wave from her seat at the table.

Since the chair next to her was empty, I decided to invite myself to sit down next to her.

As I walked toward her, Kathy quickly picked up her purse from the spare seat. I hadn't seen the purse, but I couldn't help but wonder if she had, by chance, saved the seat for me.

"Thanks," I said, setting my food and beer down on the table while trying to hide my slightly trembling hands. I slid into the chair.

"How are you?" she asked, flashing me a bright smile.

"Hungry," I responded, instantly regretting it. I should have come up with some witty or funny comeback. "Hungry" wasn't going to win me any points with this bright, intelligent woman. I took a swig of beer as embarrassment set in. I felt my neck and face growing red. I have to admit that I've never been confident around women and, with Kathy being a successful doctor, I felt even more unsure of myself.

Thankfully, Eric chose that moment to start the meeting, drawing Kathy's attention away from me.

As each of the men from Steve's crew told their stories, they emphasized their amazement at the other world. I wasn't surprised at their glowing awe. I'd been over to the other side three times now, and I still had a hard time believing it was real. However, I was surprised that they downplayed the mishaps. None of them brought up my gun firing at the feet of O-cha nor the dead Indians. *What's this about? Are they so anxious to go on the trip they don't want Eric to know?*

Sergio and Juan, the two quiet, unassuming men who seemed to have the least to say and the most original resistance to entering the portal, confessed that the opportunity for the gold was too good to pass up. Both wanted in. So did Kathy and Trish.

Listening to the talk, I had to confess I wasn't as confident about my plans now as I had been when I'd first discovered the portal. People could get killed over there. Knowing that none of this would be happening if it weren't for me stepping through the portal, I felt a heavy responsibility and wondered if I should tell them, or if it were possible to put a stop to the trip before it was too late. Still, I wanted the gold. I wanted it badly. I needed it to make my own world work. The longer I sat there and listened to the reports, the more indecisive I became about what to say.

Eric finally called on me.

I gave a brief report. I lied that everything went well. I figured if no one else was going to bring up the problems, I wasn't going to tell Eric about them either. I definitely decided to keep my encounter with Butterfly a secret, not wanting my imprudent experience with her to become common knowledge, and especially, not wanting it to get back to Kathy. "As far as I'm concerned," I finished up, "we can go ahead with the trip."

My report must have satisfied Eric and Pat. Neither one had any questions for me when I finished.

As the meeting ended, I turned to Kathy. "It was nice seeing you again. I'd stay and visit, but I'm tired and I have a horrible headache. I'm going home, take some Advil, and crash and burn."

"I don't blame you. I'm tired myself," she said as she stood up and held out her hand.

Taking her offered hand in mine, a thrill raced through my body when our skin touched. "See ya later," I said, not knowing what else to say. I released her hand and moved toward Eric. "I'm going home. I'll talk to you tomorrow."

"Okay," Eric replied. "Oh, wait. Before you go, let's take a vote. Who's in favor of going back?"

Twelve hands shot into the air.

Eric nodded approvingly. "Then it's unanimous. We start moving our gear over one week from today."

As much as I wanted to go, I didn't know why those words sounded like a death sentence to me.

Chapter 14

I spent the next week ordering, purchasing, and gathering supplies and equipment. As things came in the following week, we began making many labor-intense trips through the portal to move our gear and rations to the other side. We took turns hauling things in groups so that none of us would be prevented from getting back through the portal, due to the tricky factor with time having to catch up on our side.

The second week after the meeting at Eric's house, all of us hiked into the Indian village to settle in while making final preparations for the journey to find gold. Excitement grew among our ranks as the training of the horses got underway.

Iron Cactus and the rest of the tribe had been friendly and helpful. So far, O-cha hadn't caused any problems, but he watched me with keen, piercing eyes. I kept an eye open for him, too, and avoided him like the plague.

At the end of our first week of living in the village, I found myself marching through the scrub on the desert plain along the Colorado River, just north of the village. On this day, the two Wyoming cowboy brothers, James and Tory, four Indians, and I, made up the team to work with the herd of twenty horses that had been selected for our cross-country trip into Northern California. To my dismay, O-cha had been one of the Indians assigned to work with the group this day, and I made every effort to stay as far away from him as possible.

The iron stake I used as a tethering post had come loose while working with the last horse. I pulled it out and moved it to a new spot. There, I pounded it deeply into the hard desert dirt. Grabbing a lead rope, I headed out to select a chestnut-colored mare, my next "victim," out of the brush corral we'd built. As I clipped the rope to her halter, the mangy, mean-tempered horse tried to bite me. "Dammit," I cussed under my breath.

James, the older of the two cowboys, laughed. "Better watch out, Donny. That horse is determined ta sink 'er teeth into yer backside."

"It's not funny," I complained, keeping a wary eye on her as I led her to the stake.

"Maybe she's tryin' ta kiss ya," Tory called out as he pulled a saddle cinch tighter.

I couldn't figure out if the ever-present plug of tobacco in the mouths of James and Tory caused them to talk that way, or if their Texas cowboy twang was natural. For sure, they were always chewing.

I stared at my reflection in the horse's eyeball. *God, I wish I could go home and have a cold beer and just hang out. But that's not gonna to happen until I get the gold.* As much as I hated to admit it to myself, the gold was the only thing that kept me going every time I wanted to give up….and that was all the time.

We'd been going non-stop since we'd made our last trip through the portal and started training the horses. Just in the last few days, we finally got the horses used to bridles, saddles, and packsaddles. Most of the animals were cooperating and accepting their new accessories with ease, but a few just had to be stubborn, like this one.

Even though the tribe had quite a few horses, not all members of the tribe rode or used them. Some warriors rode them when hunting, but most of them preferred to walk. The tribe used the animals mainly for hauling things from one village or campsite to another, which was probably why we were having a hard time breaking them in for riders. Most of the horses weren't used to saddles or people and had never carried the kinds of loads we were counting on them to haul for us across the country. Not that they couldn't carry the loads. They just didn't want to.

The warm afternoon April sun, though not hot like in the blazing summer months, still caused everyone to work up a good sweat. Beads of perspiration formed on the faces of my companions. Wet spots dotted the fronts, backs, and armpits of their shirts.

I tethered the ornery horse to the metal stake and moved far enough from the four-legged demon to be well out of her reach. I tore off my long-sleeved shirt and welcomed the opportunity to start my summer tan. Wiping my forehead with the shirt, I yearned for a slight breeze to cool me off, but no such luck.

The week's growth of stubble on my face itched. Now, I wished I'd brought a razor from the other side like Eric, Steve, James, and Tory. Instead, like Pat, Chad, Travis, Juan, and Sergio, I hadn't wanted to be bothered with shaving every day. The six of us sported beards of one kind or another. Unfortunately, I found I couldn't grow a full, attractive-looking beard. The hairs came out patchy, heavy on the chin and neck, thin on my cheeks. It probably didn't look all that great to Kathy, but there wasn't much I could do about it now. Eric would have a fit if I asked to borrow his razor.

Sweating profusely, I glanced toward the river. It called to me: refreshing and cool. Looking around, I wondered if anyone would notice me sneaking down to the water, just long enough for a quick swim. Everyone else seemed to be busy with the horses, so I didn't see any harm in taking a short break.

As I started toward the bank, I suddenly noticed a pile of rocks on the edge of the hill leading down to the river. *Damn, if*

Butterfly is hunting ducks, the last thing I want to do is disturb her. True, I could go upriver or downriver from her position, but looking around again, I caught O-cha staring my way. I decided I'd better wait for a swim until we were done with the horses.

As I saddled the wily mare, I paid full attention to her behavior in order to avoid being bitten, kicked, or trampled. When I finished, I moved out of kicking range, wiped my forehead with my shirt, then headed across the field to tether another horse.

On my way through the desert scrub, I thought about Kathy. I hadn't yet had an opportunity to spend any private time with her. I meant to invite her for a walk along the river with me one of these evenings before we left the Indian village. I just couldn't work up the courage yet, especially since she seemed so eager to spend as much time as possible learning about herbs from Iron Cactus.

I loved to picture myself holding Kathy's hand as we stood on the riverbank under the moonlight. The water would softly caress the shoreline as it slid by on its journey to the sea. Kathy would draw close, kiss me lightly on the lips. I'd grab her around the waist, pull her closer, and kiss her passionately as she surrendered into my arms. Later, I'd walk her back to the village and give her another gentle goodnight kiss before we entered the hut where we were all sleeping.

A distressful yelp from one of the men caught my attention. I looked up across the field to see a saddle hanging loose under a horse's belly and an Indian scurrying to get out of the way of the four thrashing hooves. Another Indian held tightly to the horse's lead rope.

"Stupid idiots," I muttered, turning to lend a hand. As soon as I realized the Indian who had escaped the horse's hooves was O-cha, I halted in my tracks, hoping someone else would step in.

"Donny," James shouted, "go help them two before they hurt that horse." James held a horse's front leg firmly between his thighs and was in the process of working on the hoof in preparation for shoeing.

Not missing the fact that James seemed more concerned about the horse's welfare than the health of the Indians, I glanced to see if Tory could go instead.

Tory shook his head in the negative, as if he knew exactly what I wanted to ask of him.

Resigned to my fate, I trudged toward the Indians, dreading what I feared would be a nasty confrontation with O-cha.

Thankfully, Rabbit, the Indian helping O-cha, held tightly to the horse's rope so that it could only buck in a circle.

Over the last five or six days, I'd met a lot more members of the tribe and was amazed at how accurately each had been named. Rabbit, for instance, had all the traits of his namesake, including timidity and wariness. He looked scared to death as I walked toward him to take the lead rope.

Relieving him of the rope, I eased the horse toward the tie-down stake. Slipping the end of the rope through the eyelet, I backed away, pulling the rope, pulling the horse's head closer to the stake. Having less and less room to maneuver, the horse finally stopped bucking. I continued to pull the rope until the horse's head came within two feet of the stake. Wary of biting teeth and slashing hooves, I moved in cautiously and tied off the rope.

Before I could remove the saddle, I heard Rabbit call out something in a voice of terror. Not understanding the language, but certainly knowing that something was very wrong, I looked at him.

He pointed at me, jabbering away with unintelligible words, his wide eyes showing shock.

O-cha, safely out of harm's way for the last few minutes, grunted loudly from where he'd been watching. Taking long, ground-eating strides, he headed straight for me with a glower on his face that told me I needed help, and soon.

"James, Tory," I screamed as I backpedaled, keeping an eye on O-cha and maintaining a good distance from him. "Get your asses over here. *Now*."

O-cha stopped five feet from me. "Rabbit says you have a tattoo of a bear on your back. Let me see."

Confused, I stood frozen in place.

"Show me the tattoo," O-cha demanded impatiently as Rabbit and the other two Indians made their way to his side.

I slowly turned my back toward them, watching over my shoulder for their reactions.

O-cha's eyes widened in surprise, then quickly narrowed into a scowl.

I turned around. I wasn't sure what was going on, but I knew it wasn't good. With my eyes still locked on O-cha, I heard James and Tory step next to me.

"What's the problem?" Tory asked, keeping an eye on O-cha, too.

O-cha blurted, "You and your kind are the problem." Without further explanation, he spun on his heels and hurried back toward the village, as though on a mission.

"What'd ya do now, Donny?" James asked, turning to me with an accusing look.

I snapped in a defensive voice, "I didn't do anything. I came over here to help, like you asked me to."

Rabbit and the other two Indians huddled together, whispering among themselves.

"Rabbit," James said, "can ya handle things here? Looks like we need ta go find out why O-cha is on the rampage all 'a sudden."

Eyes wide with fear, Rabbit and the other two nodded nervously. They headed out toward the unsaddled horses.

"I'll never understand these people," I said, feeling a sense of doom about to come down on me. I pulled on my shirt and grudgingly walked toward the village with James and Tory. "Just when I think everything's going good, I do something that violates someone's rules or pisses someone off. I'll be glad when we're on our way north to get the gold."

"I cain't agree more," Tory said, leading the way back to the settlement.

We all fell silent. I knew we were each busy with our own thoughts about what would happen when we got to the village, but I hated the fact that I was somehow responsible for it all.

I felt my heart moving into my throat as we passed the first hut on the edge of the village and I heard a commotion of loud voices coming from the area of the communal hut. I was suddenly reminded of how sorely I missed my life back in my world with a soft mattress, comfortable couch, a big TV, and plenty of ice-cold beer in the fridge.

Chapter 15

Eric's voice rose above the din of the commotion as we entered the community hut, but I couldn't hear what he was saying.

"Oh, oh," James commented. "This don't sound good."

"Yer right," Tory agreed, more to himself than anyone. "This ain't good."

Eric and Pat stood by the fire pit with Beaver, Iron Cactus, and a few older men. In turn, O-cha and two or three Indians who seemed to be supporting him stood with them. Everyone talked loudly, waving arms to make their points.

O-cha's voice seemed the loudest and most persistent.

"Dammit, I don't know what happened, Donny," Eric cried when he saw me, "but whatever you did, you really screwed up this time."

The old anger of being blamed for something I didn't do surged through me as I walked toward him. "How come you think I did something?"

Pat, calm as ever, answered for Eric. "We were talking to Beaver when O-cha came running into the village and yelling something about you being the proof he needed to have the Gateway closed forever."

Eric leaned forward, his hazel eyes dark with anger. "What the hell happened out there?"

I let out a loud breath. "I don't know," I said defensively. "O-cha freaked out about my tattoo."

A flash of recognition glinted in Pat's eyes. "That tattoo," he said, rubbing his chin. "The charging bear on your back?"

I nodded, wondering why the hell this could cause such a ruckus.

"What is it, Pat?" Eric demanded. "Why is O-cha so upset?"

"Power."

"Power?" both Eric and I said at the same time.

"Hang on." Pat turned to Beaver, standing next to him. "Is O-cha's spirit helper the bear?"

Beaver nodded with a wry twist of his mouth.

Turning back to Eric and me, Pat said soberly, "Bad news."

Before he could say more, Steve, Kathy, and Trish broke through the crowd. A large number of Indian men, women, and children, what seemed like the rest of the village, collected around the periphery of the group, filling the hut to overflowing.

"What's happening?" Trish squealed, her green eyes wide, her face pasty-white with fear.

Two huge warriors shoved the crowd out of the way and grabbed my arms.

"Wait...what are you doing?" I yelled, struggling to get free from their fierce grips.

A foot struck me in the small of my back. As the warriors let go, I went flying into the fire pit. Luckily, no fire had been lit yet.

I landed chest first. Ashes billowed up in a cloud around me. Spitting and coughing, I rolled to my side and looked to see who had kicked me.

O-cha and his loathsome group of supporters stood over me and gloated smugly. Butterfly poised herself next to them with a satisfied smirk on her face.

"What the hell's your problem?" I yelled at O-cha. "You're lucky I don't get up and kick your ass." I knew I wouldn't stand a chance against even one of these battle-hardened men, now laughing at me, but the natural reflex made me feel better to at least make some threats. I just hoped they didn't take me up on it.

"Don't worry," O-cha taunted with his mean-looking eyes and caustic tone. "You'll get your chance." He turned and sauntered away with a slight bounce to his step, as though walking on top of the world. His warning sounded more real this time. Whatever he knew that I didn't, scared me.

Realizing the eyes of the crowd had been on me this whole time, I felt the blood rush to my face in embarrassment. I stood up and brushed the ashes from my clothes.

Kathy touched me on the arm. "You okay?" The deep concern in her eyes shot an electrical bolt through me.

Still brushing off the ashes, I nodded, afraid my voice would betray my fear. She was the last person I wanted to know how scared I was.

"If there's anything I can do for you, let me know?"

Wow. I wanted to say, "Will you walk with me along the river, tonight?" but, unfortunately, this didn't seem like the appropriate time or place to discuss it.

A commotion at the back of the crowd drew my attention from Kathy's wonderful, worry-filled eyes.

Chad, Travis, Juan, and Sergio bullied their way through the on-lookers, bringing together our entire group for whatever occurrence was about to happen. Trish stood just behind Kathy, clinging to Kathy's arm as though Kathy would protect her. Pat looked at me with a slight pensiveness on his face.

Not good, I told myself.

Eric, still glaring at me for causing this ruckus, tightened his lips and kept silent for once.

In fact, silence descended over the whole milling mass as Chief Iron Cactus and a couple of hunched-back, wizened warriors jostled their way through the throng and out one of the doors. After their passing, the crowd followed, eager to watch the action. We went along, wondering what was going to happen next.

* * *

Outside, a boy of eleven or twelve ran up to Iron Cactus and handed him what looked like a long ceremonial robe of colored woven fibers and a headdress covered in brown-and-white hawk or eagle feathers. After he donned the robe and headdress, Iron cactus and the two elder warriors climbed the ramp to the top of the community hut. There, Iron Cactus held his hands above his head, silently demanding full attention and submission from the crowd.

It was suddenly so silent that, if not for the sound of a barking dog and the cry of a hawk soaring high ahead, I thought I'd gone deaf.

Despite Iron Cactus's commanding presence on the rooftop in calling everyone to attention, a growing nervous shuffling moved through the expectant crowd and seemed to fill the air with a tension that needed release.

I gulped. The occasional thoughts that I had made a big mistake in coming back through the portal and interacting with the Indians after the warnings of my dreams, seemed to be on the verge of turning into reality. An unseen, festering black cloud loomed so large above me, I feared it was about to strike me down with lightening. Maybe God was punishing me for all the mistakes I'd ever made in my life, this one being the biggest.

Iron Cactus finally spoke. His voice, though quiet, carried far enough for all gathered to hear. Unfortunately, he spoke in his native language and I was a little worried about asking someone to translate.

I didn't see O-cha now. He had walked off too confidently, acted too cocky. He had something up his sleeve, and I dared not even think what that could be. My sixth sense kept biting me, worried about O-cha's threat and whatever Iron Cactus was saying.

"What's he saying, Pat?" Eric whispered.

Pat shrugged his shoulders and shook his head back and forth, indicating he couldn't follow Iron Cactus's speech well enough to translate.

The crowd murmured and grunted among themselves. At first, their faces gave no clue about what their leader was saying, but my gut tightened when several male Indians suddenly shot angry, menacing looks my way.

My fellow travelers seemed to be as confused and frightened as I was. They stood stoically in silence, waiting for the verdict to come down.

Up until now, Iron Cactus had played our ally, pleading our innocence before O-cha's vigilante attitude. I couldn't be sure that Iron Cactus hadn't now become an enemy and was planning my demise. And, who knew what kind of fallout would affect my innocent companions from the other world?

While Iron Cactus droned on, my mind wandered back to Rabbit's nervous reaction to my tattoo and the puzzling wrath from O-cha. Why would my tattoo bother the tribe so much? I looked around at all the men and women standing at the front of the crowd. They all wore tattoos, mainly on their faces, arms, and chests. Some of them had tattoos covering most of their bodies. Why would they care that I had a tattoo?

I studied Iron Cactus's face. The swirls and dots, mixed with chevrons, squares, circles, and squiggly lines, formed an impressive and intricate pattern. Done in a rainbow of natural colors, I didn't see how a tattoo parlor back home could have done a better job.

The younger Indians had fewer tattoos, some just on the bottoms of their chins. Maybe the Indians earned their tattoos by age. The longer they lived, the more tattoos they collected. Other than the very young children, whose faces remained untouched by added lines and colors, the few Indians who had no tattoos at all on their faces, like O-cha and Beaver, now seemed like an anomaly.

What had not dawned on me until now, was that all the patterns of the tattoos on the Indians were basically geometrical forms. None of these people sported pictures of animals, women, serpents, or birds, things of nature. I always thought Indians worshipped nature, so I didn't see why they wouldn't use animals as symbols for their tattoos. Didn't they have any good artists in the village?

As these thoughts went through my mind, I began to realize that the detailed image of the angry bear on my back had everything to do with this, and that I wasn't going to like what it meant or the outcome of the tribunal that was taking place before me.

With shaking fingers, I pulled out my pipe.

Eric narrowed his eyes at me.

I almost laughed. What difference was his opinion going to make at this point with my life on the line? Of course, maybe the glare was meant for the whole affair, me getting everyone else involved, not just the smoke.

When Iron Cactus finished his speech, he apparently opened the floor to a debate. For another thirty minutes or so, heavy arguing and yelling passed between the tribe members. It stopped abruptly when O-cha appeared at the base of the hut after having pushed his way through the crowd.

My heart sank.

O-cha pointed at me and spoke harshly in English. "Outsiders may not know our customs. That doesn't matter.

Being here among us, they must live by our law." He turned and shoved his way out of the crowd with several followers close behind.

With O-cha's constant appearing and disappearing. I prayed that the disappearance would last forever this time.

Eric took advantage of the quiet crowd and called out, "Beaver, what's going on?"

Beaver held up his palm and shook his head, plainly indicating that he couldn't explain anything at the moment. Meanwhile, the crowd began to break up, leaving only Beaver behind with us outsiders.

Iron Cactus and the two old warriors descended the ramp. The chief glanced at me before they went their own ways. I couldn't read anything from his eyes.

Beaver stepped toward us, stress showing on his ashen face. He asked, "Other than Donny, do any of you have tattoos?"

Kathy, James, and Tory shook their heads in the negative. The other six, including Trish, silently and halfhearted nodded yes.

I could feel the dread running through them that they might be in just as much trouble as I was.

"Are any of the tattoos of animals?"

All of them shook their heads no.

Beaver's face softened. "Good."

A wave of relief seemed to pass over the whole group, although this couldn't be discerned from any blatant observations of their behavior.

It looked like I was standing alone with my angry bear.

Kathy piped up, her voice tight with tension. "What does our having tattoos have to do with any of this?"

Beaver sighed heavily, as if he was having a hard time dealing with the situation. He looked at me directly. "I'm sorry.

I did everything I could to save you from this situation. Our laws and customs are clear. You've offended O-cha. Now, you must pay the penalty."

Pay the penalty? My heart went into my throat. I could barely speak. As everyone waited, I struggled to get out my question. "Is... is... is this because...because I have a bear tattoo on my back?"

"Yes." A pained look came into Beaver's dark eyes. "Our customs allow tattooing that does not offend or affect another person. We use only shapes and symbols to prevent a problem." He sighed deeply again. "O-cha claims your bear tattoo is stealing his power."

Pat quietly nodded next to me. That's what Pat had meant when he had said this whole affair was about power.

"What do you mean?" Trish asked in a high-pitched nervous voice.

"O-cha is convinced that, ever since Donny showed up, O-cha's spirit helper, the bear, has abandoned him. He claims Donny's tattoo has stolen it."

"That's insane," Eric blurted, folding his arms over his chest. "If his spirit helper's abandoned him, there's got to be a perfectly good scientific reason why."

Pat chuckled. "They don't know anything about science, Eric. They're barbarians. Plus, they're superstitious as hell. I can understand why they are raising such a fuss about this. I don't think we have any choice but to play along."

Play along? Great. I'm the one whose neck is in the noose.

"So what happens now?" asked Tory.

Beaver hesitated again, as if what he had to say was hard for him to spit out. He eyed me with a look of apology. "O-cha has called for a Warrior's Challenge."

Damn. Goose bumps raced up my back, over my shoulders, and down my arms. I choked out, "Warrior's Challenge?"

"I've heard of this," Pat broke in. "It's a method of settling disputes between two people. Or even two completely different tribes."

"How do they settle these disputes?" Eric asked, looking from Beaver to me and showing the first signs of parental concern.

Beaver said, "One warrior challenges another to a fight."

"Oh, great," I said, turning to the group. "I don't stand a chance of beating O-cha in a fight."

Their sympathetic looks didn't calm the tremors building inside me.

"Is this a fight to the death?" Eric asked. I hadn't even thought about that.

Beaver shook his head. "No, it isn't."

Relieved, I asked Beaver, "So, what happens after he beats the crap out of me?"

"You will be forced to go back to your world and never return."

Kathy's eyes, filled with compassion, glanced at me. In an optimistic tone, she asked Beaver, "What happens if he refuses to fight?".

"He'll be recognized as a coward," Beaver said sadly, "and sacrificed to the gods."

My heart skipped a beat as visions of my recurring dream flashed through my mind. Over the pounding of my heart, I heard the *what's, oh-no's*, and *you've-got-to-be-kidding-me's* come from the other members of my group. I looked at Eric.

He seemed especially perplexed. He'd always managed to be confident and courageous in the face of any conflict, even problems I brought to him that I couldn't resolve myself. Eric might scream at me and belittle me, but he always knew what to do. Now, Big Brother seemed to shrink. It looked like this was something he couldn't fix.

"I don't think you have a choice, Donny," Pat said gently. "If you want to win, you should start thinking about how you might trick or distract O-cha. You won't beat him by size or strength."

Beaver nodded in agreement. "O-cha is one of our best warriors. I'm sorry to say, you're going to need a miracle to win this fight."

I heard Kathy groan next to me. Just when I was starting to get her attention, I had a battle to fight that I just might lose. How would that look to my fair maiden? Not good.

I swallowed hard. I just hoped the hell that O-cha wouldn't *accidently* kill me, making me look like a complete fool the last day of my life.

"When are they supposed to fight?" Eric bravely asked.

"Now." Beaver motioned for me to follow him through the street.

I could barely get my leaden feet to move as my mind slipped into a stupor of silence and disorientation.

Chapter 16

Standing by myself on the inner edge of a human ring that surrounded the designated fighting area in the gully below the village bluff, I had never felt so alone and scared. Under the hot sun, I felt like I was going to be sick. I'd had only a few moments to come up with a plan to save myself, so I'd hurriedly explained it to Pat.

"I don't know," Pat had said with little conviction in his voice. "Maybe it'll work, maybe not. At least, a bad plan is better than no plan."

I looked over my shoulder at the rest of my traveling companions. They stood solemnly in a row directly behind me. To my chagrin, they were going to have a front-row view of my upcoming beating. I dared not even look at Kathy. I couldn't bear to think of the humiliation this whole affair had brought upon me, probably causing me to lose her forever. And just when she was coming around to noticing me.

I looked across the dirt ring at my opponent, standing just twenty feet away.

Stripped down to a breechcloth, his skin slick with sweat, O-cha grunted and flexed his muscles, warming up for an easy fight. His muscles seemed outrageously huge to my puny build.

I gulped. He must have pumped up with weights or something to try to freak me out. Thinking about that, I chuckled to myself, realizing O-cha's plan was working well. *Hell, he didn't have to go to all that trouble. I'd be freaked out anyway.*

Standing shirtless, I hoped my white skin made my tattoo stand out like a flashing neon sign. In defiance, I wanted every

Indian to see it and cower under its perceived spirit-robbing powers.

For the fight, I'd decided to leave on my cowboy boots and jeans. If I got knocked down, and I was sure I would be, I wanted all the protection I could get from the rocks and spindly mesquite bushes that dotted the impromptu arena.

Beaver stepped into the center of the circle.

"What are the rules?" I asked as I wiped my sweaty palms on my jeans. I felt like I might faint, but I had to hold myself together.

"Short of killing each other, there are no rules." He handed me a leather belt with a knife and a tomahawk attached. "Good luck, Donny," he whispered as he passed me. "You're going to need it."

I fastened the belt around my waist. I couldn't help but wonder why we needed the weapons if we weren't supposed to kill each other. I guess we were allowed to cripple and maim.

With a quick glance at O-cha, I pulled out the tomahawk and put my plan into action.

As O-cha stepped toward me, I tipped my head back, closed my eyes just enough to still see O-cha, and started humming.

O-cha stopped dead in his tracks.

The crowd began to murmur among themselves.

I kept standing in the same position and continued humming, now a little louder.

"What is he doing?" O-cha called out.

"He's meditating," Pat answered calmly.

"Meditating?" O-cha asked in disbelief.

"Yeah, he's calling on the spirit of the bear to help him kick your ass."

O-cha laughed.

I hummed little louder, raising to a higher tone.

"This is funny," O-cha said, circling around me. "What's he going to do next? Get down on the ground and chase me around?"

My heart sank. I'd hoped that acting like I'd been taken over by the spirit of the bear, O-cha would become leery of me, giving me a slim chance of striking the first blow. *Ah, the hell with it. I might as well get it over with.* I stopped humming, opened my eyes, threw my arms wide open, and charged. "Aaarrrrrrrrrrrrrrr."

O-cha easily sidestepped the attack.

I barreled past him and ended up in the arms of two of O-cha's cronies.

The crowd cheered.

O-cha played off the ovation by bowing repeatedly, while the two cronies roughly shoved me backwards into the ring.

Flailing my arms to catch my balance, I unwittingly slammed my tomahawk into the back of O-cha's head as he took another bow.

The crowd went silent.

O-cha dropped to the ground.

I tripped on my feet and fell on top of him. Rolling off as quickly as I could, I stood and stared at the blood running from O-cha's head. *Oh, God, I hope I didn't kill him. What will they do to me now? I wasn't supposed to kill him.*

O-cha's two warrior friends rushed into the ring and rolled him over. By this time, Iron Cactus was stomping his way across the dirt to the scene of the crime with a deadly scowl on his tattooed face.

I stood shaking in my boots, not knowing which way to turn, not knowing what I was supposed to do now, wondering if I could make it back to the portal without being caught if I started running.

My fellow companions seemed stunned, unable to move or speak. I caught a glimpse of Kathy looking at me with total shock in her eyes.

I bit my lip. *What have I done?*

Iron Cactus knelt next to O-cha and studied him closely. A few other Indians, including Beaver joined him. It seemed like a long time passed before Iron Cactus stood up. He made some kind of announcement in gibberish.

The crowd roared.

My pulse raced. I pulled out the knife with my left hand and raised both the knife and tomahawk in the air. If I had to go down fighting the whole village, I wanted a weapon in each hand.

Iron Cactus spun toward me. He pointed. "Okay. You win. Bear win." He pointed to O-cha. "Him lose." His claw-like hand took me by the arm. "You come me. Me fix you good."

Still holding the tomahawk and knife, I jerked back and looked at him warily. "Where're you taking me?"

"You good," Iron Cactus said. He licked his tongue across his tattooed lips, like getting ready for a tasty meal.

The crowd started moving in.

The hot sun beat down on my face. My eyes blurred from the sweat dropping off my brow. My mind slipped into a panic. These people wanted to eat me. It was a trick. Iron Cactus was tricking me into disarming myself.

I slowly backed up, watching all sides, ready for someone to jump me any moment.

My companions stood stiffly on the edge of the ring, doing nothing to help me.

Iron Cactus stepped forward. His lips moved.

I couldn't hear his words, but he was cornering me. I lifted the tomahawk. "You'll never know how good I'll taste, you evil son-of-a-"

A hand shot out from nowhere and gripped my wrist. The owner of the hand bent my arm down and back, forcing me to lean forward or have my arm broken. The tomahawk and knife were ripped from my hands.

Released, I slumped to the ground in defeat and cradled my sore arm. A hand fell hard on my shoulder, causing me to almost jump out of my skin.

"Donny, you did it," Eric said proudly. "You beat him."

I dared to look up to see all my companions standing around me…untied, uncooked, uneaten.

Steve nearly laughed, shaking his head. "I can't believe it, Donny. I never thought you could beat that big guy."

"Whoa, Donny…way ta go," Travis yelled.

Kathy smiled, looking relieved and concerned at the same time.

Pat stuck out his hand to help me rise to my feet. "I think Iron Cactus wants you to go with him." He nudged me in the direction of the chief.

Beaver approached. "You must come with us, Donny. We must finish this business with O-cha."

A string of tall warriors stealthily inserted themselves between myself and my group.

"Why are you taking him?" Eric asked Beaver in a demanding tone. "He won the fight, fair and square."

Even though I didn't think Eric's words were going to make a difference, a warm feeling washed over me that Eric seemed to be taking an interest in protecting me, now that O-cha was out of the way.

Beaver placed a hand on Eric's shoulder. "Nothing bad will happen. We'll bring him back soon." He turned and motioned for the warriors to bring me.

With an Indian escort on each side, I had no choice but to trudge listlessly forward with them. I might as well have been handcuffed. As I passed the place where O-cha had fallen, I saw a dark pool of blood on the dirt.

O-cha's body was being carried back to the village ahead of us by a group of his own men. With O-cha's arms hanging limp at his sides, his head bobbing loosely, and his eyes closed, it looked like he was dead.

Oh, my God. I killed a man.

* * *

I soon found myself ducking into the short entrance hole that led inside Iron Cactus's hut. I blinked repeatedly as my eyes adjusted to the dim interior after the stark brightness of being out in the sun for a long time. The cool air across the sweat on my back made me almost shiver. My energy seemed to be slowly returning.

Four raised platforms that looked like beds, hugged the curve of the wall on my left. Racks and shelves made of wood took up the rest of the wall space. The myriad of bowls, some hewn from rock and some hand-woven with reeds, probably held the chief's many medicines.

As my eyes came into full focus of the room, they settled on Iron Cactus and eight older men, sitting in a half-circle around a fire pit. No doubt, these men would be my court, jury, and judge.

With a gentle nudge on my arm by the warrior standing next to me, I moved further into the room until I stood next to Beaver in front of the fire pit. We faced the silent group of what I presumed to be Iron Cactus's aged advisors.

Beaver and Iron Cactus each took a turn speaking to the group for ten or fifteen minutes. Other than a grunt or occasional nod, the old men remained silent and immobile. When Beaver finished his final talk, one of the elderly men made a short speech.

I shifted my feet, growing restless about what was going to happen. I didn't know what kind of rules or punishment the tribe had for killing someone, especially someone of their own kind by an outsider.

After a what seemed like a long silence, Iron Cactus proceeded to call on each man in turn. That man would give a shout and a nod of his head.

They are taking a vote? My mouth went dry.

As soon as the rounds had been made with all the men giving their shouts, I couldn't stand waiting to know my fate. I leaned toward Beaver and asked, "What's happening? Are they going to kill me? Are they going to send me back home?"

"No," Beaver said solemnly. A slight smile seemed to form at the corners of his mouth. "They are going to conduct a ceremony. A ceremony to initiate you into the tribe as an honorary member."

I stared at Beaver, then shot a look at Iron Cactus. I scanned the faces of all the men sitting on the other side of the fire. *Honorary member? Did I hear right?*

Iron Cactus spoke directly to Beaver, nodded at me, then sat in silence.

Beaver motioned for me to sit down on the ground. "We've never had anything like this happen," he explained softly. "They didn't know what to do."

As I looked across the fire pit at the old men, I saw the confusion in their wary looks. Some of them began to talk quietly among themselves.

Beaver went on. "Iron Cactus and I convinced them that your bear magic was so powerful that to harm you in any way would bring down the wrath of the gods. To appease the gods, they decided to accept you into the tribe. You know what they say in your world: If you can't beat 'em, join 'em."

"But...but..." I had so many questions, I didn't know which one to start asking. I mostly feared that this honorary membership might ruin my chances for getting the gold and going back to my own world. What would be expected of me?

Beaver chuckled at my nervousness.

He reminded me so much of Pat in the way he just took things in stride and seemed confident that everything would always turn out okay.

"Don't worry, Donny. All your questions will be answered in time. For now, I must ask you an important question before the ceremony starts. Are you willing to go through with this ceremony to become a member of the tribe?"

"What if I'm not?"

Beaver's mouth pursed and his voice grew solemn. "Then the elders have no choice but to have you sacrificed to the gods."

My mouth dropped open. "But you just said, if they harmed me in any way, it would bring down the wrath of the gods. How could they sacrifice me?"

"They cannot allow your power to be used against them. If you are a member, they will trust your power to work in their favor. If not, they will risk destroying it to protect themselves and tribe."

I couldn't believe how fast things could turn around. I had to decide whether to go through some kind of unknown ceremony…and, God forbid, a grueling ceremony…or die?

"In some ways, we're a complicated people," Beaver said. "You may never fully understand our ways. Make it easy on yourself. Accept the ceremony." Despite Beaver's easy-going manner, he seemed to be pleading with me to make the right decision.

Great, here I am, about to be made an honorary member of a tribe I'll never understand. Maybe it doesn't make a difference in the long run, but my gut is telling me that my nightmares will come back to bite me tonight if I don't go along with the new plan. Also, I don't know what will happen to my companions if I get sacrificed, and I definitely won't have a shot at Kathy.

"Okay," I said grudgingly, "but everything is happening so fast. I feel overwhelmed."

"Don't worry. I'll be with you to explain things. The ceremony isn't complicated. Just answer a couple of questions and part with some blood and hair."

I shot him a look. "Part with some blood and hair? Are you kidding?"

"Nothing to worry about. I'll be there. Now, do you agree to go through with the ceremony?"

How did I get myself into this mess?

I looked around at the elderly Indians, all now staring at me. *Can you believe it? This is my new family.*

It suddenly occurred to me that being an honorary member of the tribe might have some perks, like going a long way in getting more of the Indians to help with finding the gold or making the whole adventure easier. None of my fellow companions, not even Eric, were getting this honor, so it would give me some points of authority with them. After all, the whole trip was my idea in the first place, and Eric had stolen it out from under me. My connection with the Indians would raise my status in everyone's eyes. *I'll be like a hero. Kathy's hero. Yes!*

I looked at Beaver and stated firmly, "I'll do it."

Beaver smiled and nodded to the elders.

The older men grunted their approval and stood up to leave.

"Come with me, Donny," Beaver said, pushing on my arm. "We've got a lot to do. And not much time to do it in."

Chapter 17

Feeling embarrassed and self-conscious wearing nothing but a breechcloth, I walked barefoot down the street with Beaver and the elders to the communal hut. Iron Cactus led the procession in his ceremonial garb.

It seemed like the whole community stood on the sidelines and watched the parade. The crowd seemed larger than just the local community. I wondered if word had spread to neighboring villages and some of the residents had made a quick journey to watch the ceremony. It hadn't taken all that long for the ceremony to get underway.

After we entered the hut, we stopped in front of the fire pit. Beaver and I stood on one side of the pit, while Iron Cactus and the elders circled around to the other side.

Iron Cactus remained standing while the other elders sat down cross-legged in a semi-circle, like earlier in Iron Cactus's hut. When all the surrounding observers in the hut sat down, I started to sit myself, but Beaver grabbed my elbow to indicate that we had to stay standing.

I wished I could pull my pipe out of my pocket to calm my nerves, but I didn't have a pocket or my pipe. My fingers nervously played with the fringe hanging on the side of my breechcloth as I waited for the ceremony to begin.

I glanced to my left where Pat, Steve, and Steve's crew sat tensely. They looked at me with concern. Eric gave me that what-the-hell-are-you-doing? glare. I wondered how much my friends knew about the purpose of the ceremony, and whether or not anyone had informed them I was to be made an honorary member of the tribe.

Sitting next to Eric, Trish smiled, almost bubbling over with giddiness, like she was attending a wedding or something.

Kathy, on the other hand, kept her eyes down. She tightened her lips, like she was trying really hard not to laugh. She coughed into her hand and covered her mouth.

I felt my face turning fire-engine red as I quickly turned toward the circle, hoping she wouldn't see me blushing if she looked up. I just wanted to get this over with, get the gold, and go home. This whole trip was turning out to be more than I could handle.

I thought about the portal...*Blind Man's Gateway*, as Pat's tribe had called it. How blind and innocent I had been when I had first come through. I had miscalculated that it would be so easy to come to this side, get a bunch of gold, and return home to live in comfort and luxury, never having to work again. I never imagined all the problems we'd have with the natives. And we still had a few days before we planned to leave the village. What more could possibly happen in that time? Would we ever get out of here?

No one had said anything about me killing O-cha. The elders seemed to be fine with it, since they were making me a member. I wondered if O-cha's cronies would try to get revenge.

Iron Cactus raised his hands and spoke to the crowd in his own language. After a few sentences, he motioned for me to come forward. Beaver escorted me around the pit to where I stood before the old chief.

I hated knowing everyone was staring at me and my white, almost naked body. I hoped they got a good dose of the angry bear on my back, the cause of all this commotion.

Iron Cactus chanted a few words, then stepped forward and cut off a lock of my hair with a sharp handmade knife. He lifted the lock for all to see, then dropped it in a clay pot that was being held by one of the other elders. Continuing to chant,

Iron Cactus opened my hand and put the knife point to my thumb.

I wanted to jerk my hand away, but he held tightly. It took all my will power to restrain myself for fear I might insult the tribe by acting like a baby. Sweat poured from my forehead as Iron Cactus pressed firmly with the knife, breaking the skin slightly. It stung like hell, but I wasn't about to whimper with Kathy and the whole crew watching me.

Still chanting, Iron Cactus held my thumb over the pot and allowed a few drops of blood to fall.

When he released my hand, I wanted to suck on it to make it feel better, but thought better of it in front of the crowd.

Iron Cactus raised his chant to a higher pitch and lifted his arms above his head. The old Indian with the pot mixed the contents with his fingers.

Earlier, Beaver had told me the pot contained the hair and blood of every member of the tribe who had ever lived. The idea of being a part of that heritage bolstered my ego a little.

Iron Cactus finally stopped chanting and lowered his arms. He stood directly in front of me and the corners of his mouth turned up in a kind of smile. His dark eyes seemed to dance in the maze of tattoo patterns on his face. "You part us. Need help now."

I raised my brow in bewilderment. I turned to Beaver.

He shrugged his shoulders.

Seeming to catch my confusion, Iron Cactus spoke briefly to Beaver.

Beaver's eyes flew open in shock.

"What?" I asked, suddenly terrified again. "What's wrong? What'd he say?"

"He said you are one of us now. He's going to give you status."

"Is that good?"

A strange, wary look sat on Beaver's face. "Just do what I tell you. We must see what happens."

One of the old men handed Iron Cactus a flat rock containing small dollops of nature-colored paints. The chief picked up a stick about the size of a pencil. It had been sharpened on one end. Holding my chin firmly with one of his hands, he began dabbing into the paint and drawing designs on my face.

The paint felt cool to the touch. The makeshift brush tickled a little. Even though I couldn't see what Iron Cactus was drawing, his strokes told me he was painting the same kinds of lines, chevrons, and patterns that the tribe used in their tattoos. This temporary tattoo would make me look like the rest of the tribe. I started liking the idea of looking like a fierce warrior. I found myself standing a little taller in my near nakedness under Iron Cactus's shadow.

After a short while, Iron Cactus stepped away so the rest of the tribe could see his work.

As I turned to face each corner of the room, gasps of astonishment spread throughout the Indian crowd. Stunned looks appeared on the faces of the eight elders around the fire pit. Beaver quietly groaned when I turned to him. Angry words hissed from somewhere behind me.

Before I could ask what was going on, a familiar voice called out in rage.

As the whole room seemed to exploded in turmoil, I turned to see O-cha standing at one of the entrances as a few of his buddies fanned out on either side of him.

O-cha's blazing eyes tore into me. His arm muscles bulged as he clenched his fists. An angry growl emitted from his throat. Like a dragon, he huffed fire from his nose. The image of the Incredible Hulk popped into my head.

I swallowed hard. O-cha wasn't dead. He'd arisen, angrier than ever.

Eric, Pat, Steve, and the rest of the crew shot to my side, surrounding Beaver and myself with their hands on their weapons. Trish and Kathy crowded into the circle next to me.

By now, most of the other Indians were on their feet, milling around, talking loudly among themselves as they exited through the four doors.

Iron Cactus and the elders remained in a group, all of them standing now. An aura of hardness seemed to form around the chief as he glowered at O-cha. He directed a few slow, harsh words toward O-cha.

For a moment, O-cha stood defiantly, then turned away with his buddies.

As the elders sullenly filed out of the room, Iron Cactus put a hand on my shoulder and squeezed it. He winked and smiled at me, then silently followed the others outside.

* * *

"What's going on, Beaver?" I pleaded.

"Iron Cactus didn't make you an honorary member. He adopted you as his son."

I blinked, trying to get a grasp of what he meant.

"That's good, isn't it?" Trish squeaked in an optimistic tone, not seeming to sense the danger of it all.

"It would be," Beaver stated wryly, "if it wasn't for O-cha."

"What do you mean?" Eric asked, glaring at me.

Like it's all my fault.

"By beating O-cha in the fight, Donny proved his bear spirit helper to be stronger than O-cha's. O-cha has lost face. He'll never be as powerful as he once was in the eyes of the community."

"And what about the chief making Donny his son?" Eric asked impatiently.

"By adopting him, Iron Cactus gave him more status than O-cha. Donny ranks even above me in the tribe now."

"He adopted me?" I asked with uncertainty, looking at the others, as though someone should have the answer. "Why would he adopt me?"

"The reason doesn't matter," Beaver said in a flat tone. "As far as the tribe goes, you are his son." Beaver backed away and started to leave.

"Wait, Beaver. What's expected of me? What do I do? Will I be able to go back home?"

With a dismal look in his eyes, Beaver turned to face me. "Yes, you can go back home. Your life won't change. But certain members of our tribe will treat you differently."

I didn't miss the reference to *our* tribe.

"Beaver," Pat said, stepping forward, "I'm not sure I understood what O-cha yelled to Iron Cactus. It had something to do with death, didn't it?"

Beaver made eye contact with each one of us before he spoke. "O-cha told Iron Cactus that, if it was the last thing he would do, he was going to kill you, all of you, plus everyone who helps you, including me and Iron Cactus."

"What did Iron Cactus say to him?" Eric asked.

"That he was to leave the village. That he was no longer welcome in the tribe."

Kathy put her hand on her chest. "Do you really think O-cha will go through with it?"

Beaver nodded.

Pat agreed. "I do, too."

"From now until we leave," Eric said, taking control, "I want none of us to be alone. Kathy, Trish, you are to stay together and I want one of us with you at all times. James, will the horses be ready in two days?"

"We got enough ready now. The one's we was workin' with today is extras. They ain't essential."

"That's great," Eric said. He looked around the group. "Is there any reason we can't leave in the morning then?"

Pat shrugged. "I don't see why not." He turned to Beaver. "Can our guide and camp helper be ready to leave tomorrow?"

"They're ready."

"Then it's settled," Eric stated, giving me a cold, cursory glance in my nakedness. "We leave at first light tomorrow morning. Be ready."

My ire rose. *Whatever bad happens, he blames me, even though I have no control over the events.*

As we headed out of the hut, my head reeled with the impossibility of it all. I didn't get it that I was a son of the chief and everyone's life was on the line because of me. Although, it was kinda cool to be a warrior. Even with my cowboy boots and jeans, the warrior paint would make me look as fierce as the Indians. I couldn't wait to see what I looked like. I hoped the paint wouldn't wash off too quickly.

One thing for sure, I was looking forward to getting out of this village. Even with O-cha exiled, I didn't trust the Indians after the fiasco in the hut. I didn't trust my own people. *The Indians...my own people.* Wow, that thought seemed weird.

Traveling hundreds of miles away from the portal didn't give me a lot of reassurance, but at least we would have our freedom and no one to account to. For the first time, I sort of liked the idea that Eric was in charge. He always made sure things stayed organized and knew how to handle problems that arose. He'd also had a lot more experience with backpacking, camping, and horses than I did. Maybe it was best that the rest of the group didn't know all of this was my idea in the first place.

From now on, I'll just tag along and keep my mouth shut. I'll get a good stash of gold and lie low. That way, no one can blame me if things go wrong again.

* * *

The next morning, at the crack of dawn, the twelve of us had our pack horses loaded and the riding horses saddled.

Beaver had offered to be our guide and scout. That surprised me. Maybe he wanted to get away from the uproar in the village, too. Or, maybe being a Keeper, it was his duty to keep an eye out on us outsiders.

Another Indian, Coyote, had volunteered to be our cook and camp helper. Coyote refused to ride a horse, but he agreed to lead one of the pack horses.

As I gave a last pull on the cinch of my saddle, James started handing out packages of women's pantyhose. "I want ever'body ta put these things on," he exclaimed.

Sergio held up his palms, refusing to take one.

Following in kind, Juan backed up. His scrunched face and dark eyes clearly read, "I don't think so."

I'm sure my painted face said the same thing, in concurrence with all the other macho men in the group. I had made sure not to wash my face so I wouldn't remove my warrior paint. I did, however, feel a lot more macho in my cowboy boots, jeans, and flannel shirt than in a breechcloth.

When James tried to give Travis a package of pantyhose, Travis stood his ground. "Seriously, dude...no way."

Tory chuckled. "Have it yer way, but them will keep ya from gittin' saddle sores on yer inner thighs and butt."

Eric asked, "How is wearing those things gonna keep us from getting sore?"

James handed Pat a package. "When yer ridin', jeans tend ta bunch up and rub 'gainst yer skin. The slick pantyhose lets yer jeans slide, not rub a sore on yer leg."

"Makes sense to me," Pat said, accepting the package.

Eric grabbed a package, tore it open, and held up the dangling nylon contraption.

We all laughed.

Trish giggled.

"What I want to know," Steve said with a hint of amusement, "is how you discovered this little bit of knowledge in the first place."

"Yeah," Travis jumped in. "Were you secretly wearing pantyhose under your panties, or what?"

James laughed. "No, I ain't no cross-dresser. Right after I got outta high school, my brother and me worked on a dude ranch. One just outside Yellerstone Park. The owners insisted we tell all them guests ta wear 'em before takin' 'em out on a ride."

Tory broke in. "Yup, and the next day, ya could sure tell which ones of the macho men refused ta wear 'em. They was walkin' 'round like they'd shat in their pants." His little imitation of a man trying to walk with a sore rear-end seemed to convince some of us to wear the pantyhose.

"Hell, if it'll keep me from walking like that," Steve said, holding out his hand, "I'll take one."

Smiling, and maybe a little embarrassed, both Kathy and Trish willingly accepted the pantyhose, then hurried off together behind a small hill of mesquite bushes to change.

James tossed me a package.

I'd ridden horses before, but only a few hours at a time. I painfully remembered how sore I'd been the next day. I couldn't imagine how it would feel after sitting in a saddle for eight or ten hours. I knew both James and Tory had a lot of experience with horses. They seemed to know what they were doing. I decided to go along with it. Hell, I'd wear high heels and a sun bonnet if it would help get me to the gold and back home faster. Since waking this morning from another dream, a bad feeling in the pit of my stomach just wasn't going away.

Juan and Sergio stepped forward and each reluctantly accepted a package of the women's apparel.

Only Travis and Chad, the two muscle-bound brutes, continued to refuse.

"I'm not wearing pantyhose," Chad stated again and again as he fiddled with the straps on his saddle.

Travis shook his head indignantly. "I know how to ride. I'm not putting those things on either."

"Suit yerselves," James said to the naysayers. He stuck the leftover packages in a pocket off his saddle. "But don't ya complain tamorrow mornin' when ya cain't walk, let alone sit on yer horse."

Those of us daring to take the chance and try something new, went behind the pack horses and removed our boots and jeans. Laughing and making fun, we had a hell of a time struggling into the darned things. More than ever, I couldn't understand women wanting to put up with this torture.

As we finished redressing, Beaver and Coyote headed toward us, leading Beaver's horse. We saddled up, not taking time to say good-by to anyone in the village.

I wondered if Iron Cactus was glad to see me go, being that his decision to make me his son caused such a ruckus in the community.

I sure didn't know what was going to happen ahead of us, but I was glad to leave the village problems behind. What bothered me most, though, was the unrelenting knot in my stomach from the previous night's dream of violence and death that seemed to hang over me like a guillotine about ready to fall.

Chapter 18

The next morning, rising from my bedroll in our first camp, I was glad I'd worn the pantyhose. Even though I felt bruised and sore from sitting on the hard saddle, I didn't have the classic chaffing sores that made walking difficult.

That wasn't the case for Travis and Chad. Within three hours of leaving the village, both macho men had been squirming in their saddles in discomfort. By the end of the day, they'd both gotten off their horses and duck-walked, leading their horses by hand. They stumbled into camp some two hours after the rest of us had set up and settled in. They swore they'd wear the pantyhose this day forward, but I'm sure the damage had been done. It would take time for their sores to heal.

The sun had not yet skimmed the low craggy mountains that formed the western border of the desert valley where we had made camp for the night. A slight chill filled the morning air, unusual for an April desert morning. But soon enough, the sun would be beating down on us and we would look forward to that chill again.

Already, Coyote had a fire going and food cooking in a large pot. The squirrely little man couldn't have been more than five-foot-four with only a hundred pounds of flesh and bone. I thought he was a child when I had first seen him. He had to be the runt of the entire village of giant men standing six feet tall or more.

Coyote's thin face and body reflected his quiet, shy nature. He didn't talk much and kept to himself in the little time we'd known him. He continued to refuse to ride a horse, preferring to lead one of the packhorses and walk alongside it.

I had feared his walking would slow us down, but he moved at a good pace. I couldn't figure out why someone who seemed to hate being around people would consent to spending three or four months with a group of men and women who would be together almost constantly for the sake of safety.

Kathy and Trish didn't appear to be up yet this morning. They had set their tent back a little from the others, but close enough to be within reach, should there be a problem.

Eric tended to an iron pot of coffee on a flat rock near the edge of the other end of the fire. He looked rested and energetic. His hazel eyes looked on me this morning without his typical reproach, even though he had raked me up and down the night before for forgetting to put flashlights on our list of supplies. I had been hoping he would learn to appreciate me on this trip, but already, I'd screwed up.

Pat, wearing a buckskin jacket in the nippy air, sat next to Eric and gave me a nod of recognition.

My stomach stirred at the smell of the coffee. Having gotten away from the village seemed to settle my nerves. I was starting to get hungry, as well as excited about the trip ahead.

"Morning," Eric said, handing me a metal cup of coffee.

"Thanks." The warm cup felt good to my cold hands. I sipped the drink, savoring the bitter taste that reminded me so much of home.

As Beaver joined us, Eric pulled a map from his back pocket and laid it out on the ground.

We spent the next half-hour reconfirming the direction we wanted to take and the potential hazards we might meet. Beaver added his knowledge about the various territories through which we would pass. We had talked a lot about all of this before, back at the village during the week we had prepared the horses, but now, the information seemed more important and relevant. The talk of gold revved up my spirits. Already, I felt like I was getting back to my old self.

As breakfast was served, Kathy exited her tent wearing a bulky knitted navy sweater that set off her golden-brown eyes. Even with her hair mussed and her makeup gone, she looked bright and energetic, ready for action. Her tight jeans showed off her slender curves and emphasized the seductive sway of her hips as she sauntered toward us.

She touched the side of my face with her cool hand and sent a bolt of lightning through me. "I love your warrior marks," she said softly. "They make you look strong and menacing. And I mean that in a good way. You look cool. Too bad the paint is wearing off."

I'm sure the flushing skin under my warrior paint emboldened the marks with a red background. I feared most that my feelings for her would be exposed to the other men, who I noticed were all looking away on purpose.

I just couldn't seem to get up the courage to be alone with Kathy. When she was near like this, I got so flustered, I couldn't talk.

Still, I felt thrilled by her compliment. The rest of the morning, I found myself strutting around the camp as we gathered up our things and prepared to move out. I liked being thought of as a strong, menacing warrior.

* * *

The next twenty-one days passed with hours of riding across boring Mojave Desert plains with low shrubs, scattered cacti, and sandy washes. We passed lots of Joshua trees and sagebrush on the higher desert. Taking the Indian trails through the Tehachapi mountains gave us a reprieve from the afternoon desert heat, but the nights and mornings just about froze me to death. I was glad when we finally made our way through the location on our map called Stallion Springs and exited the mountains at the lower section of the San Joaquin Valley. From there, we headed north.

With Beaver's competent guidance, we'd been averaging twenty miles a day and hadn't seen any problems so far. I crossed my fingers that our luck would hold out.

Being in close proximity with each other, stronger bonds began to form between the members of the group. We shared stories around the campfire. Fun and laughter helped to pass the time.

It had taken at least seven days of pure hell before Chad and Travis finally got rid of their leg sores and were able to ride and walk with some kind of normalcy.

For me, my body had adjusted quickly to the saddle. I'd been able to stop wearing the pantyhose completely after the first week. The hose were full of runs and holes by the time I finished with them. I buried those ungainly things in the dirt. Just for the hell of it, I marked the grave with a cross I hastily made out of two small sticks.

Eric remained ever so much the patriarch, the leader, the one to make sure everybody pulled their weight, set up and broke down the camps properly, and kept to our schedule. He kept track of the days on a calendar to make sure we didn't overrun our time.

All the men, other than Beaver, took turns leading one of the seven packhorses, which were lightly loaded with our gear and foodstuff. We had plenty of food. Eric had insisted that we take enough grub to cover the whole trip without counting on fresh meat. A lot of it was dried food and powders to make biscuits and pancakes. We managed to replenish our water supplies from the mountain creeks and natural springs.

Trish seemed to be doing well with her vegetarian diet. She'd brought plenty of granola bars, dried nuts, and dried fruits. It didn't seem to bother her when we cooked an occasional wild rabbit for dinner.

I began to relax around Kathy with her easy-going nature. She was pleasant with everyone, but it never failed to warm my heart when she smiled at me. At least now, I could get through a conversation with her without blushing or stammering. Whenever I had the chance, I rode next to her on the trail.

She told me about herself and her family. She had been an only child, always independent, encouraged by her parents to make something of herself. She had started out wanting to be a nurse, but in the middle of her training, she decided it wasn't enough. She prodded herself to become a doctor. She hadn't specialized like most doctors. Being a general practitioner gave her a wider range of patients and ailments to treat. Never once did she regret anything she had done.

I wished my life could have been as seamless and directed. I couldn't stand school, and I could never make up my mind about what I wanted to do. Mostly, I didn't want to do anything, other than avoid studies and training and avoid any job that had authority figures telling me what to do. I admired Kathy for being so independent and clear about the path she had taken.

Other than the rugged terrain, long rides, and minor discomforts from the weather, everything seemed to be working well so far. I had left behind all my problems in the village.

I turned my attention to getting the gold and pushed away the occasional thoughts of the violent dreams that poked into my imagination. Once I had the gold in hand, once I got back to my own world, everything would fall into place. I'd be in a position to ask Kathy out and treat her royally.

I decided to just bide my time in getting to know Kathy and letting her know me. The pressure of asking her to be alone with me brought up my shyness and insecurities. I'd just have to wait for the right time.

* * *

On the twenty-first day after we had left the village, I rode up front with Beaver. It was late afternoon as we came up on the first area where we expected to find gold. In my world, the area just south and a little east of us was known as Yosemite National Park. The country that spanned out before me looked more raw and beautiful than in my own world. Even though this was basically the same earth as back home, the weather conditions, lack of civilization, and a lot of other factors had probably set this world and this particular area on a slightly different course. If I could have taken photos of both worlds, I imagine I would have found some amazing differences in the way the terrain had developed.

Beaver stopped at the edge of a clearing.

I held a topo map, folded into a square about twelve inches across. Studying the map, I compared it to the surrounding countryside. "I think the river we want is coming up shortly."

"Maybe ten miles ahead," Beaver estimated from his knowledge of the area. "There's no sense going all the way to the river, then following it upstream. We'll take a shortcut, head over these hills, connect with the river twelve miles upstream. That's about where you want to end up."

I nodded in agreement and put the map away. I trusted Beaver to get us where we wanted to go, but I still preferred that he would follow our progress on the map. I wanted some tangible landmarks that we could measure, so we could find our way back in this direction, if we had to come this way again.

The countryside consisted of rolling hills, covered with summer dead grass about a foot tall. Clumps of sagebrush and scattered Manzanita trees made traveling in a straight line impossible. We wove around them like being on an obstacle course.

Several hours later, Beaver pulled his horse to a stop on a hill. "There's your river," he said.

A narrow, rolling river ran through the valley between two hills. Two banks of sand, about ten- to twenty-feet wide, sat on each side of the river, areas perfect for walking around and working the gold.

Nervous anticipation flooded through me as I thought about the gold that lay in wait for our discovery.

By now, the rest of our group had moved up beside us to look out over the stretch of valley.

Pat pointed to a clearing not too far from the sandy embankment. "Over there," he said through his thick, lush beard. "Looks like a good place to set up camp."

A large flat area had been formed where the river made a turn to the south. It had probably been shaped by years of flooding, but now, it didn't appear the water would rise high enough to touch it. Large cottonwood trees and willows shaded the grass-covered ground. The area looked spacious enough to hold the camp and the horses.

The group's mood became joyful. As we rode down the hill toward our new camp, I was sure each one of us was eager to get set up and start searching for gold. I couldn't wait.

* * *

Unfortunately, by the time camp was ready, the sun had lowered on the western horizon, making it too dark to start working the river. We ate an early dinner, then sorted through our equipment, making sure we each had everything we'd need the next day.

As I did every night since we had left the village, I watched as Kathy and Trish set their tent up. I silently wished Kathy would share mine, but it didn't look like that would happen anytime soon if I didn't get off my butt and ask her.

Not giving myself enough time to start thinking about what I was doing, I stepped over to Kathy when Trish went back to get something off her saddle. "Hey, Kathy, you want to take a walk up the river with me?"

A warm smile passed over her face. "Sure. That would be fun." She turned toward Trish and called out, "I'll be back in a little while."

Trish nodded and went on searching through her saddle bag for some item.

I silently gulped as I walked toward the bend in the river and started down the bank with Kathy.

She had rubbed sage in her hair. The scent whiffed through the air with a spicy freshness.

I wanted to hold her hand, but I stalled. My hands grew sweatier with each step.

"Great evening, isn't it?" she said conversationally, turning toward the west where the sun's last rays glowed behind the natural landscape.

I stopped next to her. "Yes, it is." I dared to slip my hand into hers, now that we were far enough from the camp that no one would see us.

Her eyes widened with mild surprise as she briefly looked at me. She didn't resist, letting her fingers grip mine.

We walked down the river a little further. Her lack of resistance encouraged me, made my feet lighter. As we reached a beautiful clearing where the water rushed past, I leaned over to kiss Kathy on the lips, but the motion turned out to be clumsy, especially since she didn't return the favor.

She gently pushed me away with her free hand. "I like you, Donny, and I like getting to know you, but I'm not one to jump into a relationship. I have to know someone pretty well for that."

"But we have been getting to know each other. In the close proximity of being on the trail, I think we've gotten to know each other pretty well."

"That's true," she countered, still holding my hand as though to pacify me, "but before we get to know each other physically, I want us to get to know each other on a deeper level, deeper than just telling where we came from or what we have done. There's lots more to a good relationship than that."

I felt the old face-burning rise again, unable to look at her. I wanted to take my hand away, but she held on.

"Anyway," she said more lightly, giving my hand a squeeze, "we need to concentrate on this trip and getting back safely. I don't want anything to distract me right now." She looked back at the darkening river. "Come on, we better get back to the camp. They don't like us to be this far away. In case of problems."

She dropped my hand and we walked back in silence.

What a doofus I am. She probably doesn't even like me. As usual, I had made a fool of myself. And I didn't see how we could get to know each other on a deeper level until we took the relationship to the next level and became more intimate. What else was there?

Like always, I remained at a total loss when it came to dealing with women, a mystery I would never be able to solve or understand. Judging from the few married couples I'd known and my own short-lived relationships, I figured the best thing I could do was to learn how to apologize with sincerity, grovel with humility, and beg like a dog when all else failed. Even knowing those things, I didn't know how to apply them now with Kathy.

As we neared the camp, Kathy stopped and looked up into my eyes. "Thanks for the walk. It was nice to take a break. Maybe we can do it another time."

I nodded.

As she returned to her tent, I walked to the fireside and sat down.

I hated to admit it, but I began to doubt that my hoped-for relationship with Kathy would ever materialize. I was such a loser. What did I have in common with her anyway? She was bright and educated. I was a dropout. She knew what she wanted and she went for it. I floundered around, wasting my whole life without ever knowing where I was going.

I began to realize that I was just kidding myself that the money from the gold was going to make any difference. It might let me buy her nice things, a nice house, a beautiful car, extravagant clothing, but it wasn't going to make me any smarter or give me a crack at an educated woman like Kathy. It wasn't going to make her like me better. Besides, she'd have her own gold, so what difference would mine make?

Feeling beaten, I went to bed early, intending on getting an early start in the morning. I found it hard to rev up any eagerness for the gold at this point. *Maybe I'm just a loser. I'll always be a loser. And, in the end, it has nothing to do with being rich or poor.*

I spent the night tossing and turning, finally falling asleep.

Chapter 19

Early the next morning, I heard people rustling around outside my tent. I rolled out of my blankets with renewed eagerness to get on with the gold hunting. I put Kathy out of my mind. Even if I'd never find the woman of my dreams, at least I could enjoy other good things in life with the money from the gold. Besides, there was no way I was going to lie around in bed while everybody else was off filling their bags with golden nuggets.

Before entering the portal for the last time, we had all practiced with the gold sluices and pans back home. We now each had our work cut out for us and knew what we needed to do.

After breakfast, Eric stood up and pronounced, "Okay, everyone, listen up. As you know, since we had to travel by horseback, we could only bring a minimum amount of tools and equipment for finding and extracting gold, so we don't have everything we would have liked if we were doing this back home. I'm going to divide you up into groups, for both use of equipment and safety. Each group will be given a sluice box, a shovel, and a pick. There will be one gold pan per person."

As he was talking, Pat and Steve had started removing some of the equipment from one of the larger packs.

"Everyone must carry a backpack containing extra clothes, food, and a basic first-aid kit. Take a solar blanket, a BIC Lighter, and your pocketknives, in case of an emergency."

Sitting on a dead log, I grumbled, "We don't need all those things. We're just going a ways up or down the river. We can get back to the camp if we need those things."

"No," Eric bellowed at me. "I want everyone to take all the necessary precautions, in case something happens and you can't get back or get lost." He stared at me with that disapproving paternal glare. "You make sure you get all your things together before we go."

Irritated, I looked around at the others. They glanced away, as though I was the only one who cared about carrying all that dead weight around for nothing. I shook my head and slumped over my knees in typical defeat.

"I want everyone to work in teams of two or three," Eric continued. "That way, you can keep an eye on each other and be available if one of you needs help. James, you and Tory stay together. Chad and Travis, you'll make up another team."

Chad slapped Travis on the back as though they were old long-lost buddies who had just found each other.

"Steve can go with Juan and Sergio. Pat, you'll partner up with me. Trish and Kathy, you stick with Donny."

What? Why do I have to take care of the women? And after making a fool of myself with Kathy? I got up off the log to protest, but Eric turned away.

"Everyone be back here before dark," he said. "Now, let's get going."

As I angrily grabbed my gear, I couldn't believe I had to spend my day alone with the women. It was embarrassing enough to be around Kathy after I had screwed up with her the night before, but now, I would have to babysit Trish and listen to her high, squeaky voice all day. I hoped she'd get so involved in hunting for gold or so tired that she wouldn't want to talk very much.

* * *

Trudging upstream, taking the opposite direction of the other groups, I led off my team. I carried the portable sluice box in one hand and my rifle in the other. On my back, I had a pack full of food and survival gear. Each of the women carried their own backpacks and gold pans. Trish carried the shovel and Kathy carried the pick.

Fortunately, we were all in better shape than when we had started the trip. We'd all lost weight, toned up, and increased our stamina. Part of this came from our diet, but mostly, it came from the rugged, hard outdoor living that exerted a heavy toll on our bodies. Even Chad, Travis, James, and Tory, who'd all been in excellent shape, had found living over here had slimmed their bodies.

About a half-mile upstream, I stopped and set my stuff down on a sandy bank. Here the river changed directions, coming from the north, running east to west for a stretch, then turning south. The water deeply eroded the bank along the turn, but directly above it, a sandbar stuck out into the river like a small dam, forcing the water into a deep, narrow channel against the opposite bank.

After making the turn, the river once again spread out, flowing across a rocky bottom only two feet deep. About a hundred yards downstream sat another sandbar. I hoped that gold nuggets, washed out of the hillside, would be deposited there. Of course, I had no idea if the hillside held gold to begin with, but I figured this was a good place to start.

I felt shy around Kathy. We hadn't really talked this morning. Just said the typical morning pleasantries.

As she set down her equipment and removed her backpack, I couldn't help but notice how good she looked, her slender body so toned, her skin so darkly tanned. I liked to see her bend over her pack in her tight jeans, but I had to be careful that she wouldn't catch me watching.

Trish dropped her gear next to Kathy's and chattered with excitement. Her voice seemed harshest when she was excited, rising to an unbearable pitch. I didn't know how Kathy could put up with her all the time.

I did notice that Trish had changed physically, too. Of all of us, she had shed the most weight, maybe twenty pounds or more. Her firmer hips, slender waist, long legs, and round curves actually made her more attractive. I could see why Chad and Travis often eyed her moving around the camp.

We set the sluice box in the water where just enough current flowed across it. Normally, as we had been taught, we would have to classify the material by sifting it through a half-inch screen before putting it in the sluice box, but since I was planning to work the sandbar, we didn't bother. I figured we could throw out any big rocks that got in our way.

The three of us pulled on our hip-waders, rubber pants held up with suspenders, which allowed us to stand in the cold water for long periods.

While we'd all watched videos of people using sluice boxes to learn how to do it, and despite the fact we'd practiced as much as we could in Eric's backyard, without traveling to an actual river, we could only learn so much. At the rate we were going, I figured it would take a couple of days to work out the bugs and get into a rhythm of working together as a team.

I put sand in one end of the sluice box and let the water wash it over a series of ripples. The concept came from idea that the ripples caught heavier materials, like gold or black sand. The heavy items would sink between the ripples while the lighter material washed out the other end.

After about a half hour of letting sand run through the sluice, we stopped and cleaned out the accumulated material, moving it into a gold pan. This was the tell-tale moment when we would find out if our efforts had paid off. We didn't see any gold nuggets among the few larger pieces of stone in the sluice, so we just pitched them.

Kathy swirled the gold pan containing the heavier sands from the bottom of the sluice. She studied the pan closely in the sun, looking for glints of gold.

I said, "Since it takes longer to pan out the gold, why don't I shovel the material into the sluice box while you two pan it out?"

"Great idea," Kathy said.

"Sounds good to me," Trish squeaked.

Even though we were involved in looking for gold, I couldn't help but feel the presence of Kathy near me. My heart palpitated when she would stand next to me. I watched her graceful fingers search through the wet sand.

She seemed friendly enough, but not solicitous or giving me much attention…not as much as I would have liked. She kept her nose to the grindstone when sloshing water around the pan to check for gold.

Suddenly, Trish yelled, "Look, there's a piece of gold."

I hadn't been expecting to find anything so soon, and was surprised to see a chunk of gold show up in the sluice.

Trish picked up the nugget, rinsed it off, and held it out for inspection.

"How much do you think it weighs?" Kathy asked excitedly, putting her own pan aside to take a look.

I shrugged. "Rough guess, I'd say about an ounce, maybe a little more."

"This is good, right?" Trish squealed. "I mean, if we found this one so soon, there must be lots more. We should be able to gather up a whole bunch by tonight."

"You're right, Trish," I said. "Let's get busy. By the time we leave here, I want to have so much gold, we'll need a horse to help to carry it back to camp."

Kathy laughed. "I doubt if we'll find that much, but I agree with you. Let's get busy and get what we can."

Hardly able to contain herself, Trish put the nugget in the special heavy-duty leather bags we had brought and got back to work.

Wow. I couldn't believe our luck. We'd actually found gold. "Right now, back in our world," I said in conversation as I fed more sand into the sluice, "an ounce of gold is worth $1,600. If we can come up with ten ounces today, that would be $16,000, or a little over $5,000 each, a nice day's pay."

As we continued to work, I silently estimated that, if I found one hundred pounds of gold, I would end up with 1.9 million dollars. This was the goal we had set for each individual in the group, to bring back one hundred pounds of gold per person. At that rate, we'd all have plenty to take back with us and be able to live more comfortably. I calculated we'd each need to average five pounds per day for two months to reach that goal. *Two months.* My back was already aching after a few hours of bending over the sluice and pans. My excitement dampened at the prospect of spending two more months doing this kind of work. Unless gold suddenly started appearing in large, easy-to-see chunks, I feared we might not all make the desired goal.

Over the next hours, we found more nuggets. By the time we stopped for a late afternoon snack, we hobbled around with stiff, sore muscles from the unaccustomed work. It looked like we had at least twelve ounces of gold. Seeing the gold sparkle in the sun, my spirits started rising again.

When Kathy walked away to make a private pit-stop behind some trees, I got the urge to lean over to Trish and quietly asked, "Does Kathy have a boyfriend?"

In a serious, modulated tone that seemed strange coming from Trish, she whispered back, "No. She told me she's been burnt two or three times by different men, either cheating on her or taking advantage of her. She was in love with one doctor during her residency, but she caught him with another woman in his bed when she dropped by his house. I think she's given up with men. Her career is now her whole life. She's married to it."

I wanted to ask Trish if Kathy liked me, but I didn't see the point if she was sour on men. With all the males in our group, Kathy was always friendly, but non-committal. *At least she doesn't have a boyfriend.*

As Kathy approached us from behind the trees, five distant gunshots, spaced about two seconds apart, echoed up the valley. Kathy's eyes shot open in surprise and fright.

"Why are people shooting?" Trish asked as she rose from the ground.

I stood up, too, wondering who the shots had come from and if they were some kind of warning. I hoped no one had run into a bear, or worse, some kind of man-made trouble.

"Maybe someone was just shooting at a deer," Kathy offered, her voice a little tight.

"Five times?" Trish exclaimed.

"Sure," I said nonchalantly, wanting to put them at ease. "Maybe the shooter missed a couple of shots before hitting the animal." If Indians or raiders were attacking our group, we didn't have all that much protection. I didn't want to scare the women by mentioning the wild possibilities running through my mind. I turned around, half-expecting to see a horde of mounted warriors lining the skyline over the ridge.

Not hearing more shots, I relaxed a little, sensing that we weren't in any imminent danger. "I hope they got a deer," I said to ease the tension. "I'd like fresh meat for dinner tonight, instead of those boring traveling rations we've been eating." I looked at Trish, hoping she wouldn't take offense at me so eager to eat meat.

My words made no impression on her as she stood wringing her hands and looking around nervously for some kind of danger.

"Maybe they got an elk," Kathy said lightheartedly, smiling at me and licking her lips. Earlier, she had admitted to craving elk ever since it had been served at our farewell dinner the night before we had left the village.

I was glad she wasn't a vegetarian like Trish. I liked a woman who enjoyed tearing into a thick, juicy steak.

The gunshots gave me reason to get us back to the group to find out what had happened. "Come on," I said, heading back to the sluice. "Let's pack up our stuff and get back to camp. We've put in a hard day."

Trish seemed to cling closer to me as we packed up our gear. She constantly looked around, as though fearing something would jump out of the trees or appear over a hill.

We stashed most of our equipment under a large bush for retrieval in the morning. I didn't see any reason to haul it all back and forth again, especially since our claim site had been fruitful.

Trish's anxiety made me nervous, too. I was glad to be heading back to camp.

* * *

As we approached camp, all seemed well. Eric, Pat, and Steve stood talking by the fire. All the other members of the group had already returned and seemed to be settling down for the evening meal. There was some buzz among them, but no one appeared particularly upset about the shooting incident. Near the fire, I saw evidence of an elk carcass. I figured that was the end of the shooting mystery.

Before I reached my tent, Eric came stomping toward me with a scowl on his face. He took on the tone of a parent talking to a five-year-old. "Where's your sluice box and your other tools?"

Feeling a lecture coming on, I spoke defensively, "We left everything at the river because I don't want to carry it back and forth every day."

"And what will happen if someone comes along and takes it?"

I exploded. "Who the hell's gonna take it? There's nobody here but us."

Kathy and Trish wisely scurried away to attend to their own business.

"Don't yell at me, Donny," Eric said, showing perfect patience with his unruly little brother.

His condescending, self-righteous attitude made me all the more angry. "Then don't lecture me." I leaned my rifle against a tree and shrugged out of my backpack.

"I wouldn't have to if you'd quit doing stupid things."

"Why is leaving my gear there stupid?"

"Like I said, what if someone takes it?"

I threw my hands in the air. "Like who? There's not another human within a hundred miles."

"Not so. Did you hear those shots earlier today?"

I nodded, looking toward the elk remains that Coyote had cut into sections. I saw two bloody arrows still sticking out of the animal's neck. Fear crept back into my mind. "What was it?"

"Two Indians. It looked like they intended to steal Chad's pack while he and Travis were working. Luckily, Travis saw the Indians before they got to the pack. He pulled out his pistol and fired shots until his gun was empty. He was too far away, though. All he did was scare them off."

Damn. I picked up my rifle and started walking upriver.

"Where're you going?" Eric demanded.

"Back to get my gear."

"Give me a minute to grab my gun. I'll come with you."

Pat joined us. "I want to go, too. I'd like to see where you're working. Did you find anything?"

"Sure did. I'll tell you about it on the way. Thanks for coming along."

During the walk, I shared with them the story of our findings, how much we had pulled out of the river. I had kept one nugget, the biggest one, in my pocket, so I pulled it out to show them.

"That's great," Eric said, studying the nugget closely in the late afternoon sun. "No one else has even come close to finding something like this."

"James and Tory got about half an ounce," Pat said. "Everyone else got skunked."

As they talked, I could hear the unspoken words of congratulations for having decided to locate my claim upstream rather than downstream with the rest of them.

I felt bad about the bad luck of the others. I thought I'd better not gloat too much about my extreme luck in picking a good site. If my team was the only one drawing out gold, we would need more than two months to accumulate our estimated goal. "Maybe you just picked the wrong places," I conceded, hoping to appease them. "Everyone will probably do better tomorrow."

* * *

By the time we returned to camp with all the gear, the sun was nearly down. My back ached and my feet burned. Eric's lavish praise for the location of my claim helped elevate my mood. The smell of cooked elk made my mouth water.

The other members of the group had already eaten. They sat around the campfire and listened while Kathy and Trish told them about our exploits.

Sitting down next to Eric and Pat, I savored my dinner. I didn't know if it was because I was hungry from working hard all day, or because the steak was cooked over a campfire, but I'd swear it was the best steak I'd ever eaten. "Who got the elk?" I asked Beaver.

"Coyote. He went hunting this morning. Dropped the elk pretty easily."

"He must have needed help bringing it back."

"The two of us managed it, but he's strong for his little size."

Coyote cooked us some kind of biscuit. He mixed dough with water, formed the batter into rough balls, flattened them a little, then cooked them on a hot, flat rock near the fire. The biscuits were okay, but without butter, I found them a little too dry for my taste. If it came right down to it, I could survive on just meat. I ate until I couldn't push down another bite.

After the meal, I gulped down one of Kathy's required multi-vitamins. Each member of the group had been forced to bring along a large supply because Kathy had insisted we wouldn't get enough nutrition. She didn't want anyone to get scurvy. Steve had argued with her, saying the natives seemed to do fine, but she replied that they were used to a diet of mostly meat, corn, and bread. We weren't.

A long day of hard work and a large dinner conspired against me. I soon found my eyes drooping. My neck could no longer hold up my head. Fortunately, I wasn't the only one ready to hit the sack.

I stumbled to my tent. I didn't even bother to strip out of my clothes. Dropping onto my sleeping bag, I was out like a light within minutes.

Chapter 20

We spent a week working our claims before deciding to move north to the next river on my list. Everyone had found gold by this time, alleviating my concerns that we might have a hard time locating it. Trish, Kathy, and I had done better than the other teams. We had pulled out ten pounds of our now carefully guarded treasure. At night, everyone slept with their gold collection and kept an eye on the horses that carried it.

It was now early May as we headed toward our next campsite. I leisurely rode with the packhorses at the back of the group. Kathy and Trish helped me bring up the rear. The three of us had formed a new kind of camaraderie after all these days of working close together. Trish no longer got on my nerves so easily with her overexcitement and squeaky voice. Kathy seemed to take a friendlier tact with me, seemingly forgetting my clumsy kiss. I still enjoyed being close to her and looking at her slender, fit body, but I didn't feel the overwhelming need to push the relationship. Well…sometimes, maybe…when my heart yearned for her beyond my mental control…but most of the time, I'd reasoned with myself that maybe I would never be in her league, and thus, I would have to accept just being her friend.

As I rode along, I turned my thoughts to the gold. Before I'd left home, I'd checked the spot price. Gold had been selling for just over $1,600 an ounce, which meant that, at twelve troy ounces to a pound, we had 120 ounces of gold. At $1,600 an ounce, that came to a respectable figure of $192,000. After dividing that three ways, my share would come to around

$64,000. *That's more than a lot of people make in a year. And we did it in a week.*

Giddy at the thought of all that money, I daydreamed about everything I wanted to do with it, like buy that big Dooley truck.

A loud shout and commotion came from the front of the pack. I couldn't see what was going on with the trees and bushes in the way.

I yanked on the reins, stopping my horse from running into the one in front of it. My normally easygoing horse pranced nervously in place. It's wide-open eyes and flared nostrils told me it was scared.

Is there a bear or something up there or what?

"Everybody stay calm," I heard Eric yell from up ahead somewhere. "Don't pull out your guns or do anything that could be taken as being aggressive."

I saw movement to my right. My heart jumped to my throat when ten warriors stepped out of the brush with bows at the ready.

Trish gasped when another group of fierce-looking warriors appeared on the left side of the group.

A sound behind me caused me to swivel in my saddle. Another group of warriors with bows drawn came up behind us, effectively blocking all avenues of escape.

I swallowed hard.

The Indians herded us into a dense clump of milling horses and nervous riders.

Beaver talked loudly and fast in another language to three chief-looking warriors with headdresses. He used a lot of hand motions and expressive gestures to make his points.

The angry faces, set jaws, and glaring eyes of the Indians told me they were really pissed off about something. These Indians were tall, stately and proud, their bodies muscular and fit. They had sharper features than those of Beaver's people, their skin slightly darker. They didn't wear tattoos, but they had marked their cheeks and foreheads with some kind of war paint. Most of these warriors had a prominent, hawk-like nose and a pointed chin. All wore long hair, pulled back in a ponytail, tied with a strip of rawhide. They wore breechcloths. Their moccasins came to just below their knees. Most were bare-chested, but a couple wore buckskin vests.

One thing they all had in common was the hate that glared back at us from their black eyes.

Beaver kept talking. Pat, leaned forward on his horse and listened intently. I couldn't wait to find out what was going on.

After what seemed like an hour, but maybe only a few minutes, one of the warriors listening to Beaver made a motion with his hand. The warriors surrounding us released the pressure they'd been holding on their strings and lowered their bows. I noticed they kept their arrows nocked and ready for a quick release.

I couldn't imagine what might have caused such intense anger from this tribe. I hoped Beaver would be able to straighten it out before we all ended up being taken back to the village, tied to a stake in the middle of a bonfire, and roasted alive. My dreams flitted through my mind, but I quickly pushed them away.

Beaver got off his horse and joined the three warrior chiefs. While they discoursed with each other in a civil manner, the rest of us fidgeted and wondered what was going on.

Finally, Beaver nodded to the Indians, turned away from them, and swung himself onto his horse's back.

At a word from their leader, the warriors vanished into the brush as if they'd never been there.

"What's going on?" Eric asked.

"It's okay now," Beaver said. "There was a misunderstanding about who we are and where we're going. I'll explain after we make camp tonight."

"Why not tell us now?" Chad asked.

Beaver's face went hard. "We must first put some miles behind us. Find a place to camp that's easy to defend...just in case." He kicked his horse in the ribs and set off at a canter.

Still bringing up the rear, I constantly looked over my shoulder, not trusting the Indians and growing paranoid about being attacked without warning.

* * *

Beaver called a halt to the party next to a cutback in a hillside, which went straight up for at least eighty feet. It looked like a location easy to defend. No one could attack us from behind with the cliff to our rear, and with a clear view in the opposite direction, no one could approach without being seen.

We picketed the horses and quickly set up camp. While we ate dinner, Beaver relayed the story of what had happened.

It seems the two Indians who had tried to steal Chad's backpack had been mere boys of twelve. They'd never seen a white person or firearms. While hunting, they had come across Chad and Travis doing something strange in the river. From their vantage point on the top of a hill, they saw another group of three people standing in the river downstream. Investigating the situation further, they found other groups repeating the same activity. Seeing Beaver and Coyote in the camp, they assumed they were slaves.

The two boys decided to count coup by stealing a valuable bag lying on the bank of the river. Unfortunately, the strangers caught them in the act. Seeing no weapons, the boys remained unconcerned until one of the men pulled something off his hip and pointed it at them. Travis had nicked one of them on the arm as they made their escape.

The boys decided we had to be watched closely. For the whole week, they tried to figure out why we were collecting yellow rocks. When we packed up and left, the boys followed, worried because we were heading straight for their village. Not wanting us to get too close to their home, they hurried ahead to warn the village people.

"Their tall tale," Beaver concluded, "of a large group of light-skinned warriors with magical weapons that, with a boom louder than thunder, could throw rocks faster and harder than any man alive, caused great alarm throughout the village. Like all rumors, the tale grew into a huge marauding army of brutal savages who took no prisoners and killed anyone they found."

The wood popped in the fire pit and filled in the silence.

"My God," Kathy said, "it's no wonder they were ready to kill everyone of us at the slightest wrong move."

"Yeah," Eric said. "I'm really glad none of us did anything to threaten them. We could all be dead now."

Sergio stroked his mustache. "It makes me wonder if we will meet other natives who will react the same way."

"Or ain't gonna give us a chance to explain," James pointed out.

Wide-eyed, Trish said, "Maybe we should go home. We all have some gold."

"Hell, no," Chad and Travis both chimed in together. Chad added, "We'll just have to be more careful about how we approach the tribes if we come in contact with them."

"That's right," Tory said. "If we ain't actin' aggressive, them'll probably leave us alone. We need ta avoid 'em, if possible."

Eric stood up. "Let's take a vote. Who wants to go back to the portal now?"

Trish started to raise her hand, but as she looked around and saw no one else joining her, she quickly put it down.

"How many want to continue?"

All hands went up, some more vigorously than others.

Both Beaver and Coyote refrained from voting.

While I'd never been more scared in my life than when those warriors had stepped out of the brush with their bows at full draw, I would never admit it to anyone in the group. Plus, the gold-fever had gotten into my veins. I wanted to collect more before we headed home. If this would be the only chance we'd ever get this opportunity, I wanted to make the most of it.

"We're gonna have to be more careful," Eric announced. "Even if we break into teams, we're gonna have to stick closer to each other and be more on the lookout for the Indians watching us. Keep your weapons with you at all times, and don't leave your gear too far away."

"Those Indians will follow us," Beaver said, "as long as we are in their territory or they feel we are a threat to them. We must not offend them in any way."

"How far does their territory reach?" Steve asked. "Will we be leaving it before our next stop?"

"It's hard to say. There are other tribes that live in these hills and mountains, too. Some are related to them."

I didn't really know much about Indians. Now, I wished I had researched the area more thoroughly and had learned which tribes had lived along our trail. I knew the more well-known tribes like the Sioux, Cheyenne, Crow, and Blackfoot had existed further north and east of our destination, but I wasn't sure about the Indian population in this particular area. Knowing their customs and their potential aggressiveness would have helped in planning to meet them.

I convinced myself that, as long as we paid more attention to the environment around us and took more precautions, we'd be okay.

* * *

Days passed as we slowly made our way north and worked the rivers for gold. We remained on alert. Coyote required little sleep. He would get his rest during the day when we weren't traveling and kept watch at night. We saw Indians at a distance on several occasions, but they never came close. I'm sure they were tracking our progress through their territory.

We stopped for a week or two at each location I had mapped out. We could have stayed in one spot to collect our gold, but it seemed like the further north we went, the more gold each group found, that is, each group except Travis and Chad. They collected about half of what the rest of us gathered. It wasn't that they didn't work hard, they'd just been unlucky at picking good spots for their sluice box. I wasn't sure, of course, but I suspected they hadn't learned how to operate their equipment correctly, missing most of the gold that passed through.

The shiny golden nuggets began to weigh down the pack horses. It would only be a matter of time before the horses wouldn't be able to carry much more. Occasionally, James and Tory would bring up their concern for the welfare of the horses and remind us that we shouldn't force them to carry more weight than they could handle.

Although Kathy, Trish, and I had started out with the most gold, as time went on, the other groups surpassed us in their takes. James and Tory, Eric and Pat, and Steve, Sergio, and Juan, all had at least double our amount. I estimated my team's stash to be around two hundred pounds. Splitting our take three ways would give us each a little over 1.2 million dollars. Not bad, but I still wanted to collect a little more before returning home.

While we had all found the work to be exhausting at first, as time went by, our physical stamina grew with our riches. By the time two months had passed, those of us who had grown beards looked like rugged mountain men, especially in the heavy buckskin coats we'd traded for with Iron Cactus's people. Those coats kept us toasty warm during the cold mornings and nippy nights. Luckily, over the weeks, we only met with occasional thunderstorms that forced us to find shelter from the rain.

Though all of us were used to the hot, simmering summers of Arizona, none of us complained about the cold mornings. With no apparent danger from the Indians, nothing could dampen the high spirits that ran through the camp as we continued to build our piles of gold and share our dreams of all the things we planned to do with our portions when we got home.

As the weeks passed, I knew that our time on this side of the portal was growing limited. We would have to start back soon to make it through the portal before it closed with the eclipse. I silently prepared myself for the announcement of our departure to come soon, and I didn't have long to wait.

Chapter 21

One night after dinner in early July, a good month before the portal was to close, Eric called us all together. He looked lean, tanned, and clean-shaven as he stood before us to make his announcement. "I think we've just about gathered as much gold as the horses can carry." He paused, looking around at everyone and letting the idea sink in. "We should head back to the portal and home. Anyone have any objections?"

Chad shifted restlessly near the fire. "Hell, I'm not ready to go yet. Travis and I don't have our millions. We need more time."

"Yeah," Travis jumped in. "We were hoping we could take back double what we have now."

The two muscle-bound men had lost some of their muscle mass from not lifting weights regularly every day, but other than that, they looked fit and healthy with beards and long hair.

"Granted, you and Chad have had some bad luck," Eric stated, "but we need to get moving. We've got a long trip back and the horses won't make it if we load them down with too much gold." Ignoring the two whiners, Eric glanced around to the rest of the group. "Anybody else have a problem?"

"I have no problem," Pat said idly, running his fingers through his beard. "We don't want to cut it too close and get trapped over here when the portal closes."

"Whoa," Steve blurted. His buzzed haircut had grown out, but still looked out of place compared to the long, unkempt hair the rest of us had grown. "Wait a minute. What's this about the portal closing?"

Pat's eyes flickered from Eric to me. The realization he'd said something he shouldn't have showed on his face.

Seeing it was too late to keep the secret, Eric explained, "There is something we neglected to tell you about the portal." He went on to describe how the opening and closing of the portal was controlled by eclipses, and that at least two years would pass after the portal closed in August. "We have plenty of time to get back if we start out in the next couple of days."

Shock, anger, and disbelief radiated from the rest of the group.

I hoped nobody would create a scene by freaking out. What was the big deal, anyway? We already had our gold.

Tory spoke in a low, mean voice as he rose from his seat on a log. "That's somethin' ya shoulda told us from the beginnin'. If I woulda known, I ain't sure I woulda come along."

"Me either," James said, his blue eyes forming narrow slits, dark with anger. His once neatly trimmed mustache now almost completely covered his mouth, making it difficult to see his lips moving when he talked.

"Exactly how long do we have until the portal closes?" Kathy asked Eric. She sat pensively on a log with a look of worry on her face.

"Our goal is to be back thirty-five days from today," Eric said. "That gives us six days leeway before the eclipse.

"That's only a month," Sergio cried. "It will take us that long to get back with the horses carrying all this gold."

"You should have told us," Trish squealed. "Now we definitely need to head back. I won't stay here for two more years. I've had enough of this living in the wild. I want to go home." She folded her arms across her chest and huffed.

Growing murmurs of griping and disapproval rose among the group.

Kathy turned to me with a look of hurt and betrayal. "You knew about this, Donny?"

Feeling like I'd been caught doing something bad, like cheating on her, I looked at the ground and shifted my feet in shame. "Yeah, I knew about it."

"You could have told us. If I would have known, I don't think I would have come, either. I've got a practice to run, and I don't like worrying that it could be two years or more before I can get back to it."

"When you go back," I said, trying to pacify her fears, "you'll be right where you left off. No one will know the difference."

"That's not the point. *I'll* know the difference. This was just supposed to be a nice long outing for me, an adventurous vacation. I like hiking and camping and backpacking, but I don't want to make a career of it. Not two more long years of it."

"People," Eric shouted, holding up his palms. "Listen, people. We have plenty of time to get back before the portal closes. True, maybe we should have told you, but we thought it would be one less thing for you to worry about while you were over here. And to tell you the truth, it's not a big deal anyway."

The angry murmurs quieted a little.

"Chad and I haven't gathered enough gold yet," Travis grumbled. "We want to find more...at least as much as you have."

"Yeah," Chad agreed. "It won't take us but a couple of weeks to get back. We have time for a little more panning. At least another week."

James glared at him from across the campfire. "The horses cain't carry any more weight. They carryin' too much as it is."

Tory jumped in to support his brother. "And they cain't go very fast with all that weight neither."

"So? We'll get more horses," Chad suggested.

In a disbelieving tone, Sergio asked, "And where do you propose we get them?"

"We'll trade with those Indians who've been watching us. I'm sure they'd love to have all our prospecting gear when we're done."

"No way," Eric growled. "We're not leaving our gear behind."

"Why not?" Travis asked. "It's not like we're gonna need it again."

"This is expensive equipment. It came out of my pocket. It's going back with us."

Tory said, "I don't know 'bout the rest of ya, but I ain't comin' back. I got enough gold ta last me the resta my life."

"Me, too," James said.

Like Trish, Eric folded his hands over his chest. He said calmly, "I think all of us have enough to last us the rest of our lives if we don't blow it all in the first year. There's no reason for us to come back."

Chad mumbled something to Travis under his breath. To Eric, he said, "Then Travis and I will get a group together and come back. You can't stop us from getting more gold. I'm sure the Indians will help us again." He turned to Beaver, who sat silently near the fire and watched the group without any expression on his face. "Won't you?"

"It depends on the council of elders. If they agree, I would help."

"There you go," Chad bellowed, his voice full of hope as he looked around the group. "We can come back if we have to."

No one showed any signs of being all that enthused about making another trip. I sure wasn't.

"Okay," Chad added, "then maybe we don't have to come back. How about getting some extra horses so we can stay another week and get more gold? With more horses, we can travel faster to the portal when we're done."

"What do you think, James?" Eric asked.

James gave Tory a silent look. The brothers nodded to each other. "If we kin lighten them loads on the horses," James said, "we kin move faster. We kin probably stay one more week and still make them miles to git to the portal in time."

Steve said, "I have no objection to staying another week if we can get the horses. I could always use more gold."

Eric glanced at Juan and Sergio. "What do you think, Sergio?" he asked. "Do you want to stay another week?"

"If you think we can make it on time, Eric, I'll trust your judgment."

"Same with me," Juan said.

I could feel the reluctance in Eric to make the decision to stay. He finally looked at Pat and opened his hands, silently saying, *What do we do now?*

Kathy piped up. "As long as you're positive we can get back before the portal closes, I'll go along with it."

Chad and Travis mumbled their approval of her choice. I wasn't sure, but it seemed like everybody had a touch of gold-fever. They all wanted just a little bit more.

Personally, I was tired of panning for gold and looked forward to going home and having an ice-cold beer. My scruffy beard itched and caught the dribble of my food when I wasn't watching. Like Eric and Pat, I felt concerned about making it to the portal before it closed. Still, I wasn't going to vote against the decision to stay if the majority wanted to go at the gold another week.

"Okay," Eric said, "I'll go along with staying another week as long as we can get more horses in the next couple of days. Each day we stay means time is running out at the portal. Make use of your gold panning while we wait. If we don't have more horses in two days, we're packing up and going home. How's that with you, Beaver? You think you can get some horses?"

"I'll see what I can do," he said nonchalantly.

"How will you get the horses?" Trish asked. "What can we trade? Will they take gold?"

"Gold has no meaning to them." Beaver waved his hand toward the packs. "I brought trade goods. Knifes, hatchets, mirrors, beads, and ribbon. The same things fur trappers brought two hundred years ago in your world."

Travis laughed. "They'll really trade horses for that kind of junk?"

"To them," Beaver replied seriously, "this stuff is more valuable than a horse."

"It's a matter of supply and demand," said Steve. "They have plenty of horses, but they have no way of getting certain weapons, tools, and materials, other than by trading."

"Do you think you have enough junk in there to trade for three or four horses?" Chad asked.

"I'm sure he does," Travis offered. "If not, we can always steal a couple of horses."

Beaver looked alarmed. "Do you have a death wish? These northern tribes are known for dealing with horse thieves harshly."

"They kill them?" Trish asked timidly.

"They burn them at the stake," Beaver responded bluntly.

Trish's face paled. "Trade only then," she squeaked, looking at Travis. "I don't think I could stand to see either one of you burn."

* * *

Two nights later, while everyone was eating dinner, Beaver rode into the camp. We all looked up, anxiously awaiting the news about getting more horses. Pat, Eric, and I had reservations about staying much longer. We wanted to head home, but the other men seemed to burn with gold-fever and worked hard to extract as much gold as they could these last two days.

During these two days, Kathy and Trish had stayed around the camp while I did some gold-panning on my own. Kathy would only speak to me if she had to and, most of the time, didn't acknowledge me at all, as though it was all my fault that everyone hadn't been told that the portal would be closing. Her avoidance of me made me feel like a total jerk.

"I talked to one of the Indians watching us," Beaver said as he made his way to the campfire. "He spoke to his tribe. They have agreed to let us camp near their village to trade for horses."

A bad feeling washed over me. I didn't like how these Indians had so aggressively approached us the first time with their bows and arrows. I didn't trust them. I wasn't sure why, but maybe it had to do with how similar they looked to the Indians in my recurring nightmare.

Eric and Pat passed each other knowing looks, not happy ones. I'm sure they had been hoping we wouldn't get more horses so we could begin our trek back to the portal. Also, camping near the Indian village didn't bode well for a quick getaway if things went wrong.

I was starting to feel the pressure of the portal closing if anything happened to delay our return. None of the three of us, Eric, Pat, and myself, wanted to be stuck on this side, nor be responsible for the others being stuck, either. Steve's crew had stopped listening to Eric as Chad took on a more forceful stance in the group.

"Okay," Chad said gleefully, "we got our horses. In the morning, let's move to their village and make the trade. Anybody disagree?"

"Yeah," Eric said. "I want to remind you, we need to start back as soon as possible. We don't know what kinds of problems we'll meet. The longer we stay, the greater the chances are that we might miss the portal closing."

"I've changed my mind," Kathy said as she stood up. "I don't want to stay here. I'm in favor of returning home."

"Me, too," Trish added, wrenching her hands.

"Damn, if we get the horses," Chad interjected, "we can shift the weight of the gold and the lighter load will allow us to move faster. We took our time getting here, so if we push harder going home, we can make more miles in a day. We could easily make it back to the portal, even if we stay here another week."

"I don't like it," Eric reiterated in an angry tone. "I don't like this whole situation with the Indians. I think we should just pack up and leave now."

"Yeah, 'cause you have a stash of gold," Travis accused. "If you were in our place, you'd want to do more panning, too."

A heated argument ensued. Chad and Travis continued to insist they needed more time to get their fair share of the gold. Sergio and Juan nodded their heads in agreement with Steve, who felt that we should take as much gold as possible so we didn't have to come back. James and Tory seemed to think that more horses would do the trick in resolving everyone's problems. In the end, Steve and his crew outnumbered the dissenters seven to five, with the two women on our side to go home.

Finally, in exasperation, Eric turned to James and Tory. "Can you two guarantee us that, if we have four or five more packhorses and a few more days of gold panning, we'll be able to get back before the portal closes."

"Absolutely," James stated. "With less weight, them horses kin outrun us all the way if they hadta."

"With more horses," Tory added, "another five or six days of pannin' won't be no problem."

Eric sighed heavily, looking around the group. His eyes settled on Pat.

Pat shrugged his shoulders, then nodded his agreement to go along with the majority.

In defiance, I wanted to stand up, say a few cuss words, pack my horse, and head back to the portal alone. Maybe the others would wise-up and follow. Maybe I would end up being a hero for saving them all, for getting us all through the portal just before it closed. Maybe Kathy would begin to appreciate me.

As everyone else rustled around getting ready to turn in for the night, I got up off my log and ambled toward my tent. I was not looking forward to meeting those scary Indians again.

Chapter 22

Bright and early the next morning, after packing up and breaking camp, we arrived at the outskirts of the Indian village, a small contingent of warriors came out to meet us. Beaver had a brief conversation with them. I admired him for seeming to know their language, although at times, he appeared to struggle to find words. They used a lot of wild hand gestures to communicate.

The village sat in a large meadow, sprawled out along the northern bank of a small stream with plenty of room for our group. Knee-high grass with scattered elms and oak trees formed the main vegetation.

When the Indians turned away, Beaver said, "They want us to set up camp in the meadow, downstream. Some think you're unclean."

James lifted his arm and sniffed. "Wheeww, I think them Indians is right."

Chad laughed.

"After we set up camp," Eric said, standing in his stirrups to get everyone's attention, "I think it would be a good idea for all of us to wash in the stream. We don't want to offend our hosts by stinking up their lodges." He turned and we followed him and Beaver past the teepees toward the downriver section.

After unpacking and setting up my tent, while most of the others went down to the river to clean up, I walked to a small hill behind the village and studied the Indians while I smoked my pipe.

This tribe lived in teepees, which looked just like the ones I'd seen on T.V. and in movies. Each teepee had been painted with the same kinds of geometric patterns Beaver's people used for their tattoos. Additionally, there were also paintings of animals and birds. On each teepee, one animal seemed to be dominant, like the spirit-helper of whoever lived there.

It was difficult to tell how many people actually lived in the village. I counted twenty teepees. If only one warrior lived in each teepee, I wondered how so many more warriors had shown up that day they had pulled their weapons on us. Even if there were only twenty warriors here, I didn't think it would be much of a contest if we had to fight them.

Although I found myself totally curious about this tribe, an uncomfortable feeling continued to run through my mind. In the past couple of weeks, my dream of being burned at the stake had increasingly interrupted my sleep. I wondered if that dream was triggered by the similarity between these Indians and those in my dream. I did not like being so close in proximity to these warriors and their home. Something was going to happen. I could feel it in my bones.

After I made my way down to the river with a small stick of Coastal soap, I took off my outer clothing and waded along the edge of the river. I shivered at the first touch of the icy-cold water, but the day was turning out to be pretty hot, so the cold water felt good on my skin as I got used to it. I cleaned up the best I could.

When I returned to camp Beaver, Eric, and Pat, took Steve, Chad, and Travis into the Indian village proper to meet with the leaders of the tribe.

James and Tory stayed back to check and repair their tack. Sergio and Juan just wanted to rest. They retired to their tents.

This left me sitting alone under a tree with Trish and Kathy. The others had pulled a number of fallen logs together to form a conversational semi-circle. It felt good to sit in the shade.

Coyote had not yet lit the campfire, probably because of the heat. He busied himself with various goods he had removed from a pack.

Kathy seemed different today, not so cold, more friendly. I guess she had come to terms with the situation. She even looked up at me and smiled.

Sensing a crack in her resolve, I piped up quickly, "Would you like to go for a walk along the river?"

An amused look came over her face, like she was remembering the failed kiss I had given her.

Damn. Will I ever live that one down?

"Yeah," she said, getting up and whisking the dirt off her hands. She had obviously washed up earlier. Her damp hair fell into soft waves and gave off a fresh scent of shampoo. "Let's take a walk." She gave a little wave to Trish as she stepped over a log and headed toward the water.

"I'm sorry for not telling you about the portal closing," I said. "We didn't think it would be a big deal, as long as we got everyone back on time."

"That's just it," she said. "I'm concerned about getting back to my normal life. Though this has been an extraordinary adventure, I miss my real life, my real work, and my real friends. This isn't how I want to spend the next years. And, in this world, how would we find out when the next portal opens? What if we miss it? How do we keep track of the days without a computer or a calendar? The longer we put off leaving, the more nervous I get."

"Well," I said in appeasement, "when we get the extra horses, we should be set to make it back on time, even if we take a couple more days to pan for gold."

We walked along in silence. I had such a compulsion to hold her hand, but feared she would slap me this time. "I'm sorry about the kiss that night," I stammered. "I guess I thought maybe you thought the same about me, going for the walk with me and all."

She smiled and took my hand in hers.

Wow. My whole body tingled. I struggled to prevent showing any reaction, hiding my surprise and the thrill she would make such a move.

"It's okay, Donny. I'm just not ready for a relationship. I just need a friend right now." Her dark eyes looked up at me with gentleness. "I like you as a friend."

Oh, great. That's what all women say when they mean, "I'm not going to bed with you, so forget it." Well, if this was all I was going to get out of her, then I decided to enjoy her company for what it was. The smell of shampoo in her hair seemed familiar and reminded me of home.

Kiddingly, she reached up and pulled on my beard. "I really wish you'd shave off this stupid thing. I think you look much better without it."

I laughed, trying to hide my self-consciousness. "You're probably right. I don't like it either. Just wish I would have been smart enough to bring a razor like Eric." I decided the first thing I would do when I saw Eric next time would be to ask to borrow his razor. I'd do anything if it made Kathy happy.

On returning to camp, we grabbed granola bars and trail mixes from our packs and sat around talking about what we were going to do when we got home with our gold. James and Tory joined us and contributed to our mutual dreams. The tone among us had lightened considerably.

For the moment, I forgot about the stirrings in my mind that seemed unsettling. A silent part of me waited anxiously for

Eric and his group to return from the village. I hoped we could trade for some horses and get the hell out of here as soon as possible.

We spent part of the afternoon unpacking and rearranging things in our packs, since we had pretty much hurried off in the morning rush to get to the village.

I grabbed a handful of my golden nuggets from my saddlebag to feel the richness of its worth. I couldn't believe that my dream had actually come true. When I got this load back to my own world, I really would be rich. Somehow, though, the feeling of being rich wasn't as dazzling or thrilling as I thought it would be. It was more like a sense of relief, knowing that my financial situation would be secure for the first time in my life. I wouldn't have to worry about how I was going to pay my bills.

* * *

An hour before dusk, Beaver, Eric, and the rest of the group finally returned from the Indian village.

"We've got good news and bad news," Eric said as he settled down on a log and poured himself a cup full of coffee.

"The good news is," said a smiling Travis, "we got us four horses. We pick 'em out in the morning."

And the bad news? I wondered.

"The bad news," Beaver said somberly, "is we've all been invited to a ceremonial feast in the village tonight."

"Why is that bad news?" Trish asked.

Beaver seemed edgy, out-of-character for his usual laid-back nature. "I don't trust this tribe."

Pat added, "We got the distinct feeling we're being set up for something."

A chill ran up my spine. *Please, God, don't make my dream a reality*. "Why do think that?" I asked. "What'd they do?"

"They didn't do anything. Nothing like that," Pat said. "I just have a gut feeling that if we go tonight, we need to stay together and keep our eyes and ears open for trouble."

"Should we take our guns?" Sergio inquired, his dark eyes round with fear.

"Definitely," Eric stated, taking a sip of his coffee. "Otherwise, we don't go. Right, Pat?"

"That's right."

Beaver remained standing. "We must have everything packed and ready to go. Only keep out what you are using tonight. Make sure it will fit on your saddlebag. In case we have to leave in a hurry."

"Good idea," I said, nodding toward him.

"Do you really think that's necessary?" Trish asked in a whiny tone as if she was the only one being put out by Beaver's demand. "We just finished unpacking everything."

Feeling edgy myself, I wanted to tell her to shut up and do what she was told, but Eric spoke first.

"We don't know what will happen, Trish. But I agree with Beaver. I think we all need to be prepared for the worst. There's something eerie about this tribe."

She frowned, but at least she stopped arguing.

It was getting dark, but we all jumped up and pulled our things together. Since I had organized my gear earlier in the day, it was pretty easy for me to pack it away. Whatever I needed, I left where I could get to it in a hurry. The rest got packed. All of us left out our tents and sleeping bags.

On the way to the village, we hiked in silence through the knee-high grass of the meadow. The grass ended at the edge of the village where a stretch of packed dirt formed the dimensions of the village area.

I walked in the rear of the group, not paying much attention to where we were going. In the growing darkness, the flickering light of a large campfire ahead gave us a direction to follow through the village. The sound of soft, steady drums and chanting grew louder as we drew nearer to the center of the village. The celebration seemed to already be underway.

Suddenly, everyone stopped in front of me as we came near the fire, surrounded by the Indian community standing and sitting in groups. Looking around, my eyes about popped out of their sockets when I saw the fire pit from my dreams. At the far end of the large fire pit stood a tall stake about a foot around and ten feet tall. A chill ran down my spine. This part of the pit had no fire burning in it at the moment, but the scorched, black wooden stake had only one obvious use: human sacrifice.

Oh, my God. I stood frozen in place. Unable to speak, I finally stammered out a few words in a whisper to Pat. "We need to leave this place. Now."

Pat's eyes narrowed. He looked around. "Why? What did you see?"

I pointed at the stake. "I think they're planning to burn someone at the stake."

Kathy clamped a hand over her mouth in horror. "They're going to burn some…"

"Leave it alone," Beaver cut her off. "It's here, but it doesn't mean it has anything to do with us. The tribes in this world still torture and kill people. There's nothing we can do about it. Just forget about it and have a good time."

Before Kathy could respond, her eyes still full of indignation and fright, one of the tribesmen approached and spoke in his own language to Beaver.

Nodding to the Indian, Beaver turned to us and said, "They want us to sit on that side of the fire pit." He pointed to an area furthest away from the blackened stake.

With the others, I slowly moved forward. The tribe members, scattered around the area, watched us closely with cold, curious eyes. I saw no friendly smiles. The drums continued to beat. An old man chanted in a low tone.

It was obvious this area was well-used for ceremonies, parties, informal gatherings, and whatever other occasions the tribe had for coming together. The full fire pit was about ten feet across. The scorched stake stood about two feet from one edge while the campfire had been built on the other side. Opposite the stake, the large, hard-packed dirt area where we were sitting showed evidence of much use. I gulped, trying not to let my imagination run wild.

As we sat down, the drums stopped. It looked like the ceremony was about to begin.

Chapter 23

After all the Indians sat cross-legged on the ground, the ceremony began with a speech from an old Indian named Flows Like A River. He just happened to be the chief. He droned on and on, ending at least an hour later. It had never occurred to me that Indians could talk this long. I always thought they were short on words.

While the chief ranted on, the glaring black eyes of the community, the whites of their eyes standing out against their dark skin and dark irises, watched us closely.

After a while, my legs started aching. I shifted to ease the pressure.

Everyone, except the chief, turned their eyes on me. Eric gave me a fierce glare.

I felt my face turning red and quickly went back into the Indian formation of crossed legs.

Pat chuckled to himself.

All of the men of the tribe, even the young boys, wore some kind of celebratory war paint in colors of white, black, or red. For most, heavily beaded ornaments hung from their necks and over their chests. Bird feathers often decorated the edges of the ornaments.

The women, most of them dressed in colorful woven skirts, had braided beads into their hair. Many of them wore inch-wide beaded bands across their foreheads. The favored colors seemed to be red and white, which reminded me that I had missed the Fourth of July Celebration back home. We were now into the second week in July.

As soon as Chief Flows Like A River ended his agonizingly long speech, the Indian women served dinner. An old woman with no teeth and stringy, sparse gray hair handed me a shallow woven basket about ten inches across. It contained various pieces of meat and corn on some kind of tortilla. There was also what looked like a salad made up of wild greens. We'd eaten earlier, so I wasn't starving and the food didn't particularly appeal to me. I let out a loud sigh.

Eric, sitting to my left, said in an annoyed tone, "What?"

"I can't wait to get back home so I can have a big, juicy hamburger, loaded with onions, tomatoes, and lettuce."

"Don't forget the fries," Pat threw in.

Kathy, having chosen to sit next to me on my right, said, "I want a pizza. With everything on it. And a cold beer to wash it down."

I conjured up in my mind a hot, flavorful pizza with gooey cheese and lots of meat. Saliva flooded my mouth, threatening to overflow my lips and run down my chin. I had to swallow hard, twice, to get rid of it.

"Not me," Trish said from the other side of Eric. "I want a Caesar salad. Umm-umm."

I laughed. "Yeah, this salad looks like a combination of dandelions, grass, and leaves. I hope this meat is elk or deer, not squirrel or porcupine." Thinking about the possibility of eating squirrel made me tentative about taking a bite.

Pat said, "I'm sure it's okay, Donny."

The meal had barely started when a hush suddenly descended across the crowd.

A slender young girl strutted into view. About fifteen or sixteen, her long pure-white hair and pale skin contrasted starkly with her dark-skinned fellow tribe members. She seemed out of place, yet unnaturally beautiful and graceful in a soft woven dress, cinched at the waist with a colorful beaded belt.

When she looked toward us, I recoiled in shock at her blood-red eyes. Against her fair skin, they made her look like a zombie from a cheap Hollywood movie.

"What the hell?" Chad said, his mouth hanging open in awe. "Is she like an albino or what?"

"I would say so," Kathy said in curious amazement. "Wow. I've never seen one with such red eyes."

"What would cause her eyes to be that color?" Eric asked.

"Normally," Kathy explained, "the human eye produces enough pigment to give the iris it's color. Albinos usually have white or pale blue eyes, but there have been rare cases where the red of the retina shows through the irises, making the eyes appear to be red."

"Now, how would you know that?" Steve challenged. "Did you learn than in medical school?"

"Not exactly. When I was in medical school, my mentor's niece had the same condition. She told me about it."

"She looks like a freak," Travis said with a low chuckle, his mouth full of food.

I expected Chad to come back with a smartass remark, but he seemed to be too busy ogling the girl.

"Jeez, Chad, don't drool on yourself," Steve remarked.

"You've got to admit, she's hot," Chad replied without taking his eyes off her.

I found Chad's interest disturbing, especially when I noticed the dark eyes of the male warriors nearby had suddenly focused their attention on Chad as he watched the girl.

The chief and two warriors arose to meet the girl. They accompanied her to where our group sat. They stopped in front of Beaver, who rose to meet them face-to-face. We all stood up in turn, somehow sensing that this was considered an important event, like meeting a V.I.P. Unwinding my legs, I sighed in relief as I stood up. Wincing as I worked the cramps out of my thighs, I smiled at the strange-looking girl.

Beaver translated for us as the chief spoke to him. "Her name is Fire Eyes," he said. "She is Flows Like A River's grand-daughter."

I studied her as the chief continued to speak to Beaver. Small bones made her look delicate and fragile. Though her red eyes gave her an eerie look, an aura of confidence surrounded her, an air of importance.

Beaver turned to us. "According to their legends, there was another Fire Eyes. She also had white hair and red eyes. She helped their ancestors defeat a rival tribe that was threatening to wipe them out. They believe this girl is a reincarnation of that woman."

The chief spoke to the girl. As she turned and walked away with the two warriors, the chief turned and stared hard at Chad, whose eyes hungrily followed Fire Eyes.

The chief relayed to Beaver more words that sounded a little harsh.

"She's a living priestess," Beaver translated. "The chief says she's watched constantly. Any member of the tribe would die to protect her. He says any attempt to approach her without his approval will be met with instant and severe punishment."

Chad continued to stare, not seeming to notice the chief's observation of him or to pick up the implications in his words.

"Hey, dumbass," Steve said sharply while popping Chad on the back of his head, "don't even think about it."

"What?" Chad complained, finally making eye contact with Steve when the girl disappeared out of sight.

"Trying to bed her. I get the distinct feeling that, if you even try to talk to her without their permission, we'll all be in deep shit."

"Yes," Beaver said. "The quickest way to get there," he added, nodding his head toward the stake in the fire pit, "is to mess with that girl."

"Okay, okay," Chad said, putting up his hands to get the rest of us to back off. "I promise I won't go anywhere near her."

For some reason, his words didn't sound convincing to me.

"Well, you'd better not," Eric warned. "If you do, I'll help them tie you to that stake myself."

Judging by the glares from the rest of our group, I didn't think any one of us would hesitate to help.

As we sat down again to finish our meal, I could see that the Indians kept watching Chad more closely than the rest of us. The whole tribe was clearly protective of her. Only a man with a death wish would dare to be foolish enough to get involved with her.

I ate a piece of meat that tasted like freshly smoked elk. *Umm.* I took a sip of my drink out of a small stone-hewn bowl that had been set beside me. I almost spit the bile-tasting liquid out of my mouth, but fearing I might offend the community, I choked it down. Looking at the clear liquid closer, I checked it with my finger. *What the hell is this stuff?*

I had thought it was water, but it tasted like a bitter wine. I took another tentative sip. Either my taste buds had been deadened, or the drink wasn't as bad as I'd first thought. The bitter bite turned slightly sweet after swishing it around in my mouth a few times. *Not bad.* Taking another sip, I idly wondered about the potency of the stuff. I looked around.

The members of Steve's crew were downing it like it was Kool-Aid.

I shrugged. *What the hell? It's really not that bad.* After downing my cupful, I held it out and let the Indian woman, who just happened to be passing by with a leather container, fill it up again.

Fifteen minutes and two cups later, I re-evaluated my opinion of the homemade brew as I suddenly felt lightheaded. A creeping numbness slowly spread throughout my body. *Son-of-a-bitch, have we been poisoned?*

I blinked my eyes, trying to focus on the middle of the fire. When I glanced around to see if any of my companions were concerned about the effects of the drink, I saw Steve's crew smiling, laughing, and generally, having a great time. None of them seemed to be worried about the drink.

By this time, Kathy and Trish had moved off with Beaver, using him as the translator while they talked to an old Indian who appeared to be the tribe's shaman with all the paraphernalia of feathers and beads he wore.

Pat and Eric, looking sober and serious, didn't appear to be partaking much of the drink. Steve and his crew, though, continued to have their fair share of the liquid and were having a grand time telling jokes, making fun, and laughing loudly. Chad kept staring off into the direction that Fire Eyes had disappeared.

The drums had started up again. Many of the warriors, women, and young children began dancing to the steady beat or watched as others participated.

I set my cup down. Even though something about the drink seemed addictive, I was determined not to drink any more. I didn't normally drink hard liquor, so I figured the alcohol might be hitting me harder than the others in the group. My head swam. I was having a hard time focusing my eyes on any one spot.

I had this increasingly bad feeling, like we were all in grave danger. My paranoia grew as I watched the other members of our group, who seemed totally oblivious to the fact that we were completely at the mercy of the Indians.

Some of the warriors still watched us with their menacing black eyes, which only made my fears worse. They drank, too, but gave no indications that the liquor had any effect on them.

Realizing there was nothing I could do and trusting Beaver and Eric to spot trouble, I decided to lean back and enjoy the high. If we were going to be rounded up and burned at the stake, I might as well enjoy my last moments. At any rate, in this condition, I wouldn't have enough energy to fight off the Indians if they did decide to kill us.

I must've fallen asleep, because the next thing I knew, Eric was shaking my shoulder. "Come on, Donny. We're going back to camp."

I had no idea how long I'd been asleep. I struggled to my feet and looked up. A quarter moon sat in the night sky, filled with brilliant stars. The fire in the pit had burned down to a glowing bed of hot coals. Most of the Indian community had disappeared by now, with only a few warriors watching the last of us head toward our camp.

Stumbling through the dark with my head spinning, I feared I wouldn't make it back to camp.

Kathy helped me keep my balance.

Gaining confidence from the liquor, I asked her boldly in my drunken stupor, "You want to sleep in my tent tonight?"

She laughed. "I don't think so."

When we reached camp, she said good-night and left me to fend for myself alone in my tent.

Not bothering to undress, I crashed on top of my sleeping bag. *Wow,* I suddenly realized, *I'm still alive. The Indians didn't roast us.*

In seconds, I fell fast asleep.

Chapter 24

I awoke to Eric shaking my shoulder. It seemed like déjà vu, him waking me in the Indian village after the potent drink. When I groggily opened my eyes, I could see I was in my tent and it was still dark.

"Get up, dammit," Eric demanded. "Something's got the village in an uproar. We're leaving. Get your stuff together." He ducked out of my tent.

I sat up on my elbows and cracked open one eye. Through the partially open flap, I could see a bare hint of morning light. My head pounded, keeping perfect rhythm with my heart, as if it was counting down the seconds of my life. I lay back down, longing for more sleep.

Voices, yelling from the direction of the village, slowly seeped into my consciousness. When the voices changed from calls of inquiry to shouts of anger drawing closer, my eyes flew open. *Damn. This doesn't sound good. I think we're in deep shit.*

Panic rushed through me as I threw off my sleeping bag and sat up. My head spun like a top. I grabbed the edge of the tent to steady myself as I got to my knees. At least I didn't have to worry about getting dressed. I hadn't taken anything off last night, not even my gun. My hat was lying next to my bed. It had apparently fallen off my head sometime during the night. Feeling slightly nauseous, I put on my hat, quickly rolled up my sleeping bag, collapsed my tent, and carried it to my horse as fast as I could move my feet.

The others already had the horses loaded and were mounting their saddles.

James said, "Throw that stuff where ya can find space, Donny. Let's git the hell outta here."

As I lashed the tent and bag onto one of the packsaddles, Travis said in a worried tone, "We have to wait for Chad." His bloodshot eyes scanned the area. He had obviously packed up Chad's gear and had his horse ready to go. I climbed on my horse and looked around to see if anybody else was missing. I was relieved to see that, with the exception of Chad, all the other riders were accounted for.

In the dim light of early morning, it was hard to see beyond the shadows. The voices from the village had quieted, but a troop of Indians marched toward us across the grassy field. Their angry grunts and pounding feet gave me the impression they were on the warpath.

"Where the hell is Chad?" Steve asked impatiently. "He could endanger us all."

"I don't know," Travis said, frantically looking around, pulling his horse in a circle. "Last time I saw him, we were going to sleep in our tent."

Pat shook his head. He spoke in a low voice. "I really hope he's not the reason the Indians are pissed off."

"It wouldn't surprise me a bit," Steve said with annoyance, running a hand across his crew cut. "That guy is always getting into some kind of trouble."

"I don't see Coyote, either," Kathy said.

"Gone," Beaver stated. "He disappeared when he heard the villagers yelling. He's probably halfway back to my village."

"Oh, great," Steve observed. "A cowardly Coyote."

"I think we're about to find out what the ruckus is all about," Kathy said, pointing to the approaching group of twenty-some warriors now halfway across the field. Chief Flows Like A River walked in the lead. Most of the Indians carried bows with arrows already nocked. A few held spears, ready to be thrown.

My hand drifted to the pistol strapped in the holster on my hip. I unsnapped the strap, ready to pull out the gun in a hurry. Resting my hand on the cool butt of the gun, I was glad all of us had gotten so used to wearing them that we always had them strapped to our sides for emergencies…like this.

The warriors stopped a hundred feet from our horses. In his native tongue, Flows Like A River yelled a few callous words to Beaver. As the dawn sky became lighter, I could see his angry face. The other Indians had sloppily donned more war paint, mostly in thick lines of black. They looked furious and wicked.

Beaver turned to us. "The chief wants to talk to me. All of you, get off your horses. Wait here." Staying mounted himself, Beaver rode out halfway to meet the spokesman.

I got off my horse along with the others. We waited tensely, our hands on or near our guns with the women behind us.

A flurry of back-and-forth banter exploded between Beaver and Flows Like A River. When Beaver returned to meet us, his tall form seemed slightly humped and fear etched his face. He dismounted as we all waited in tense silence. "All of you must do exactly as I say," he said in a grave tone. "If you don't, we will all be killed."

"What happened?" Eric demanded, stepping forward.

"Why are they doing this?" Steve blurted, standing close to his horse, his hand caressing a bag of gold.

Questions erupted from everyone in the group all at once.

Beaver held his hands up, deflecting the questions and silencing us. "Chad returned to the village last night to see Fire Eyes."

"Oh, shit," Steve muttered. "I should have known he'd try to go back and have sex with her."

"He did more than have sex with her," Beaver said grimly. "He killed her."

Gasps of astonishment burst all around me as the vision of us all being tied to the stake and burned alive came blaring vividly into my mind. My breath came in short puffs. I thought I was going to throw up. How could Chad do such a thing? How could he be so irresponsible and foolish?

Eric seemed to get hold of himself first. He spoke almost too calmly. "So, what do they want us to do?"

Beaver made eye contact with each of us. "We must leave all of our weapons here and follow them into the village."

"No way," James and Tory said in unison. Both backed up, showing their decisiveness about not being a part of this angry scene.

After getting a nod from Juan, Sergio said, "Ditto for us."

Kathy, her body tense from the direness of the situation, said, "Even though I hate guns and won't have anything to do with them, I don't think it would be wise to leave them behind."

"Could you just take your pistols?" Trish asked, shifting nervously and wrenching her hands. "Maybe you could keep them hidden?"

Pat glanced at the waiting warriors who still had their arrows nocked. "How much do they know about our weapons?"

"What do you mean?" I asked.

He turned to Beaver. "Do they even know what guns are?"

"Other than the two boys Travis shot at, probably not. I have not seen guns in my world, other than those brought through the portal. I cannot be sure this tribe has had such an acquaintance, but I doubt it." Beaver looked at our holsters dubiously, as though having to make a hard decision about the reactions of the Indians, were they to know the power of our weapons.

On one hand, if Beaver allowed us to take the handguns, we might stand a fighting chance of escaping whatever awaited us. On the other hand, if the Indians thought we were trying to sneak weapons into the village when they'd told us not to, they might be inclined to just kill us outright and be done with it.

We stood in silence, letting Beaver make the decision.

I kept an eye on the Indians, who seemed perfectly happy to keep us at arrow-point in readiness to attack, should it look like we were going to bolt.

"Take your pistols," Beaver finally announced. "But keep them hidden until you need them."

"Couldn't we just jump on our horses and run away?" Steve asked. "Hell, look at 'em. They only have bows and arrows and a couple of spears."

"Don't underestimate their 'primitive' weapons," Beaver said, looking directly at Steve. "They'd have arrows in everyone of us before we went ten feet."

An impatient shout from the waiting warriors put an end to our talk. They began to march toward us.

Discreetly, we slipped our handguns into our waistbands and covered them with our shirts.

As a group, we moved toward them. The warriors surrounded us and motioned us toward the village.

Steve resisted at first, as though he refused to leave behind his gold. Maybe he thought the Indians would steal it.

They prodded him at spear-point to move away from his horse.

By now, the stars in the sky were disappearing and the shadows around us began to lighten. The black paint on the warrior's faces looked all the more ominous.

As they herded us toward the village, Beaver walked at the head of the procession and talked quietly with Flows Like A River.

I could feel myself panting as we shuffled through the grass. My mind moved in slow-motion, like being inside a dream and slowly crossing railroad tracks when a train was barreling down. I couldn't quite grapple with my growing fear that surfaced from my recurring nightmares, nor could I seem to get out of the way of some tragic event about to strike us down.

Kathy walked next to me, glancing at me with worried eyes, yet I saw in her a strength that I didn't feel in myself. A rush of caring flowed from her touch as she reached out and put her arm in mine.

I'd never known such comfort in a time of need. It was as though her strength poured into me. I clung to her support with hope and gripped the possibility that we might live beyond this moment of fate.

* * *

We came to a stop a short distance from the community center and fire pit that had, only a few hours before, been the scene of celebration, dance, liquor, and laughter.

A cold shiver went up my spine when I caught sight of Chad's white, near-naked muscular body tied to the charred post. His legs had been bound to the stake from the ankles up to his waist with a long strip of leather. Surprisingly, his hands were tied behind the stake with only a single band of leather. A stack of wood, piled in a neat pyramid around the bottom of the stake, indicated that the worst was about to happen. A small campfire burned a short distance from the pyre.

Four massive Indians standing to the side of Chad, held unlit torches made of tied bundles of sticks and weeds.

My mouth went dry.

Seeing us, Chad wrestled against his bindings and yelled, "I swear, I didn't do anything. I didn't touch the girl."

"Don't answer," Beaver cautioned us. "No one is allowed to talk to a condemned man."

"That's stupid," Steve whispered.

"I know," Beaver responded. "In your world and in my tribe it is. But here, we must play by their rules."

Kathy clung to my arm.

I could feel the tension running through her body and mine. I wanted to wrap her in my arms and hold her tight, turn her face away so that she didn't have to see this horror, but I didn't want to make a move that might offend the Indians. I'm not sure I could move anyway. I felt frozen in place.

"You've got to believe me," Chad screamed, his arms and shoulders squirming against the stake. "They've got the wrong person. I didn't do it."

Deep down, something told me Chad was telling the truth. Feeling that an awful mistake was being made here, I turned to Beaver. "What did Flows Like A River tell you? Why do they think he's guilty?"

The sadness in Beaver's dark eyes reflected the sadness in his voice. "When Flows Like A River woke early this morning, Fire Eyes was gone. Her aide, Morning Glory, came to get her before the break of dawn. That's when they realized she was missing.

"He told me Fire Eyes can never be left alone. From the day she was born, she has never been alone. Overseers, like her parents, her grandfather, and Morning Glory, have been assigned to watch her and protect her. When she went missing, they knew something was wrong. They started a search in the village, then moved out into the woods.

"In the trees, one warrior heard the sound of snoring. They found Chad, sound asleep, next to the dead body of Fire Eyes."

"How was she killed," I asked, not sure I really wanted to know.

"Her neck was broken," Beaver replied flatly.

I shook my head. No matter what anybody said, I couldn't picture Chad doing such a thing.

Eric shook his head. "I'm having a hard time believing Chad would do something so cruelly as kill her, then fall asleep next to her. That doesn't make sense."

"I agree," Pat said with a skeptical look. "Especially after we had warned him to stay away from her. Hell, he'd have to be an idiot to go back into the village knowing how the Indians felt about her."

"An idiot," Steve added, "or so drunk he didn't know what he was doing."

Chad thrashed back and forth, trying to break free of the leather straps binding him to the fire-blackened stake. He stopped voicing his innocence and was, instead, concentrating on freeing himself.

"Guess they ain't ever heard 'innocent till proven guilty,'" James said.

"What now?" Kathy pleaded, still hanging on my arm. "There's got to be something we can do."

Beaver shook his head. "I told Flows Like A River we would see to the justice of our own, but he would have none of it."

"Do we have to watch?" Trish asked, biting her lip and looking away from Chad.

"This is the price we must pay for our association with Chad," Beaver stated. "It's their way of justice to teach us a lesson."

"Maybe Chad did do it," Steve declared. "He's been in and out of trouble as long as I've known him. I don't think he's ever paid for any of his sins with the law. Maybe it's all catching up to him."

"Even if he did 'do' it,'" Kathy shot back at him, her voice full of disgust, "he doesn't deserve to die such a horrible death. No one does." Her sharp glare warned Steve he'd better not respond.

He shrugged it off.

"So, we're just supposed to stand here and let 'em kill him?" Tory asked.

"We have no choice," Beaver stated. "If you interfere, you'll be tied up there with him, too."

"What about us?" Eric asked. "What's gonna happen when this is over?"

"We are free to go. But we will never be welcomed back."

"They'll let us go, just like that?" Travis said nervously. His face and manner looked broken, shaken to the core at seeing his friend's heinous predicament. "I would think this tribe of savages would kill all of us for what Chad did."

"They're not savages," Beaver said firmly. "They have laws and rules, just like you. The rest of us did nothing wrong. They will not hold any of us responsible for Chad's actions, but neither do they want to have further business with us."

The warriors with the bows and arrows moved us closer to the pit as a string of Indians with Chief Flows Like A River in the lead worked their way through the crowd.

A terrifying dread rose in my bones as I knew the ceremony was about to commence.

Kathy stayed close to me, her hands gripping my arm more tightly. She closed her eyes and put her head against my shoulder.

I didn't see how the Indians could force us to watch, but even with closed eyes, it would be impossible to escape the impact with our close proximity to the fire pit.

Worn out from his fight with the bindings, Chad hung limply against the stake. In a low, weak tone, he pleaded, "Please, won't someone help me?"

Kathy began to cry softly.

Ashamed at our inability to help him, I turned my head so I could avoid looking at his pleading eyes.

Trish stood behind Kathy, leaning against her for support, her eyes looking down.

Flows Like A River stepped in front of the fire pit and held up his hands to get everyone's attention. He spoke to the crowd.

"He's stating the facts about how Fire Eyes came up missing," Beaver translated. "He's telling how they found her dead next to Chad. He's asking if anyone can prove Chad is innocent."

Kathy, tears streaking her face, looked up at Beaver hopefully.

The Indian women, children, and warriors began to chant.

Beaver shook his head. "They're shouting, 'Let him burn.'"

Flows Like A River shouted a command.

The crowd fell silent.

The four powerfully built warriors holding torches stepped forward. They lit their torches on the small campfire. They formed a circle around Chad as the crowd fell silent. As one, all four warriors lowered their torches to the stacked wood piled up at the base of the stake. The dried pyre instantly flared up in roaring flames, as though something flammable had been soaked into the wood.

Kathy flung her face into my shoulder. I wrapped my arms around her as she wept.

Trish's wailing and Kathy's sobs mingled with the hissing, popping, crackling sounds of the fire.

Chad bellowed in rage. He renewed his fruitless struggle against the bindings. His face red, his neck and arms bulged from exertion. His cries finally faded as smoke and heat scorched his lungs.

My mind went numb. My eyes blurred. I could hardly breathe. The smoke and odor of burning flesh set me on the verge of fainting. Holding Kathy helped ground me, giving me a reason to stay on my feet. I watched as my dream manifested into reality, a burning, vivid reality, but not with me at the stake. Something even more horrible…watching someone else die.

A light breeze whisked across my face, carrying the odor away as the worst of the flames burned down, leaving the charred remains of a man's life.

We all stood in stunned silence for what seemed like a long time, as though paying our last respects in a stupor of horror.

The Indian crowd broke up. The family units headed together toward their teepees.

Flows Like A River gave Beaver a terse nod, then turned away.

"We can go now," Beaver said softly.

"We're heading back to the portal right now," Eric said. "No more gold. It's time to go home before anybody else dies."

Steve turned with the rest of us. "Yeah, let's get our gold and go home."

I turned Kathy away from the scene, preventing her from seeing the remains of the fire. She broke free of my arms and walked out of the village with Trish, the two supporting each other, arm in arm.

The sun had risen just above the horizon. Probably not an hour had passed since Eric had awakened me.

No one spoke as we headed back to collect the horses, already packed and ready to go. Our steps quickened the further we got from the village, each of us growing more anxious to leave behind the scene of Chad's gruesome death.

A steady tremor shivered through my body, like taking in too much caffeine at one time. My mind floated in a daze. Moving more slowly through the grass than the others, I brought up the rear.

I couldn't help myself. I turned and, walking backwards, looked one last time at Chad's remains. The bindings had burned through his hands, allowing what was left of his body to slump down into the smoldering wood.

The members of the village community had all disappeared from view, except for one Indian, who suddenly stepped out from behind a teepee. His familiar face locked eyes with me.

I stopped in shock. *O-cha? What's he doing here?*

O-cha held up one finger. He followed the gesture by making a fist with his thumb sticking upward. When he inverted his fist to point downward, he grinned.

I got the message loud and clear. *One down.*

Instantly, I knew the truth. Chad had been set up.

Chapter 25

Since the horses had been loaded and saddled, it took only a few minutes to get mounted and head southwest down the trail. Needless to say, our trade with the Indians for the extra horses had fallen through. We had only our original seven packhorses and now Chad's saddle horse, which we used to carry some of the gold from the packhorses.

O-cha's appearance in the village brought up a lot of questions and set my mind to a great uneasiness. I was still having a hard time dealing with Chad's death and the relevance to my dreams, but now, with O-cha in the picture, the whole affair was taking on a dark aspect that could be even more foreboding for the rest of us, and particularly for me, his nemesis.

As we clopped along, I moved up next to Beaver in the lead. "I need to talk to you," I said to him quietly. "In private."

Beaver nodded.

We urged our horses ahead into a trot across the tree-covered hills. The other riders and packhorses followed along at a slower pace. By the time we slowed down, we were well out of earshot.

"I think Chad was set up," I began.

"Why?"

"As we were leaving the village, I saw O-cha."

Beavers eyes widened. "O-cha? Are you sure?"

"Positive."

Setting his eyes dead ahead, Beaver hesitated before he spoke again. "You think he killed Fire Eyes? You think he got Chad to go back to the village?"

"Listen, I don't know how he did it, or even if he did, but just the fact he was there means he's up to no good. Why else would he have been there?"

Beaver seemed to ponder the situation. "Did you see anyone else you recognized?"

"No, just O-cha." I paused, waiting for a response. Finally, I broke the silence. "I thought you should know before I tell the others, being that you and O-cha are from the same tribe."

"Yes. We must share this with everyone. O-cha would not have come alone. He would bring at least two or three warriors with him." He swung his horse around sharply and trotted back to gather up the other riders.

I stayed where I was, willing to wait until the rest of the group caught up to me. Feeling nervous, I pulled out my pipe and filled it with tobacco. It had been a while since I had smoked it, I'd been trying to avoid the nasty tobacco smell around Kathy. At the moment, however, my nerves buzzed with anxiety. This was my only way of finding relief.

Exhaling my first puff, I scanned the trees in the distance. A movement caught my eye. Digging out my binoculars from my saddlebag, I focused on the trees. Figuring to see a deer or an elk, I was shocked to see a string of three Indians, all on foot, making their way through the trees ahead of us. I couldn't identify them from the distance, but the uneasy feeling that it was O-cha and his cronies crept over me.

"Whatcha lookin' at?" James asked as he rode up next to me.

"Indians." I pointed to the trees. "Three of them. Moving single-file."

James grabbed the binoculars from my hands and scanned the area. "I ain't seein' nothin'."

"Their gone now," I said.

Trish, her eyes wide with concern, came up next to us. "Do you think Chief Flows Like A River is having us followed?"

"We think it's O-cha," Beaver said calmly as the whole group gathered around.

"O-cha? Here?" Eric exclaimed. His eyes scanned the area, as though expecting to see O-cha standing on the horizon.

I described what I'd seen back at the village.

"So, let me get this straight," Steve said in a cynical voice, "you think, based on nothing more than a gut feeling, that O-cha brought a couple of his friends 700 miles just to set Chad up?"

"No," I snapped. "I think he brought them 700 miles to kill all of us. I think Chad was just the first. That's the message O-cha was giving me."

Steve laughed. "I think you're full of it, Donny. Chad was guilty. The Indians were right. You're letting your paranoia run away with you. I think we should keep moving, put as much distance between us and this crazy tribe as possible before we make camp tonight." He reined his horse away from the rest of us and started down the trail.

"I agree with puttin' miles behind us," Tory said. "We cain't trust them Indians. Let's git to our camp for the night, then discuss the rest of this." He trotted off after Steve.

One by one, the others followed Steve and Tory.

Kathy, the last one to leave, smiled at me as she gently kicked her horse and followed suit behind Trish.

Dismayed at their lack of belief in my story, and feeling that it was up to me to take responsibility for O-cha's reappearance, I kept a nervous watch to the rear.

Luckily, we were traveling through thin, sparse timbers where it would be hard for an enemy to hide.

In the late afternoon, Beaver led us to a small, willow-lined stream that sat on the edge of a meadow. Darkness fell by the time we got the camp set up and dinner started. Without Coyote's cooking skills, we pretty much fended for ourselves this first night by eating dried beef strips and whatever else we could forage from the food packs. Other than Steve, none of us seemed to be all that hungry after the grisly events of the morning.

Eric kept a full pot of coffee brewing near the campfire. He seemed quieter than normal. Chad's death must have weighed heavily upon him. He also seemed to be avoiding me.

Just as well. At least, he wasn't bossing me around and treating me like a child.

Kathy didn't interact much with the others, either. She sat staring at the fire until she retired to the tent with Trish. I would have liked to invite her to sleep in my tent so that I could watch over her and give her comfort, but that was never going to happen. Despite her own struggles, Kathy had taken on a motherly attitude with Trish, who seemed lost and distracted since the morning events.

As I sat alone off to the side of the roaring fire, I kept getting the uneasy feeling we were being watched. I looked around often, wondering if O-cha would appear out of the darkened shadows of the willows or through the thick vegetation that covered the hill on the other side of the creek.

Pat sat down next to me with his tin mug of coffee. "We all discussed your suspicions as we rode today."

I winced at the thought of them secretly talking about me. "What did they have to say?"

"They all think you're paranoid. Except Beaver."

"And you, too?"

"I'm not so sure. I trust Beaver's instincts."

But not mine? What's new?

Truthfully, I wasn't totally convinced myself that I wasn't just being paranoid. I felt like something else was going to happen.

* * *

I woke up in a bad mood the next morning after a sleepless night. The sun was already up. Without talking to anyone, I hurried off into the willows to take care of my morning duties. Skittish, I jerked at every sound of rustling leaves and twigs, expecting to be attacked by O-cha at any moment. Not wanting to go very far from camp, I found a suitable location and, after a quick look around, dropped my pants and squatted. My view of the surrounding area diminished immensely from this angle, so I pushed hard, trying to force things along.

The sudden crunching of footsteps on dry leaves and twigs did what my forcing couldn't. I finished in record time and was just buckling up my belt when a huge grizzly bear lumbered around a thick patch of brush.

Frozen in place, bowels threatening to release again, I didn't know whether to stand still or move to get out of the bear's sight.

Too late.

The bear stopped, lifting his head. He sniffed the air, his beady eyes coming to rest on me. He huffed as if clearing his throat. His dish-shaped face swung side to side as he took each slow step forward.

Backing away, I pulled out my pistol. I fired a shot into the ground between the bear's feet, hoping the noise would scare him.

Halting, the bear stood up to his full height of some seven feet. He opened his mouth and let out a roar I was sure would be heard in camp. Dropping down on all fours, the bear huffed, as if to say, "You're too puny to bother with." He ambled off to my left.

As soon as the bear was out of sight, I scurried back toward camp.

"What were you shooting at?" Eric asked, coming to meet me with his gun in his hand. He was closely followed by Pat, Beaver, and Kathy.

"A bear," I replied breathlessly, my body trembling. "A big grizzly, to be exact."

"Did you kill it?" Pat asked as we continued on to camp.

"No, I didn't kill it. It came out of the underbrush about twenty feet away and about scared the crap out of me. When it started toward me, I fired a shot and frightened it away."

Kathy held her hand over her mouth, probably frightened by the whole idea of a big bear hanging around the premises.

"You were lucky," Beaver said. "Grizzlies will attack with no warning."

"You can't kill them all that easily with a pistol, either," Pat added.

"Which way did it go?" Kathy asked as her eyes searched the surrounding bushes.

"I wouldn't worry about it," I said bravely. "I'm pretty sure it's a long way from here by now."

A loud pop, like the sound made when bursting a big plastic bag, discharged from the area of the campsite. A scream followed that sent chills down my spine. All of us sprinted into camp.

The bear now stood on its hind legs above the tent that belonged to Kathy and Trish. My mouth dropped open as the bear came down on its front paws, flattening the last of the smashed tent, but for the fact that Trish was still in it.

Kathy let out a scream.

"Shit," someone said behind me.

I watched in horror as the bear's head dropped, his jaws clamping onto what might have been Trish's head. Standing on his hind feet, the bear shook Trish and the tent back and forth in his mouth.

A hunting rifle blasted from somewhere around me.

A spray of blood erupted from the back of the bear's head. The bear toppled backwards, like a felled tree, its head bouncing off the dirt. The tent slid off the bear's chest and fell to the ground with a sickening, dull thump.

"Trish?" Kathy hollered as she shakily walked forward, her eyes locked on the destroyed tent that showed no movement from within.

I reached out and took her by the elbow. "Let's make sure the bear is dead first," I said gently, sensing Kathy must be in shock.

James and Tory cautiously moved toward the bear, their rifles butted up against their shoulders, their fingers ready to fire at the slightest movement.

James circled around the animal until he stood near the bear's head. With his rifle, he poked the bear in the eye a couple of times. "It's dead," he called out, propping his gun up against the bear's body. "Tory, help me see if Trish is okay."

Yanking free, Kathy covered the ground between me and the bear before Tory could put his rifle down to help James. "Trish?" she called out as she frantically searched for the opening to the tent.

I moved in to help her.

"Here," said Tory, flipping open his folding knife. He split the tent down the middle, revealing a bloody mess inside.

"Oh, God," Kathy choked out. She stumbled backwards, running into me. She slid to the ground at my feet, tears streaming down her ashen face.

In a daze, I watched the rest of the men walk toward the tent in silence. I saw enough to know that the bear had bitten Trish's neck, nearly severing her head from her body. My stomach lurched. I had to look away.

I knelt behind Kathy and put my arms around her, resting my hands over her belly.

She placed her hands over mine and lowered her head, sobs shaking her body.

I laid my rough-bearded cheek against her hair and whispered, "I'm so sorry. I wish I would have killed the bear."

Her weeping increased.

I held her while Eric began to give orders to the others. He had James, Tory, Juan, and Sergio each grab an edge of the tent and move it out of camp. They took care of the body while I stayed with Kathy and while the guilt ate away at me.

* * *

Later that morning, we all stood around a freshly dug grave, which we had taken turns digging while Kathy had rested. I was glad for the heavy physical work. It helped me forget about the deaths of our two fallen comrades, at least for a while.

By the time of the funeral service, Kathy had halfway regained her composure.

Nobody had brought a Bible on the trip, but Sergio and Juan recited a few scriptures they remembered from their youths. After the service, Travis, Sergio, and Juan volunteered to fill in the grave.

While packing up my own stuff for the next leg on our journey toward home, I helped Kathy get her things together.

Lucky for her, she'd taken all her belongings out of the tent before the attack.

Rubbing my rough beard, I thought about asking Eric if I could borrow his razor, but he walked around in a remote, somber mood...all business-like. I didn't think he would be happy about me requesting to use his razor at this point.

Like Chad's horse, we used Trish's horse to help distribute more of the load of the packhorses.

It wasn't until late morning that we were able to leave camp.

Kathy insisted on bringing up the rear. "I need to be alone for awhile," she told me.

"Tell you what," I said, "I'll stay at least fifty feet behind you. That way, you'll still have your privacy and I'll be able to cover the rear."

I stalled until everyone else had moved out of the camp on their horses. James and Tory took control of the pack horses this time. Kathy followed behind the pack horses.

About fifty yards away from camp, I stopped my horse and looked over my shoulder one last time toward Trish's grave.

I was shocked to see an Indian standing next to the bear's carcass.

I turned my horse around and stared.

The Indian raised his right hand above his head with two fingers exposed. He raised his left hand and made a slashing motion across his throat.

Two dead.

I had no doubt it was O-cha. I had no doubt he was indicating that two of our party were dead.

My hand moved toward my pistol, but before I could pull it out, O-cha disappeared into the brush as though he had never been there.

I turned my horse around and urged it forward to catch up with the others. *There's no way O-cha could have orchestrated the bear attack,* I thought. *Then again, he doesn't care how we die…just that we die.*

* * *

When we made camp that night, Pat took charge of roasting two large rabbits we had been lucky enough to shoot along our trail. As we sat around the campfire, I hesitated to bring up my new sighting of O-cha, but I couldn't hold it back any longer. "I saw O-cha again," I blurted.

Everyone looked at me.

"Yeah, where?" Steve asked.

"Where we left the bear. He was standing over the carcass and formed two fingers over his head, then made a motion like this." I swiped my hand across my throat.

In a condescending tone, Steve retorted, "You're mind's making you see things that aren't real. It's probably just some of Flows Like A River's warriors following us to make sure we're really leaving the area."

Kathy looked down, showing no expression. I don't think she was really paying attention to what I was saying. She was still bummed out by Trish's death.

I pressed on. "I also saw O-cha again today, here and there along our trail. He has two warriors with him."

"Why didn't you tell us so we could see them, too?" Steve asked facetiously.

I snarled, "There wasn't time. They disappeared as soon as I saw them."

Steve laughed. "Well, there's your answer. It's all in your mind."

Travis's former arrogant attitude had shrunken into a silent state since Chad's death. At least until now. "If they don't have horses," he asked, his haunted eyes looking around, "how can they stay up with us?"

Beaver said, "Most of my people travel long distances by foot. We can move further and faster than horses because of our endurance. When we want to kill a deer, we chase it down until it's too tired to stay on its feet, then kill it. Indian messengers run hundreds of miles on foot between villages to relay news. They do it in a short amount of time."

"Yeah," Pat said, "there's this tribe in New Mexico that's known for their long-distance endurance running. They can run a hundred miles in twenty-four hours. The ranchers out there hire them to run down wild mustangs and capture them."

Just the thought of walking the twenty miles the horses traveled each day made my feet ache. I knew I couldn't handle a hundred miles.

Beaver stood up. "I think we should all be on the outlook for trouble. Keep your eyes open." He went to check on the horses.

Steve and his crew murmured among themselves, shaking their heads, chuckling, obviously disavowing everything I had said about seeing O-cha.

Eric, sitting with Pat, stayed out of their circle. I didn't get a reaction from either of those two. I could still sense that Eric had begun to feel the weight of the responsibility for this trip. What was he going to say to people when we returned? How was he going to explain the deaths?

The same thing passed through my mind. How much of this was I responsible for? I no longer felt proud of the fact that it had all been my idea to get the gold. In fact, the gold didn't seem all that important at the moment. Chad would never be able to enjoy his riches. Neither would Trish.

I got up and sat down by Kathy. "Would you like to share my tent tonight? You can have one side and I'll take the other."

She put a hand on my arm and gave me a weak smile. "Thanks, Donny, but I'd rather sleep by myself in one of the spare tents."

Tory jumped up. "I'll git it ready fer ya, young lady." He strode off to the area where the packs were stacked.

Not wanting anyone to see my disappointment in Kathy's rejection, I said goodnight to the group and ambled off to my own tent. The night was warm. I lay on top of my bedroll and wondered if I would always be alone. I thought about Kathy being alone in her tent, too. I wished I could bring Trish back to make her happy again. I wished I could find some way to comfort her.

Exhausted from the wariness and tension of the day, I turned over and went to sleep.

Chapter 26

The next morning, we all had pancakes for breakfast, courtesy of James, who had squirreled away the mix in his pack. He had brought it intending to use it on a day when we could all use a lift in our spirits. Travis slept in late, his tent still silent while the rest of us finished our meal and packed up our belongings.

Eric growled, "Where's Travis? How come he's sleeping in so late this morning? We need to get going."

Steve roughly shook Travis's tent. "Travis, get up. It's time to hit the trail. Come on."

Not getting a response, Steve unzipped the tent flap and peered inside. "Son-of-a-bitch," he exclaimed, staggering backwards. He tripped on a rock and fell on his butt, his eyes wide with terror.

Pat ran toward Steve with his pistol in hand. "What's wrong?"

"He's dead." Steve's blue eyes looked dazed. "Travis is dead. Someone killed him."

Pat pushed back the tent flap and squatted down to look inside as the rest of us gathered at the site to see what was happening.

"He's right," Pat said, rising to his feet. "He's dead. It looks like someone cut open the back of his tent and slit his throat."

Everyone shot a look at me with accusing eyes.

I put up my hands and backed away. "I didn't do it."

James took a peek inside the tent. Turning to me, he said, "I think ever' one here wonders if ya weren't right about O-cha. I know I am."

Feeling a little vindicated, I squared my shoulders. "Damn right, I'm right. It's just too bad Travis had to die before you'd believe me."

Remorseful eyes turned away, looking toward Travis's tent.

"Are you sure he's dead?" Kathy asked, approaching with her doctor's kit.

"Positive," Pat said, stopping her from going further. "You don't need to see it."

"I'm a doctor."

"There's nothing you can do now."

Hesitating for a few moments, she relented fairly easily. The mounting bodies had to be getting to her. For sure, the doctor in her wanted to do something to help keep people alive. Unfortunately, all three deceased members of the group had died in ways that made her doctoring skills irrelevant. She took a deep breath, turned, and headed back to the horses.

We quickly dug a grave and reverently placed Travis's body in it. His funeral took half as long as Trish's.

Before leaving the campsite, we decided we would have to do a better job of standing watch at night, all of us taking turns. Kathy refused to be left out. Even with the long days on the horses, it would mean breaking up our sleep at night, a necessary routine for our safety.

This time, when we left the camp, I dared not look back, but my gut told me I hadn't seen the last of O-cha.

* * *

Back on the trail again, we headed southwest through a thicket of trees and brush. No one spoke as we rode, but I noticed the men looking around more often, looking over their shoulders for Indians hidden in the trees or behind the hills and mounds.

After a few hours, we travelled across a sloping hillside covered with light grass. A line of trees interspersed with heavy brush ran just to our left, while a cliff that dropped about eighty or ninety feet to the riverbank sat twenty feet to our right. As had become my habit, I brought up the rear. Instead of Kathy riding in front of me today, I watched the back of Juan. We were moving at a fairly steady pace, not wanting to wear out the packhorses and the three extra saddle horses carrying gold.

As Juan passed a particularly thick stand of brush, two Indians suddenly stepped out of nowhere and shoved his horse hard, toppling it over sideways. I stopped my horse and watched in horror as both Juan and the horse fell toward the cliff. The Indians disappeared just as suddenly as they had appeared.

It happened so fast, I didn't have a chance to react as Juan landed five feet from the edge of the cliff, his momentum propelling him toward the drop-off. He slid to a stop with his feet hanging over the edge. He would have been fine, but the horse slid into him. Screaming, Juan and the horse both went over the cliff.

Numb with shock, I stared at the spot where Juan had just disappeared.

"What's going on back there?" I heard someone holler. It sounded like Pat.

Sergio, who had been in front of Juan, came back on his horse and looked around in confusion. "Where did Juan go?"

I couldn't speak. I lifted my arm slowly and pointed.

Sergio's eyes got wide. "What?"

By now Eric, Pat, and Beaver had arrived on foot to see what was going on.

"Where's Juan?" Pat asked.

Still mute from shock, I repeated my actions. I slowly lifted my arm and pointed.

Eric studied the ground where the obvious slide marks showed in the dirt. His eyes narrowed at me in confusion. "Why? What happened?"

Beaver and Pat carefully stepped toward the edge.

"We need a rope," Beaver called out.

"Can you see him?" Sergio pleaded in dread. "Is he okay?"

"Not yet," Pat said. "We can't get close enough to the edge to see the bottom."

James, on foot, came sliding to a stop next to me with a hundred-foot rope. "I figured ya might need it." Holding one end, he threw the rope out over the cliff. It uncoiled and disappeared from sight. He tied his end to a stout tree five feet from the edge, made a loop, then twisted the rope around the loop twice. He slipped the loop across his back and used the twisted portion of the rope as a brake by letting rope out as he slowly walked backwards toward the edge of the cliff. Standing on the very tip of the ledge, he said, "I see 'im. He ain't movin'. I'll go on down and check 'im out."

While we waited for James to return, I got off my horse and told them what I had seen.

"I don't believe it," Steve said derisively. "Nobody could shove a horse over like that. It's not possible. His horse probably just slipped."

"Oh, it's possible ta tip a horse over," Tory said in response. "When we was kids, we used ta go cow tippin' at night. Two of us would sneak up on some unsuspectin' sleepin' cow and shove it over. It's not as hard as ya'd think." He indicated the hillside with a sweep of his hand. "It'd be even easier on a steep hill like this."

A yell from James drew our attention back to the tragedy at hand. We couldn't see James, but we could hear him.

"He's dead. I'm gonna tie us up. Tory, tie off on a horse or two. See if ya can pull us up. I'll try ta keep us from snaggin' on the rocks."

Tory and Beaver quickly rigged a make-do pulley using two horses and another rope.

Five minutes later, Juan's broken, bleeding body lay atop the cliff next to a breathless, tired James.

Kathy knelt down next to the body. She checked Juan's pulse as though hoping he might still be alive.

"I'm too tired ta go down again," James said between deep breaths. "Someone else is gonna have 'ta go this time."

"Why?" Kathy asked,. "Why does someone have to go back?"

"We ain't gonna leave no supplies and stuff down there," James stated. "We need everthin' we got to make it home."

"Not to mention whatever gold he had in his saddlebags," Steve added.

Sergio's gaunt face, contorted with the loss of his friend, gave Steve a hard look. "I care nothin' for that cursed gold. I want his personal effects."

"Sure, no problem," Steve replied nonchalantly, as if he could care less about the gold. He turned away and headed back to his horse.

I'd noticed a change in Steve's attitude. He seemed harder somehow. At first, I thought it might be the way he was handling the deaths of his crew members, Chad and Travis, but now, I could see he had become overly protective of his gold and making it back alive, even if it meant sacrificing the other members of the group. I made a mental note to keep an eye on him. To put it bluntly, I didn't trust Steve anymore, and maybe I never did.

"I'll go down," Tory offered.

"Eric and I will start digging a grave," Pat said.

I helped Beaver lower Tory down the cliff. We hauled up Juan's saddlebags and supplies. We left the saddle, since we had no need for it and didn't want to further burden the packhorses.

As Sergio said a sad prayer over Juan's grave, I held Kathy. My mind boggled with the dwindling number of our group. I wondered if any of us were going to make it back alive.

As we headed west a little while later, we rode closer in proximity, all of us edgy. Even the horses seemed wary of the surroundings. As much as possible, we stayed in open clearings and avoided places where we might be ambushed. Now, every single one of us, even Steve, stayed alert. We kept our weapons at the ready.

* * *

Two hours later, as we crossed a knee-high river, tragedy struck again. Sergio's horse slipped on a loose rock as it entered the water from the rocky river bank. Sergio didn't have time to jump clear. He slammed into the rocks, his head hitting the sharp edge of a boulder. He died instantly.

Steve sneered at me. "Are you gonna try to blame this on O-cha, too?"

"Of course not," I shot back, irritated by Steve's tone of voice and general attitude. "This is obviously just an unfortunate accident."

We buried Sergio on a small hill overlooking the river. Now, there were only eight of us left: Eric, Pat, Beaver, Steve, James, Tory, Kathy, and myself. No one cried, not even Kathy, as though we had no more emotion left in us.

We used Sergio's backpack and saddle bags to shift some of the weight from the more stressed pack horses to Sergio's horse, then headed out, a silent group of mourners with very little to talk about.

It ran through my mind how Eric and Steve would handle telling people about the deaths of Trish and Steve's crew members. When I considered the fact that maybe none of us would make it back to tell our stories, the thought flitted away quickly. I wondered what people in our world would think if we never showed up again. Would the world go on without us?

Chapter 27

Morning dawned bright and clear, but the day didn't promise to be a good one. As we wearily sat around the morning campfire and drank coffee in anticipation of starting a new day, James came rushing into the camp. "The seven packhorses is gone."

Steve shot up from his seat on a stone. "What do you mean, gone?"

"Gone. As in no longer here." James looked pissed and I feared Steve would be foolish enough to argue with him.

"How could they be gone?" Steve pressed. "Did you forget to tie them up last night?"

James's eyes narrowed. "I tied 'em up like always. They was stolen."

"What makes you say that?" Kathy asked.

"Rope was cut. Plus, they was footprints in the dirt that don't belong ta any of us."

"O-cha," I said with conviction. "He's playing with us now."

"O-cha, my ass," Steve bellowed. "I'm sick and tired of you blaming everything on O-cha when nobody's seen him but you."

Tired of taking Steve's crap, I shot to my feet. "I'm sick of you calling me a liar. I know what I've seen. Sooner or later, O-cha's gonna screw up and somebody else will see him, then you'll believe me."

"I believe you," Kathy said, placing her hand on my arm to calm me down.

"Weren't you supposed ta be on watch this morning?" James said to Steve in an accusing tone.

"I was on watch. You're damned right. And I was awake the whole time. It had to be Tory's watch."

We all looked at Tory.

"The horses was fine when I give the watch over ta you, Steve. Don't ya blame me. You was the last one up."

All our eyes turned back to Steve.

He clenched his jaw and angrily strode toward his gear, tearing down his tent and starting to pack up his things.

Beaver spoke to the rest of us. "I have no doubt O-cha is responsible for the deaths of Chad, Travis, and Juan. I also believe he took the missing horses."

"If he was gonna take something," Steve interjected heatedly, "wouldn't he take the gold?"

"Gold has no meaning to him," Beaver said.

"In a way," Eric said, "he did steal gold from us. By taking the packhorses, he limited what we can carry." He emptied the coffee pot into his tin cup. "We still have the extra saddle horses from Chad, Travis, Sergio, and Trish." He turned to James and Tory. "Can we put the packsaddles on them and use them for our packhorses?"

"Don't see why not," Tory replied. "Don't have much choice, anyway."

"How much can we take?" Kathy asked.

James said, "A horse kin carry one-third its body weight comfortably. All these horses weigh in at about a thousand pounds, maybe a little more, so we'd be safe puttin' around three hundred pounds on each one, including our own weight." He looked at Tory for confirmation.

Tory nodded. "Yeah, but we'll probably have to leave some of the gold behind."

"No way," Steve blared. "We'll leave anything we have to, but not the gold. Tents, food, clothes. We can get by without any of that stuff, but we take the gold."

"You've changed, Steve," Pat said, watching Steve throw his things together. "You've got gold-fever. You'll do anything to make sure you get your gold home. I assume you're also thinking we'll split the gold of the people who've died?"

Steve didn't deny Pat's accusation. He kept packing, shifting the gold he had shared with Sergio and Juan closer to his own satchels. "What else would we do with it? Leave it behind?" He guffawed, as if the thought of leaving gold behind was ludicrous.

"We'll give it to their next of kin," Pat affirmed.

"Does anybody else agree with Steve," Eric asked, "or are you with me and Pat on this issue? Shall we take the gold to the relatives?"

"I'm with you," I said.

"Me, too," Kathy agreed.

Tory answered for James. "Us, too."

"I'm glad I'm just the guide," Beaver said, trying to ease the tension. "I'm glad I don't have a say in this."

"You are all fools," Steve declared. "Go ahead, give it away, just don't touch mine or, I swear, I'll kill all of you."

Shocked at the hatred in Steve's voice, I watched as he stomped off toward the saddle horses. The gold-fever had taken over his personality. I decided, then and there, to stay as far from Steve as I could. I didn't think it would take much for Steve to accuse one of us of trying to steal his gold. I know I didn't want to get shot.

Interrupting my train of thought, Pat said, "Let's go through the packs and decide what to leave behind."

"Seeing as how we only have eight people from our original group of fourteen," I ventured, "we can leave half the food, I suppose."

"Yer probably right there," Tory said. He looked questionably at Beaver. "Do we even need ta take half?"

"Depends. If we're heading straight back to my village, then no. We can take just enough food for four weeks. We can also live off the land, if we have to."

"Personally, I'd rather take enough food so that we don't need to stop and hunt," Kathy said. "I'd rather spend as many hours on the trail as we can. The longer we linger, the more likely we might not all make it."

Eric grimaced as he looked around at all the packs and expensive gear that we would no longer be able to carry with us. "We have to at least take the gold sluices and panning equipment."

Nobody argued with him, but I was pretty sure we all knew that wasn't going to happen.

We spent the next hour repacking the packsaddles, starting with the gold. Despite Steve's bitterness about taking all the gold, we'd all worked hard to get it, so even though we didn't see ourselves willing to give up a life for the gold, none of us wanted to leave it behind when it came down to it.

Still, it meant that the four extra horses could carry nothing else, and we would still each have to bear over forty pounds on our own horses. That didn't leave any room for bedrolls, tents, food, and other gear, let alone Eric's sluices. Something had to go.

James shook his head. "With them horses carrying so much weight, we have to go slower. Rest 'em more often. This ain't good."

I figured we still had a good four-and-a-half weeks before the portal would close. That was my main worry…getting to the portal on time. I wasn't sure how I would feel if I had to make a choice between getting to the portal and leaving the gold behind. We were already having all kinds of problems with O-cha following us and putting obstacles in our path. If our horses broke down, I couldn't imagine being forced to stay in this world another two or more years, even if I was now the adopted son of Chief Iron Cactus. The comforts and safety of home in my world meant a lot more to me now.

"I think we should leave some of the gold and hightail it back to the portal," I said. "We can bury the extra and come back to get in a few years, when the portal opens again."

"I'm with Donny," James readily agreed.

"Let's leave the shares of those who are no longer with us," Eric stated, trying to be fair.

All reluctantly voted to leave the extra gold, except Steve who turned away as the voting started. I felt certain he would secretly keep a share of what his two dead team members had found.

We dug a hole and buried the food, gear, and all the other stuff we had to leave behind. Along with it we buried about 400 pounds of gold.

In the end, we still had to abandon the gold sluices, pans, and all but two shovels. Eric moaned and complained, but he really had no choice. The horses couldn't carry it all. It was either leave his sluices or leave his share of the gold. He wasn't about to let his gold go.

After stashing our stuff into the hole, we laid three-inch-diameter logs across the expanse, then piled dirt on top of the logs. We studied the landscape and talked about the obvious landmarks. Eric made markings on several trees to help us identify the spot. None of us knew for sure if we would ever come back this way or need to retrieve our things, but if something happened, if we couldn't get back through the portal, at least the items were there. Knowing that gave me a small comfort.

* * *

That evening, as we sat around the campfire eating dinner, I realized I hadn't seen O-cha all day. I knew he was still following us. It almost frightened me more not seeing him, not knowing when or where he would pop out from some hidden place when we weren't looking. All of us continued to be more and more wary, especially now with our packhorses gone. We couldn't afford to lose any more horses.

Although we had ridden fairly close together all day as we slowly made our way south, Steve kept his distance, holding to the reins of one of the extra horse that carried his gold. He didn't trust any of us with his cargo.

As we sat around the campfire, my mind wandered to the breakfast altercation with Steve over O-cha's involvement. Kathy had been the first one to step forward and defend me, to stand by my side. It warmed my heart to think of that now, to remember the feel of her soft touch against my arm. I liked it that she chose to sit next to me during the meal this evening. Even if we didn't speak, I liked her presence and the feeling that she had begun to trust me.

All this was new to me, having a woman want to be near me without feeling that I had to have sex with her to keep the relationship going. I felt a special kind of respect for Kathy, a deeper connection with her that came without spoken words. Maybe this was what real friendship was all about. Maybe it was what people called love. Whatever the name of the feeling, it impelled me to want to do anything for her, even give my own life, if necessary.

After dinner, Kathy agreed to take a walk with me, not too far from camp. We all needed to stay near each other, within calling distance, for protection.

As we walked, Kathy again put her hand in mine. The sun was disappearing over the mountains to the west, turning the wispy clouds above it into brilliant shades of red and pink.

I still hadn't shaved. I found myself self-conscious of it, hoping it wouldn't put her off if she wanted to kiss me, by chance. "How're you holding up?" I asked.

She snuggled up close to my side. "I'm okay, I guess. I still can't believe everything that's happened. I keep wanting the cops to come roaring in and arrest people." She laughed. "I was naive to think this trip would be fun. I should have seen the potential for danger and just stayed home."

"If you're referring to Trish. I think she would have come anyway, even knowing the dangers. She was so excited about it."

Kathy's breath caught in her throat. "But maybe not. Maybe I could have…"

"Don't let yourself think that way," I said, stopping in my tracks and turning her toward me. "You didn't do anything, and there's nothing you could have done to save her."

She shrugged. "I know, but it doesn't make it any easier. She's been with me since I started my practice. I'm going to miss her. I don't even know what I'm going to tell her parents when we get back. I mean, how do I explain this world and Trish's disappearance? There's not even a body to prove she is dead." She dropped my hand and walked to a nearby willow tree. Looking toward the sunset, she sighed.

Not knowing what to say, I stood beside her and fidgeted with the willow branch in front of me, picking off leaves. As the sky turned to deeper pinks and purples, I realized my own guilt in this whole affair.

"Well, I have to confess," I said timidly, "that I'm carrying around a lot of guilt myself. Chad, Travis, Sergio, Juan, and Trish would all be alive if I hadn't found the portal in the first place, then gone to Eric with this great idea to search for gold. It was a selfish thing, me wanting to be rich so I wouldn't have to work. If anybody, I'm the one directly responsible for their deaths." I chuckled to myself. "Hell, I'll probably have to spend all the money I make from my gold on shrinks to get rid of all the ghosts floating around in the back of my mind."

Kathy laughed and took my hand again. "Well, I'll make a deal with you. I promise not to let Trish's ghost interfere with my life, if you'll promise your ghosts won't cause you to go insane and hack someone to pieces with a tomahawk."

My heart swelled at her sweet smile and teasing words. "Okay, I promise."

"We better get back. It's getting dark. We'll be safer at the camp."

Walking hand in hand, I felt a closeness that I couldn't explain. It seemed strange to me, yet thrilling, too. All my experiences with women had ended after short affairs or angry differences over my behavior. For the first time, something else was happening.

As I held her soft, delicate hand, my hope soared that maybe we could have a relationship when we got back to our own world. Of course, maybe I was just kidding myself, too. Maybe we just needed each other now to share our grief.

"You want to sleep by yourself tonight?" I asked timidly.

She squeezed my hand as if pacifying me. "Yes, I need to be alone."

I nodded, refusing to let my desire to have her in my tent ruin the pleasant evening. For now, I'd just bide my time and let the images of her keep me company all night.

* * *

The next day passed with no problems, other than a broken packsaddle. Tory repaired it quickly.

By late morning, we finally broke out of the trees and rode into a flat, grass-covered valley where Sacramento existed in my world. I breathed a sigh of relief to be out of the trees and thick brush. We could see a long expanse around us.

Once we reached the open territory, O-cha and his followers weren't as careful about staying out of sight. Now, everyone in the group could see them.

I wanted to say to Steve, "See, I told you so," but we weren't on speaking terms. In fact, Steve didn't seem to be on speaking terms with any of us. He kept to himself, even in camp.

While O-cha and his buddies kept their distance, usually showing themselves just ahead of us, I wondered what they were up to.

Beaver had gone out on two occasions and tried to make contact with them, but neither O-cha nor his two warriors would talk to him.

Eric had set up a new schedule for guarding the horses, so we would all get shorter hours on duty and more hours of sleep. We didn't have a way of keeping time at night, so we had to watch the moon, estimating it's distance to a certain location to tell us when to call the next guy for the shift. Being that the moon was waning in the last quarter, I wondered how we would tell time when we saw no moon at all.

That night, our camp sat in a clearing with a few trees and low grasses. We kept the horses close to the tents, with all of the packs inside the tents with us.

I took the second shift, the one following Eric. As the night passed slowly, the sound of crickets rose and fell. At one point, I heard the horses moving around, shifting restlessly on their tethers.

I checked them closely, squinting my eyes in the dark, scanning the horizon. *Damn. I wish I had a flashlight.* I saw no movement, nothing that seemed out of place. I wondered if I should wake Tory, the one assigned to take the next shift, but when I couldn't see anything and the horses settled down, I figured a raccoon or ground squirrel had touched off their reactions.

Sometime later, a slight breeze had come up, rustling the grass and leaves. The horses shifted and pulled at their tethers again. The idea of O-cha being near the camp while I was on duty scared the hell out of me. I cautiously walked to the far side of the horses and saw nothing that I could identify as worthy of making the horses anxious.

When I figured the time for my shift was up, I awoke Tory. "The horses seem restless tonight," I told him. "I don't know if they smell something or what, but I didn't see anything."

Tory yawned. "Okay, I'll keep my eyes and ears open fer anythin' outta the ordinary."

Hardly able to keep my eyes open, I climbed into my tent, fell on my bedroll, and passed out.

* * *

I'm not sure how long I had been asleep, but the clatter of running horse hooves entered my consciousness. I awoke to Tory's scream.

"Ya theivin' SOB's, get back here."

Throwing my tent flap open to an early dawn, I tripped on a pack in my tent and fell flat on my face. My arm landed on a rock. I grunted in pain, massaging my arm as I rose.

Beaver, Eric, and Pat exploded from their tents.

"What happened?" Steve asked, running up out of the dark.

"I don't know," I said, looking toward the horses. "But I think we just lost more horses."

Kathy stumbled out of her tent, her sleeping bag wrapped around her shoulders like an overstuffed, down-filled coat. "What's going on?"

Tory came storming toward us. "They got three horses," he said with disgust, kicking the dirt with his boot, seemingly blaming himself. "I knew they was out there. I thought I could handle 'em myself." He shook his head and hung it like a shamed puppy. "I shoulda yelled a warnin'."

James ambled up beside his little brother and slapped him on the shoulder. "He'll beat himself up fer the resta his life over this."

"He should," Steve growled. "Now, we have to leave more stuff behind. I'm not leaving my gold. I'm using the extra horse. The rest of you can decide what you're gonna do with your own stuff."

Kathy suddenly tore into him. "Hey, if you were so damn worried about getting your stupid gold home, maybe you should have been sleeping with the horses yourself. Then maybe you could have stopped O-cha from stealing them."

Steve scowled and took a step toward her, his hands balled into fists.

My hand shot to my gun as James and Pat placed their hands on their gun butts, too.

Steve stopped in his tracks.

"Not a smart thing to do, my friend," Pat warned.

Steve glared at us. "Let me know when you're ready to load up," he spat, then turned on his heels and slithered away toward his tent like a demon.

"We might as well get breakfast going," Beaver said, looking up at the stars, fading now as the sun lightened the sky to the east. Being mid-July, the sun came up early, giving us longer, hotter days for travel.

At breakfast, we discussed what to do now with our gold and gear.

Tory explained what we could carry on our own horses. "Take yer body weight, add fifteen pounds fer clothes and thirty-five pounds fer yer saddle and the rest of yer tack. The difference of three hundred pounds a horse is what ya kin take in gold."

I made a quick calculation. I weighed 135 pounds. Adding fifty for my clothing, saddle, and tack, it came up to 185. That meant I could take an extra 115 pounds. Some of that had to be guns and ammo, but I figured I could still take a good hundred pounds of gold.

"Remember," James cautioned, "we'll each have extra clothes, tents, sleeping bags, and food ta carry. I'm figurin' around fifty pounds fer all that."

That brought my base total to 235 pounds, which meant I could take sixty-five pounds of gold. *Perfect. My share of the gold amounts to around sixty-six pounds anyway.* I didn't have much stuff, just my pipe, a shirt, socks, and underwear. I could take all my gold. The riders that outweighed me and had collected more gold, would be out part of their shares. The spare horse could carry some of it, but that argument had to be settled with Steve.

Kathy sighed. "I'll heat up leftovers from dinner last night. The rest of you can start sorting through things."

"I'll help you, Kathy," I offered, knowing it wouldn't take five men to decide what to take and what to leave. Eric would take charge anyway. He could argue with Steve over having to leave more of the gold behind.

We still had almost three and a half weeks of travel ahead of us, but I was sure the gold was going to get priority over what would stay. More and more, the gold didn't seem all that important to me anymore. If we all made it back alive, that alone would count for something.

As before, we dug a hole, buried the supplies we couldn't take with us, and this time, left nearly 350 pounds of gold behind. Digging graves was getting to be a habit, only this time, we didn't bury a body, just more of our earthy treasures.

The day passed sluggishly under the hot sun with the slow-moving horses. We had forced them to carry heavy loads.

That night, I was glad I wasn't on guard duty. After dinner, I tumbled onto my bedroll, alone again, and fell into a deep asleep.

Chapter 28

We all must have slept deeply, because the next morning, I was the first to awake after sunrise and noticed two of the horses were gone. And so was Steve.

"We never should have trusted him with guard duty," I complained to the others after I got them up.

"How did he get out of camp without anybody hearing him?" Eric demanded, his face twisted in rage.

"Who the hell knows?" Pat replied. "But, now we don't have any way to carry our extra stuff."

"Meaning we cain't take nothin' but bare minimum survival supplies," James told us. Like that was something new.

At this point, according to Eric's calculations, we still had about 560 miles to Beaver's village and the safety of his community. None of us wanted to talk about the consequences of losing more horses. As it stood now, we'd need to continue to make at least twenty miles a day in order to be back before the portal closed in mid-August. Twenty miles a day for twenty-eight days came to 560 miles. That only gave us four extra days for unforeseen problems, like losing more horses…or people. We were cutting things close.

"Is there any way we can get more horses?" Kathy asked as she set the coffee pot on the fire to heat up.

"I know a tribe a hundred miles south of here," Beaver said. "I'd be gone at least four or five days with no guarantee they would loan them to us."

"That won't work," Eric countered. "We need to keep going, or we'll never make it back in time to get home before the portal closes. We can only take what we can carry. We'll have to bury the rest, which isn't all that much anymore. We can come back in a couple of years and get what we leave behind."

"We could split up," Pat offered. "Half of us head for Beaver's village, the other half can head for this other village and try to get more horses. We could meet up on the trail later."

"How would we know when or where to meet?" Kathy said.

Pat shrugged his shoulders. "I don't know, it was just a thought."

"We don't have time to go after more horses." I said. "Plus, I doubt if the horses we've got can make it to this other village and then all the way home before the portal closes. If we can't get replacements and these horses give out, we'll be down to walking. I don't think any of us can walk clear back to Beaver's village."

"So, what do you think we should do, Donny?" Eric asked.

"I don't know," I confessed, "but whatever we do, we need to do it as a group and not split up. We need to work together. We've been riding and camping together for a long time now. We're like a team. We need to stay together and do whatever we're gonna do as a team. Not only that, but with O-cha out there, we'd be a lot safer if we stayed together."

Kathy passed me a look of admiration.

I felt my face flush.

Eric studied me for a moment. "You're right. I think we need to stay together and keep heading for Beaver's village. As it stands now, if we don't lose anymore horses, we can make it back before the portal closes." He winked at me. "As a team."

I about fell over.

"Here," Kathy said, "coffee's ready. We might as well have some while we decide what to do."

We all brought out our tin cups and filled them with the dark, comforting brew. Even though the air wasn't cold, we sat around the fire and continued to discuss our plans.

"So, what options we got?" Tory asked.

"The way I see it," Pat said, "we only have three."

When he didn't continue, Kathy asked, "And they are?"

"One...we continue on and hope we make it back to Beaver's village without losing any more horses...or more people," he added quickly. "Two...we try to make it to this other Indian village on the off-chance they'd be willing to loan us some horses."

"Those are the obvious options," Beaver said. "What's the third one?"

"We remove the threat."

His words were met with silence as we all assimilated what he meant.

Kathy finally spoke. "You mean, go after O-cha?"

"Exactly. Eliminate him so he can't steal more horses or kill us."

"We can't just go out and hunt him down in cold blood," she cried out. "That's murder."

"I ain't likin' that idea, either," James said, looking at Tory, who nodded his head in agreement.

"It's not murder," Beaver said. "It's survival. Over here, it's a fact of life."

Kathy shook her head. "I can't be a part of this."

"You don't have to be," Eric stated dispassionately. "It's not gonna happen. There's no way seven of us can hunt and kill O-cha and his two companions."

"Why not?" Pat asked.

"Well, they know the country better than we do. How do we find them? Then, they're much more experienced at stalking and hunting than we are. They could set us on a false trail, hide, and ambush us easily. Also, they're in better shape. We might be slimmer and more fit than when we had started, but we don't have the strength and endurance they've gathered through years of living like this. We wouldn't stand a chance."

"That's kinda what I was a thinkin'," James said, his blue eyes looking relieved.

Pat swirled the coffee in his cup and looked down at the ground. "Okay, fine. Now, the question is, do we go southwest and try to borrow horses, or head southeast, and hope to make it straight to Beaver's village?"

"Let's vote on it," I said. "All in favor of Beaver's village, raise your hand."

Six hands rose, Pat being the lone man out.

"Looks like yer headin' fer home, Beaver," James said, getting up and starting to roll up his sleeping bag. "Let's git the extra stuff buried and git goin'."

Even though we buried another couple hundred pounds of gold and some supplies, our saddlebags and pockets were still filled to overflowing. We each carried the maximum amount of gold our horses would allow. Even then, when I swung into the saddle, my horse turned its head and looked at me with one eye, like, *You've got to be kidding.*

I felt guilty for a minute, then shrugged it off. This was survival. Even though this would be hard on the horses, I was sure James wouldn't let us push them so hard as to endanger them. Right now, the horses were in better shape than when we'd left Beaver's village at the beginning of the journey. All the hard miles had toughened them up, seemingly preparing them for this last challenge before they'd have a much-earned rest. At least, that was my reasoning to push the guilt out of my mind.

* * *

Within an hour, my horse was wheezing and panting, soaked with sweat from the heat and exertion. Even I could tell these horses were loaded down too heavily.

James called a halt next to a small stream, lightly lined with trees. Clumps of brush were sparsely scattered along our side of the stream, while the other side looked near-impenetrable in places. "We need ta lighten the loads," James said, "otherwise we is gonna kill the horses and end up on foot."

Kathy, dancing from foot to foot, said, "I'm going behind that bush." She hurried away while the rest of us dismounted and loosened our saddles.

I heard a *ffftttthump* and turned.

A puff of dust rose from behind the right front leg of James's horse. The horse grunted and stepped to the left, knocking James off his feet. A three-feathered arrow stuck out of the horse's hide.

James, not knowing his horse had been hit, shook his head. "Stupid damn horse," he muttered as he stood up and dusted off his jeans.

The horse whinnied and coughed, spraying blood out in a wide arc.

"What the hell?" James exclaimed as he moved in front of the horse to figure out what was wrong.

"James," I yelled. "Someone shot it with an arrow. From over there." I pointed across the stream toward the brush from where the arrow must have come.

Ffftttthump. Another arrow passed. This one made a wet smacking sound as it buried itself into James's neck, rocking him back on his heels.

My heart stopped.

Eyes wide in shock, James put his hands up and traced the arrow to where it had entered his neck, just below his left ear. He tried to talk, but the only thing he could manage was a wet gurgle as the blood from his severed artery drained into his throat.

"Kathy," I screamed. "We need you, quick. Get out here."

"I'm kinda busy for a minute," she sang back.

"Put a cork in it and git your ass out here," Tory screamed as he pumped bullets into the brush along the far creek bank with the hope of hitting the shooter.

I joined him and emptied my pistol into the brush.

The gunshots must have convinced Kathy to wait until later to do her business. Running out of the bushes, she finished zipping up her jeans. Seeing James lying on the ground with an arrow in his throat, she immediately ran to him.

Eric and Pat were now shooting at the bushes.

"Stop," Beaver shouted from behind his horse. "By now, they're either gone or dead. No sense in wasting your ammo."

Tory ran to his brother.

I reloaded my pistol with shaky hands. I didn't know if they were shaking because of the adrenaline running through my body, or if it was caused by the fear that James would die.

Pat and Eric headed toward the bushes as I replaced my gun in its holster. I kept a nervous eye out as I walked toward Kathy to see if I could help her with James. It only took one look to know there was nothing she could do for him. The arrow had passed through his throat from left to right just under his jaw, probably severing both arteries.

Kathy left the arrow in place, and rightly so. I didn't know much about emergency medicine, but I knew that if she pulled it out, James would bleed to death almost immediately. Seeing the arrow on both sides of his throat didn't seem real, like those trick arrows they use in movies. My mind sort of drifted off into a daydream as I tried to deal with the reality of another impending death. The arrow had done its job with deadly efficiency.

Tory sat next to James, holding his hand. Tory kept a grip on his emotions as he looked lovingly into his brother's eyes. It was as though he wanted to be strong for his brother in their last moments together.

Kathy gently wiped James's brow with a bandana she had been wearing over her hair.

His body jerked and twitched. He tried to say something, but he could only make gurgling sounds.

I turned away. I couldn't bear to watch James's futile struggle to live. I joined Eric, Pat, and Beaver, still searching the bushes.

"One Indian," Beaver said as he studied the ground.

"O-cha?" Eric ventured.

"Probably."

"He's torturing me," I exclaimed.

"What makes you think that?" Pat asked.

"He's killing us off one-by-one and letting me know he's doing it. He's gonna keep at it until I'm the only one left. He's saving me for last. I can feel it in my bones."

"I don't know," Eric said skeptically. "You think he'd really do something like that?"

"Yeah, I do. With the exception of Steve, I notice he's saving the people I'm closest to until last."

Eric gave me a skeptical look.

"I've been thinking about it a lot." I continued. "True, I was upset when Chad, Trish, and Travis were killed, but I wasn't particularly sad because I didn't feel that close to them. In a way, I guess I didn't really like any of them that much. Sergio and Juan, I liked." I looked in the direction where Tory sat next to James. I couldn't see them behind the bushes. "I really like James. I admire him. I fear that Tory will be next."

Eric looked at me doubtfully, giving me his old familiar stare of disapproval for my words and actions.

"I believe it," Beaver stated. "It's a form you call 'psychological warfare' in your world. O-cha starts killing off your friends one by one, taunting you as each one dies, knowing there's nothing you can do about it." He looked at me expectantly. "Except…"

I had a bad feeling. "Except what?"

"Call him out."

"You mean fight him again? Yeah, right," I spat. "We all know how well that went the first time."

"Just a thought. That's how we would do it in the tribe."

"Forget it." I tried to picture such an event. I might have been lucky against O-cha the first time, but I didn't want to chance another shot at him. "Besides, O-cha would never go for it. He wants me to watch and suffer as he kills off everyone else."

"Well, I'm not going down easily," Eric declared.

A cry went out from Tory.

"I think James is gone," Pat said softly.

"We'd better get back," Beaver said. "We've got a grave to dig."

"And a good friend to bury," Eric added quietly.

James's death weighed heavily on my mind as we dug the grave and laid him to rest with his personal things.

Because of the hardship on the horses, Tory only allowed each of us to keep about ten pounds of gold, which was worth around $192,000 apiece. I figured I could live on that while I looked for a job. I was no longer sure I wanted to come back in another two years when the portal opened again, *if* it opened again.

We dug another hole and buried the cache we had to leave behind, then headed back out on the trail. With the lighter weight, we began making better time. The horses moved along at a good speed.

At one point along the trail, Eric stopped his horse and waited for me to catch up. "You're awfully quiet, little brother. What's on your mind?" He'd never seemed to take much interest in my thoughts before.

"Death. The future," I said.

"You feeling guilty?"

"Yeah. If it wasn't for me finding the portal and wanting to come on this journey, James, Sergio, Trish and everybody else would still be alive."

"They knew the danger. They all freely chose to come. You can't blame yourself."

"I know, but I'm gonna anyway. None of us had any idea it would be *this* dangerous." Well, maybe I did, I suddenly realized. Maybe I should have listened to my dreams at the beginning. The idea increased my belief that the tragedies were my responsibility and made me feel all the worse.

"This whole trip's been a failure, Donny," Eric remarked. "Hell, we're not even gonna get home with much of what we came for…the gold. Still, none of it was your fault. I doubt anybody blames you for anything that's happened. They all wanted adventure and they all wanted gold."

"I don't even care about the gold anymore. I just want everyone left to make it home alive."

"You're still bringing some gold, right?"

"Yeah, some. But it doesn't feel right. I feel like this gold is tainted, like having it is bad luck. Maybe if we left it all behind, we could get back home safely, like a bargaining chip."

Eric shook his head. "Don't be a dickhead. It's not the gold. It's O-cha, for one thing. O-cha wants us dead for no other reason than because we're from the other side. The other deaths…well, they were just bad luck. This is a hard, unforgiving world over here. You and I were foolish to come into it so unprepared. We should have taken more time to study the situation and the potential hazards, even if it meant waiting two and a half years before we started north for the gold."

"I don't think it would have made a difference," I said, not convinced that Eric had all the answers this time. "I wish now I would have never told you about the portal in the first place. I should have walked away and forgotten about it." I smiled at Eric to placate his concern for me. "But, I can't worry about it now, can I? Once we're back home, I'll have to come to terms with all of this. And I will…in time."

Eric studied me. "You know, you surprise me. This trip's been good for you. You've changed. I like the stance you're taking with the group and all that's been happening. After we get home, I'd like to sit down with you and talk about your future employment plans. I see some good potential coming out of all this." He kicked his heels against his horse's ribs and rode ahead.

I stayed back, wondering what he meant, yet feeling surprised and happy for his compliment. Eric had always tossed me to the wolves when it came to making my own living, like he didn't want to have anything to do with me. Lately, on this trip, he hadn't been getting on my case. It seemed to me, Eric was the one changing.

Chapter 29

The next twenty-three days passed without incident. I think all of us were surprised to wake up each morning and find our horses and ourselves intact. There had been no sightings of O-cha and no more deaths as we made our way south down the San Joaquin Valley and through the Tehachapi mountains. I was feeling optimistic the rest of us would make it home alive.

As we now made our way across the Mojave Desert, I estimated we'd come some 480 miles since James's death, which meant we had less than eighty miles to go. We'd been making our twenty miles a day, sometimes a little more. We could have pushed harder, but the August heat and night shifts took a toll on us, so we kept to our planned pace.

As we clopped along the desert plain, a large thundercloud moved in. The late-afternoon sunshine changed from an eye-hurting glare to a dusk-like dimness. The bleak, harsh desert softened in the muted light.

We had been watching the storm move in from the south. The southern mountains had been covered with clouds all morning. Wispy tendrils of rain reached for the ground, giving us the impression we were going to get wet before too long.

We made our way down a forty-foot embankment into a wide, dry wash that stretched some hundred yards across. The dry sand flew up at the feet of the horses as we ambled our way lazily to the other side. Having stayed up late with guard duty the night before, I dozed off and on in my saddle.

We had about thirty or forty yards left to get to the other side of the wash when I heard Beaver yelling.

"Get out of the wash now. Right now. Come on. Hurry. Get out." He pushed his horse into a gallop.

I looked around for the danger, forcing my tired horse to follow the rest of the group. The horses had a hard time running in the loose, rock-studded sand.

Suddenly, I heard a distant rumble, a roar that grew louder and louder. Something drawing close.

I pressed my feet against my horse to keep it moving. It kept stumbling. I feared it would trip and fall. At the same time, not knowing what the danger was or where it was coming from, I hung on and prayed.

Kathy was behind the others, but well ahead of me.

At the head of the group, Beaver glanced up the wash.

My eyes followed his.

A wall of roiling, dirty water, ten feet high and stretching the width of the wash, obliterating everything in its path, surged toward us.

My mouth dropped open. *Oh, my God*. I was the last in line. I urged my horse to go faster as my mind tried to comprehend what was happening. I'd only covered half the distance to the bank and to safety when Tory's horse went down, its right front leg bent and flopping as it tried to stand again.

Tory had jumped clear and landed on his feet in a dead run. It was a valiant effort, but I knew there was no way he could outrun the fast-approaching wave.

Slowing my horse as I came along side him, I held out my hand.

"I'm fine," Tory yelled without slowing down. "Go, go, go." He waved me away, veering off toward a Palo Verde tree sitting on a small hillock twenty feet down the wash.

Shit, he was going to try to survive the wave by holding onto the tree.

I had no choice. If I wanted to survive, I needed to continued on without him.

The roar grew so loud, I could hear nothing else. I pounded my heels against the horse's ribs and raced to the bank with the rest of the group.

Beaver made it up the steep embankment first, followed by Eric, Pat, and Kathy.

My horse seemed to sense the danger. Like a race horse coming into the final stretch, it refused to slow down. It hit the last yards at a dead run and lunged upward to the top of the bank.

A spray of water hit me as the wave thundered past.

I swung the horse around to search for Tory. The top of the Palo Verde tree thrashed violently back and forth. I feared it would get washed away.

"Do you think he'll make it?" Kathy shouted as she rode to my side.

"I don't know." I swallowed hard, my mouth dry. "I really doubt it."

The roaring sound abated as the front wall of the flood wave rushed past. I scurried off my horse and tied it to a scruffy mesquite bush. By now, we could talk in normal tones.

"How is this possible?" Eric demanded, scratching his long unkempt hair. He seemed rattled. "Where did that water come from?"

"It's a flashflood," Beaver explained. "It happens when it rains hard."

"But it hasn't been raining," Eric pointed out, looking at the dark sky.

"Not here," Pat said. He nodded toward the south. "It's been raining in those mountains most of the day. Look at the lay of the land. All the rain from the north-facing slopes of those mountains gets funneled into this wash. The water probably got backed-up by debris, which acted like a dam. When the dam broke, it released all the water at once. I've seen these floods before. Usually, they don't last long."

The water level lowered quickly. Lightning reached out and tickled the earth a few miles south of us. Moments later, a deep rumble of thunder followed.

"We should make camp before this storm hits," Beaver suggested. "We'll look for Tory's body tomorrow."

We all knew Tory couldn't have survived, but I couldn't force myself to leave the scene until my eyes verified that he was no longer there. I stayed where I was. "Go ahead," I told the others. "I'm gonna sit here for a little bit."

Plopping my butt down in the dirt, I stared at the top of the tree as it slowly appeared above the lowering water level. I didn't even know if Tory had made it to the tree or not.

He had probably intended to climb the tree as high as he could to keep his head above the water. But even if he would have made it to the top of the tree, the power of the water probably would have yanked him off and washed him away.

The water receded faster now.

My heart almost stopped when I saw a hand, then an arm appear. I jumped to my feet and yelled, "I see him." The water was still too high to get to the tree, but I hurried down the bank.

"Where is he?" Pat called out above me.

"There," Kathy shouted. "In the tree."

I threw off my gun belt and hat, then carefully waded into the flowing water. It came to about mid-thigh, not as deep as I'd thought it would be. I struggled to stay on my feet with the fast-moving current and loose sandy bottom.

"Dammit, Donny," Eric shouted. "Wait until we can tie a rope to you. We don't need you to drown, too."

I ignored the order and surged ahead. My eyes locked on Tory's head, which now hung limply above the water. My foot hit a large rock. I fell. The current caught me up and swept me into its torrents.

"Donny," Kathy screamed.

I bobbed up and down, flailing my arms to stay above water, trying to get my feet back under me. I gasped, taking in mouths full of dirty water. As I planted my foot, the moving water knocked me off balance again.

Facing downstream, I saw a thick bush sticking above the water. I reached out and grabbed a double handful of branches as I flew past. I screamed in pain as thorns dug into my fingers and palms. Clenching my teeth, I forced myself to hold on, desperately shifting my legs to get a foothold.

Once I got my feet under me, I was able to stand up. I moaned in pain as I opened my hands and tried to remove them from the bush. This happened to be one of those cat's claw bushes, growing sharp, curved thorns that looked like a cat's claw and felt just as piercing.

Damn. The thorns stuck into my skin from every direction and I couldn't remove my hands. I tried to use my right fingers to pick off the thorns from my left, but I couldn't detach myself.

"Here, let me help," Beaver said behind me, traipsing through the now knee-high water.

Pat waded out toward Tory.

It took a minute to free my hands, then Beaver and I went to help Pat.

"Look at this," Pat said as we joined him. "He used his belt to tie himself to the tree."

"He must have known he wasn't going to make it," Beaver said sadly. "He didn't even get off the ground."

Sure enough, Tory had cinched his belt around his left wrist. He'd used two half-hitches on the other end to secure himself to the tree as high as he could reach.

"He didn't want his body to be washed away," I said, feeling a sense of awe. Tory's thoroughness, even in death, touched me.

"Help me get his hand free," Beaver said. He straddled Tory's body and wrapped his arms around his chest.

Pat worked the knot in the belt, but the water had caused the leather to swell. He couldn't loosen it.

"Let's just cut it," I said. With my sore, bleeding hands, I knew I wouldn't be able to hold onto my knife.

Pat pulled out his pocketknife. He selected a blade with a serrated edge and easily cut through the tough, wet leather.

Beaver eased Tory's body to the ground, which now held no more than a couple of inches of water.

Eric and Kathy arrived with a horse.

"We can carry him on the horse," Eric said.

Beaver looked up at the darkening sky. "I don't think the rain will hold off until we get Tory buried."

Already, the air smelled heavy with rain.

"Then, let's wait until morning," Pat suggested, "We should get camp set up and dinner over with before it starts pouring."

"I don't think Tory would mind waiting," Kathy said, her face drawn and tired.

I wondered how much more of this she could take. Hell, I wondered how much more any of us could take.

Beaver and Pat threw Tory's body over the saddle. Eric led the horse.

Back on the upper plain, we placed Tory in an extra blanket and bound it around his body with a rope.

From the lip of the wash, we looked for Tory's horse, but as far as we could see it had been washed completely away.

In silence, we set up our tents, built a fire, and fixed a quick dinner. We finished just as the rain started to fall.

As I listened to the steady beat of the rain on the roof of my tent, my hands still stung from the cat's claw needles. Kathy had given me a salve to help reduce the inflammation and numb the pain. The numbing part wasn't working all that well.

I knew we only had another three or four days of travel to reach the village where we'd be with Iron Cactus and the safety of numbers. We had lost time today because of the flood and the need to make shelter for ourselves before the rain fell on the open desert. We would take time in the morning to bury Tory's body, then pack up and get moving. Being so close to the end, I suspected we would push to try to make it back to the village as soon as possible.

The closeness of the village gave me mixed feelings. One was of hope that the last of us would make it back without harm. The other was an ominous fear that something would bar our way in this last leg of our journey.

* * *

Three mornings later, with less than twenty miles of travel left to reach the Indian village, I awoke at the crack of dawn with an excited, light-hearted feeling. Not only because we would arrive back at the village on this day, but the last two days, Kathy had been spending more time with me, riding along side of me, even taking short walks with me away from the camp. I felt more and more confident that we would begin a new phase of our relationship as soon as we returned home.

I pulled myself out of the sleeping bag, dressed, and ducked out of the tent. The sun was just clearing the horizon. The clouds of the last few days had given way to a clear sky.

I stretched, then rubbed my scraggly beard, realizing that Kathy had said nothing about me not shaving. Maybe she was getting used to it. Or, maybe she didn't want to nag me. I liked that. I hated it when women nagged me to do things. It reminded me of my mom nagging on me when I was younger. I liked the idea of spending my life with someone who wasn't constantly after me to change.

"Is anybody else up yet?" Kathy asked sleepily from inside her tent, which she'd set up next to mine.

I knelt down and opened her flap.

She looked beautiful with her sleeping bag pulled up to her chin and her dark hair loosely scattered over the tent floor.

"It doesn't look like it," I said. "I'll take care of my morning business, then I'll start a fire and make coffee."

She mumbled something unintelligible and snuggled down into her sleeping bag again.

I smiled. I wanted to crawl under the warm covers with her, but that would have to wait a few more days. Right now, my bladder couldn't hold out any longer.

We had camped between two hills about fifty feet tall on each side, sparsely covered with mesquite bushes, Palo Verde trees, and various kinds of cacti. One of these Palo Verde trees sat about fifty feet from camp and made a good screen to hide our private duties. That's where I headed.

As I walked back to the camp, I was surprised to see Kathy emerge from her tent.

"I thought you were going back to sleep," I said, taking her hand and helping her rise to her feet.

"Nature calls." She brushed past me and headed away from camp for the pit-stop tree.

I turned to tell her to hurry back just as an Indian warrior stepped out from behind another Palo Verde and raised his bow.

Kathy stopped in her tracks as I screamed, "Look out!"

The arrow left the string, covering the distance between the bow and Kathy's chest in nanoseconds. The bloody arrowhead punched through her back. She stiffened and slowly sank to her knees.

"*No!*" I screamed, rushing toward her.

Men yelled all around as they poured out of their tents, but I heard nothing they said.

I slid to a stop and caught Kathy as she dropped. Gently laying her on her side, I brushed the strands of hair away from her face.

Her brown eyes, wide open and blinking rapidly, focused on mine. "I...I..." She coughed. Blood speckled her lips. "I wish I would have come..." More coughs. "...to your tent." Blood trickled from the corner of her mouth. "I wish...we could have...made love."

"Shhh, don't talk," I murmured, wanting to caress her but feared I would do more harm. Helplessness overwhelmed me. I didn't know what to say or do.

I heard a commotion all around me, but I could only see Kathy.

Suddenly, her body went limp.

Silent tears ran down my face as I moved mechanically, putting my fingers against her neck. I prayed for a pulse, but found nothing.

A pair of moccasins stepped in front of me, on the opposite side of Kathy.

My eyes slowly moved up the dirty brown legs and came to a stop at the Indian's belt. There hung a scalp with short blond hair. More skin than hair. It was Steve's.

Unable to take in all the implications, my eyes continued moving upward until they came to rest on O-cha's sinister black eyes and grinning face.

"Looks like your girlfriend had an accident." He held a bow in his left hand. His right hand rested on his tomahawk.

Looking over my shoulder, I caught a glimpse of his two friends holding Eric, Pat, and Beaver at bay with drawn bows.

Fear coursed momentarily through my body as I realized I'd left all my weapons in the tent. But as I stared into O-cha's cold, dark eyes, a growing fury began to overtake me. This man had killed my friends and the woman I loved.

Rage flooded through me as I exploded off the ground and slammed my shoulder into O-cha's stomach. He gasped an exclamation of surprise as he landed on his back. Before he could react, I straddled him, holding down his arms with my knees while pounding destructive fists into his face.

O-cha squirmed beneath me, trying to cover himself, but I fiercely held him locked under me. One by one, my senses shut down. I heard nothing. I saw nothing. I felt no pain, smelled no fear. The feeling of power urged me on. A primal scream of rage burst from my throat. My knuckles punched wildly at O-cha, breaking his nose, splitting his lips, and pulverizing his face.

Blood flowed freely into the sand beneath us.

I slammed a rock-hard fist into his neck, crushing his windpipe. As tears of anger, frustration, and sorrow blinded me, O-cha struggled for air. My arms felt like lead, but I kept swinging. I wasn't about to let him live to kill again.

Hands reached out toward me, grabbing me, pulling me away from my quarry.

I swung my heavy arms at everything, knocking the hands away.

"Donny, stop," I heard as if from a great distance. "Stop it, Donny. He's dead."

Slowly coming to awareness, I realized Eric was standing over me. I let my arms fall limply to my sides. I bowed my head and took deep breaths. My senses slowly returned.

A bloody mass of flesh and bones lay beneath me. I stared at the unrecognizable face, slowly remembering that it belonged to O-cha. "What happened to his two friends?" I asked stoically.

"They got scared and ran off when they saw you throw O-cha on the ground. I think they knew it was over for him."

I suddenly remembered what had happened to spark the attack. Struggling to my feet, I tried to compose myself. I choked up. A deep sob escaped my lips when I saw Kathy's lifeless body. What had all this come to? For what purpose?

Eric put an arm around my shoulder. "Hey, Little Brother, why don't you come with me? I'll help you clean up your hands. They look like they hurt pretty badly."

I dumbly stared at my hands, covered in blood, knuckles torn, skin split, tissue bruised. I didn't know how much of the blood belonged to me and how much belonged to O-cha. I dropped my hands and let Eric lead me away.

In a stupor, I sat next to the fire pit while Eric got a fire going and put on a pot of coffee.

He heated a pan of fresh water for me to clean up my hands. "Just think, tonight we'll be at the Indian village and, tomorrow, we'll go through the portal. Your hands will be as good as new then. I'll bet you're looking forward to that, huh?"

I knew he was trying to keep my attention away from Beaver and Pat, who were taking care of Kathy's body.

"Yeah, I guess," I answered unenthusiastically.

"I'm looking forward to seeing Cindy. We've haven't been apart this long since we got married." Eric rambled on, making small talk. "What's the first thing you're gonna do when you get back home, Donny?"

"Start my life over. I'm gonna make something of myself. I'm tired of the way I was. It's time for a new me."

Eric pulled the pan of water off the fire and set it at the edge of the fire pit. He picked up the boiling coffee pot and set it next to the pan. After rustling around for our two metal coffee cups, he filled them with the hot brew.

When he handed me my cup, I winced at the pain in my hand as I reached out for it.

"You know," he said, "I've been thinking. The last six months before we left home, I'd been in the process of starting a new business, and I need a partner. You think you'd be interested?"

I took a sip of coffee, but it was too hot to drink. I set it down to cool while I processed what Eric had said. "Business? What kind of business?"

"Installing swimming pools. I'm buying the business from a guy who's retiring. He has no kids to leave it to. I was thinking I'd put you in charge of the every-day affairs. I'd be kind of like a silent partner...behind the scenes. Whadda ya think?" Eric set his coffee cup down, probably waiting for it to cool off, too. He dipped a bandana in the pan of hot water and carefully dabbed it over my knuckles to wash off the blood.

I gritted my teeth, determined to get through the pain without crying out or telling Eric to stop. "Yeah," I said, "I think I'd like being your partner." I almost pulled my hand away at the stinging, but I held on. "And, Eric?" I waited until he looked me in the eyes. "I won't let you down this time."

Eric seemed to have a frog in his throat when he said, "I know you won't." He went back to cleaning my hands. After a few minutes of silence, he said, "You really loved her, didn't you?"

"Yeah, Bro," I whispered as I glanced to where Beaver and Pat were digging Kathy's grave. "I did. For the first time in my life, I was really in love."

Chapter 30

Exhausted and forlorn, we made it back to the village that afternoon. The Indians welcomed us with open arms, almost as though we were celebrities. Maybe it was just their familiarity with us that brought out their warmness. Maybe they accepted me as the honorary son of Chief Iron Cactus. Maybe they had heard about O-cha's death at my bleeding hands. Whatever the reason, the animosity that we had felt from many in the tribe members before we had left was now gone.

Coyote had safely returned, but kept to himself during our short stay for the night.

Butterfly was nowhere to be seen, for which I was grateful.

The news of O-cha's death brought a hint of sadness to the eyes of Iron Cactus, but he didn't dwell on it, nor did he take it out on me. Before he retired that night, he stood next to me and put his strong arm around my shoulders and said, "You brave, my son. Always welcome. Your home."

After we said our goodbyes to him and the general community, I felt at a loss as to what to say to Beaver for so courageously sticking with us, showing us the trail, and paving our way with the Indians. I was going to miss him.

He asked us, "Will you come back when the Gateway opens again?"

Pat shook his head. "Not for gold."

Eric laughed. "I might come back and retrieve some of the gold, but I'm gonna be more prepared next time. Not expect so much of the trip. Enjoy the adventure more."

"What about you, Donny?" Beaver asked.

"I don't know," I said. "I certainly got more out of this trip than I bargained for. I think I'm just gonna straighten out my life and make a go of it that way. I lost a lot over here…and I'm not talking about the gold I couldn't bring back with me."

Beaver gave me a strange, knowing smile as he patted my bruised hand. "The portal will take care of all your wounds," he said. "Go home in peace."

His words gave me hope that the portal would heal, not only my hands, but the wounds in my broken heart. All I could do was wait and see.

We all slept with our personal gold and the last of our possessions that night. The gold had pretty much lost its meaning for me. I would have given it all up to have Kathy back.

* * *

By the time the three of us, Eric, Pat, and myself, walked though the portal the next day, I realized how much we had changed as we took on the weight and appearance of our former bodies.

Eric suddenly added twenty pounds and looked five years younger. The harshness of the trip and the loss of our companions had weighed heavily upon him. Now, his long, thick hair shortened and the weathered cragginess disappeared from his face.

Pat didn't change as much, but it was strange to see the beard and mustache fade away.

I could see from the looks on their faces, they saw changes in me, too. My scrubby beard was no longer there. My hands and knuckles were no longer cut, bruised, and swollen. But more than this, I felt different, like I had lost that vigorous, hearty feeling of being in good shape. My old form didn't have the same stamina or strength. Worse yet, I still ached for Kathy. My heart hadn't healed like I'd hoped.

As we walked downhill with our gold in our backpacks, I found it comforting to see airstreams overhead and hear the sound of a jet.

I found myself out of breath. My legs tired easily. I decided then and there I would give up smoking and start exercising.

When we moved out of the canyon, Pat asked, "How are we gonna handle telling the relatives about the people who died?"

"Good question," Eric replied, his brows rising. "I'm not sure. We've got to tell them something, though."

"What about the cops?" I interjected. "Won't we need to give them information, in case they need to do an investigation or something?"

Eric shook his head. "Not a good idea. How would we explain the portal? Besides, it's supposed to close in four days when the eclipse occurs. How can we bring them up here and show it to them? We'd have to explain about it closing."

If we went to the cops and told them about the portal, all three of us would probably end up in a state mental hospital for a few weeks. "Maybe we should think about it tonight," I suggested. "Remember, today is the same day we left, so I doubt anybody is missing them yet."

"That's true," Eric said. "Why don't we get together tomorrow morning and see what we can come up with. I'm not gonna say anything to Cindy either. She'll just worry about it all night."

Pat stopped, a startled look on his face. "It's not true," he said. "The portal won't close in four days."

"What do you mean?" I asked.

"This is March. The portal doesn't close until August."

Damn. I didn't think about that. "That means other people can go through, but we can't."

"Yeah," Eric said, "and how will that sound if we try to explain things. They'll think we are crazy."

"Let's leave it alone for now," Pat said. "Tomorrow is soon enough to decide what to do."

When we got to our vehicles, I was shocked to see only two vehicles, my truck and Pat's Jeep. "Where's Steve's truck?" I asked. "And James's truck?"

Eric's brow furrowed. He scratched his head and looked around as if someone had hidden the trucks behind a bush. "I don't know."

Pat walked down the wash and studied the ground. "I don't think they were ever here," he called out. "The only tracks I see come from our two trucks."

Not believing that was possible, I studied the tracks myself. Sure enough, only two sets of tracks came up the wash. We found no footprints, other than our own. For a moment, I thought I was in the Twilight Zone, like someone was playing a cruel trick on us. It was like the other nine people in our party had never been there. I couldn't have dreamed it all. I stuck my hand in my pocket and pulled out the gold nugget I had kept there. The nugget was as real as my hand.

"I don't know what to say," Eric said, spinning around, making sure we hadn't missed something. "I don't think I can deal with this right now. I want to go home and see my wife."

* * *

After riding the horses for so long, it seemed strange to sit in my truck again. I felt like I was flying once I hit a paved road. Coming into town, I realized it was going to take me a little time to adjust to this world and it's masses of humanity.

Back in my apartment, I threw my gear on the floor and the bag with my ten pounds of gold on the table. I took a long, hot shower and scrubbed my body from head to toe. Even though my body wasn't that dirty before I had passed through the portal, in reality, I hadn't taken a shower for over four months. Finally feeling clean, I popped open a beer and flipped on the T.V. Just as I got comfortable in my chair, my phone rang.

I shut off the T. V. and picked up the phone. "Hello?"

"Donny," Eric said breathlessly, "you're not gonna believe this."

I sat forward, concerned that something had happened to Cindy. "What? What's going on?"

"They're alive."

"Who?"

"James, Tory, Steve….everybody who died over there."

Chills ran down my spine. "No way. I don't believe it. It's not possible." *How can this be?*

Eric rattled on. "I was telling Cindy about the trip. She said she talked to Steve not five minutes before I walked in the door. She's gonna have him do some work in our yard tomorrow. I didn't believe her, so I called him. He thought I was nuts when I told him about the trip to find gold. He said he's never heard of the portal and doesn't believe in that alternate-world stuff."

My mind raced for an explanation. We had been there. I knew it wasn't a dream. We had brought back gold. How could I explain the leather bag of gold sitting on my table if we hadn't been there?

I looked at my hands. The portal had healed my hands and changed all of us back to the way we had been just before we had stepped through for the trip.

Eric interrupted my thoughts. "Remember when Beaver said there were other things about the portal that he wouldn't tell us? Maybe the portal manipulates time in other ways…ways that we don't know."

A light went on in my brain. "I just remembered. Beaver had told me that if we got killed over there, we stayed dead over there. He didn't say we died over here."

"Well, I guess that makes sense when you look at what's happened. I wonder if the people who died over there can ever go back through the portal."

"I don't get it. Why wouldn't they want us to know that if we died on that side, we would just go on as normal on this side?"

"I don't know," Eric said softly. "Maybe they thought we would be more careless."

I suddenly thought of Kathy. My voice caught in my throat as I asked, "Did you call anybody else?"

"Yeah, I did," he said with a chuckle. "She's alive, Donny. I just got off the phone with her."

"No way," I said, my mind trying to cope with the fact she was alive and well after I had held her while she was dying."

"By the way," Eric stated, "she also thinks I'm nuts. She said she's never heard of the portal."

"Maybe we *are* nuts," I replied. "How can this be?"

"I don't know," Eric said in an incredulous tone, "but it is."

If Kathy had never heard of the portal, maybe she'd never heard of me, either. That means, I would have to start all over with her, if she would even have anything to do with me.

"Donny," Eric said, "the question is…what are you gonna do about Kathy?"

Fear gripped me. The prospect of talking to Kathy now scared me to death. Even though she and I had been just on the verge of making our relationship work before O-cha shot and killed her, she wouldn't remember any of it. She might not even be interested in me.

"I'm not sure," I finally said to answer Eric's question. "I need time to think about it."

"Okay, but I have to warn you, if you talk to her or any of the others, try not to mention anything about the portal or what happened on the other side. We don't want them to think we've gone off the deep end."

"Don't worry," I blurted, "I won't."

"I'll get a hold of you tomorrow. We'll talk then about our new company. Okay?"

"Sure, Bro, sounds good. Talk to ya later."

I hung up the phone and sat staring at the blank T.V. screen and numbly sipped my beer. Wow, this was about the biggest challenge I'd ever faced. Not only did I have to talk to Kathy, but I needed to get her to fall in love with me...again.

"I can't deal with this right now," I said aloud, rising from my chair and going for another beer. I stopped to open the leather bag and look at the gold nuggets. Sure enough, they were still there. They were real.

"Maybe in a couple of weeks," I told myself. "I'll find some excuse to go into Kathy's office. Pretend I'm sick or something."

I knew I would put it off. I just couldn't bear to face her yet. In my mind, she'd died a violent, bloody death only the day before. I had held her in my arms as she took her last breath. I would have to wait until I was sure I could look at her and not rush to take her in my arms. Plus, I couldn't bear to think she might reject me.

"Patience, Donny," I told myself. "If it's meant to be, it will happen in its own good time."

Six months later...

The week after returning from the other side, I'd quit smoking completely and started running almost every morning. Today, a warm, sunny morning in mid-September, I ran along one of my favorite paths next to Havasu's lake. It was already eight-thirty. Normally, I made my run much earlier, like when the sun came up, which was around six-thirty this time of year. But this morning, I'd had a seven a.m. meeting with one of my customers about his new pool, so I had put off running until now.

At a steady pace, I followed the sidewalk that arched up through the lush Rotary Park area where various exercise stations, spaced out along the paved path, had been installed. I passed the parallel bars, which were being used by an older man, and moved on to the rowing machine. Sitting down on the metal seat, I started pulling, counting my reps. Closing my eyes, I blocked out everything around me to concentrate on my workout.

The portal had closed by this time. For the time being, I had no inclination to hike up to the Mohave Mountains to check it out, even though enough time had passed to catch up with the months I had spent on the other side. My life here was working out just fine. I liked being part-owner of the pool-installation business. Eric had given me full authority to run it, and it was doing well.

I heard the pounding footsteps of someone on the path approaching my station. The footsteps stopped next to me. I hated it when somebody stood and waited for me to get done with my workout. It made me feel pressured to hurry up and get finished. Annoyed, I opened my eyes and turned to give the offender a dirty look.

My mouth dropped open in surprise when I saw Kathy standing before me. I'd been putting off going to see her, telling myself I'd go the next day. In truth, I didn't think I would ever be able to face her.

Now, she stood directly in front of me, studying me intently. She looked as gorgeous as ever, her cheeks shiny with a healthy glow, her warm brown eyes full of life. "Hey, don't I know you?" she said. Her eyes suddenly lit up with recognition. "You're Donny, Eric's brother, aren't you?"

My mouth went dry. "Um, yeah," I stuttered. "I am." I wondered how she knew me.

"I thought so. I remember Eric introducing us."

I racked my brain, but I couldn't remember meeting her, other than the time we'd talked to her and Trish about the portal.

Seeing my confusion, she said, "I met you about six months ago. You'd brought Eric in for his appointment."

Wow, in her timeline, that's how it had happened.

"Oh, yeah, right," I said as if I remembered now.

She cocked one hip to the side and tilted her head. "Don't you run one of Eric's companies?"

I got the feeling she was flirting. "Yeah, I do. How'd you know about that?"

"Eric told me. He said you were doing a great job."

I nodded, glad for the compliment, but not knowing what to say.

"I hope this isn't too forward," she said coyly, "but I was wondering if you are married or anything." Her cheeks flushed.

Wow, she's embarrassed. Her discomfort gave me confidence. "No, I'm not. Why do you want to know?" I smiled and found myself winking. I couldn't believe I was being so forward.

"I think you're cute," she said shyly.

My heart flip-flopped in my chest. I dared to ask, "Would…would you like to go to dinner with me tonight?"

She hesitated a moment, then smiled devilishly. "Only if you can catch me." She turned on the path and trotted off, looking over her shoulder expectantly.

"Shit," I grunted, struggling to extract myself from the rowing machine, which conspired against me by snagging my sweatshirt. When I finally got free, I took off on a dead run, laughing at Kathy's shrieks of joy.

Although the gold from the other side had been tainted by the deaths of my fellow travelers, as I chased after Kathy, I realized that I had found an even greater treasure on the other side, my soul mate.

They said it wouldn't
happen in his lifetime,
but it did.

On December 21, 2012, the Yellowstone super-volcano erupts.
Everything within 50 miles is instantly vaporized.

150 miles to the East in Buffalo, Wyoming, Sam Jones is watching the evening news when he's suddenly thrown across the room by a violent earthquake that quickly reduces the surrounding countryside to something resembling a war zone.

Sam flees, intent on getting his wife and two teenage kids to safety, but things go horribly wrong when his wife is shot in Casper, Wyoming.

A feisty Wyoming woman, a country in turmoil, and bad luck all conspire against Sam as he's

Escaping Yellowstone.

Look for this and other books
by Layne Walker at amazon.com

Gold Balls of
Fur and Other
Snapshots of Life

LAYNE WALKER

This short story collection, *Gold Balls of Fur and Other Snapshots of Life,* contains eighteen stories ranging from 250-word flash fiction to 3,500-word short stories. The stories cover a variety of topics and genres, including humor, science fiction, and romance.

Gold Balls of Fur involves three kids trying to manipulate their parents into adopting a Golden Retriever puppy. The parents play along with the kids, knowing full well they are being manipulated.

In *Tainted Reflection*, a man wakes up on his wedding day to find his bride-to-be not the woman he had been dating the past several years, but instead, his best friend, now his gay boyfriend. Confused and thinking everyone is playing a mean joke on him, he comes to realize he had been transported into an alternate dimension and, now, cannot get back to his former life. Despite the problems he meets, a surprising outcome awaits him at the end of the story.

These and the other stories show brief snapshots in the lives of the characters as they deal with their issues and conflicts.

Look for this and other books
by Layne Walker at amazon.com